SPQR XI

UNDER VESUVIUS

SPQR

Senatus Populusque Romanus

The Senate and the People of Rome

Also by
JOHN MADDOX ROBERTS

SPQR XI

UNDER VESUVIUS

NORTH END

JOHN MADDOX ROBERTS

THOMAS DUNNE BOOKS
ST. MARTIN'S MINOTAUR
NEW YORK

This is a work of fiction. All of the characters, organizations, and events portrayed in this novel are either products of the author's imagination or are used fictitiously.

THOMAS DUNNE BOOKS.
An imprint of St. Martin's Press.

www.thomasdunnebooks.com
www.minotaurbooks.com

MYSTERY FIC

Library of Congress Cataloging-in-Publication Data

Roberts, John Maddox.
    SPQR XI : under Vesuvius / John Maddox Roberts.—1st ed.
        p. cm.
    ISBN-13: 978-0-312-37088-6
    ISBN-10: 0-312-37088-1
    1. Metellus, Decius Caecilius (Fictitious character)—Fiction.   2. Rome—History—Republic, 265–30 B.C.—Fiction.   3. Private investigators—Rome—Fiction.   4. Murder—Investigation—Rome—Fiction.   I. Title.   II. Title: SPQR Eleven.   III. Title: SPQR 11.   IV. Title: Under Vesuvius.
    PS3568.O23874 S679 2007
    813'.54—dc22
                                                                    2007035399

First Edition: December 2007

10 9 8 7 6 5 4 3 2 1

1/15/2008

For Debbie Standifer and Gayle Maggard,

sisters-in-law for thirty-odd years

with affection

DRAMATIS PERSONAE

Metellus, Decius Caecilius, the younger: now *praetor peregrinus* for Campania

Julia, his wife

Marcus Caecilius Metellus: young relative, about eighteen years old

Circe: nickname for Julia, friend and cousin of Decius's wife; beautiful; courted by but refused Marcus Antonius, Gnaeus Pompey the Younger, Catullus, Marcus Brutus, Cassius Longinus, King Phraates of Parthia

Antonia: sister of Marcus Antonius; friend of Decius's wife

Hermes: Decius's freedman

In Baiae

Diocles: Last in a long line of priests of the Temple of Campanian Apollo

Gorgo: His daughter; not as virtuous as her father thinks.

Charmian: Greek slave owned by Diocles.

Gaia: German-looking slave owned by Diocles.

Leto: slave owned by Diocles.

Gaeto: wealthy Numidian slave trader; reluctantly accepted by the local notables

Jocasta: his beautiful, Greek, red-haired second wife

Gelon: his handsome son by his first wife; in love with Gorgo

Diogenes: from Crete, perfume importer and manufacturer; partner of Manius Silva.

Manius Silva: perfume importer and manufacturer, partner of Diogenes; *duumvir*. Married to Quadrilla.

Quadrilla: wife of Manius Silva; wears large jewels in her navel; rumored to have been forced into prostitution after her father's financial ruin.

Lucius Lucillius Norbanus; *duumvir*; master of vintner's guild; married to Rutilia.

Rutilia: wife of Lucius Lucillius.

Regilius: Spaniard, ex-cavalryman, works at Villa Hortensia; expert tracker

Quintus Hortensius Hortalus: friend of Decius's father. Wealthy lawyer, jurist, orator. Lends his villa near Baiae to Decius. Hortalus raises ornamental fish, waters his olive trees with wine.

SPQR XI

UNDER VESUVIUS

SPQR

Senatus Populusque Romanus

The Senate and the People of Rome

1

It was a good year for me, even if it was a bad one for Rome. Caesar's actions had everyone on edge and the City was full of talk of civil war. It was getting difficult to accomplish anything, whether in the way of business or pleasure, so nervous was everyone. Luckily for me, I didn't have to stay there.

It was the year of my praetorship. Had I been elected *praetor urbanis*, I would have had to stay within the walls for the whole year, but it had been my good fortune to be elected *praetor peregrinus,* in charge of cases involving foreigners, and all Italy was my province. So I had cleared my City docket in short order and prepared to travel. My first destination was Campania. With my wife, Julia, a gaggle of slaves, friends, and freedmen, and preceded by my lictors, we set out for Italy's most popular resort district.

After the endless duties and tedium of the junior magistracies, the praetorship was like a vacation with duty hours. You got to lounge around in a curule chair while somebody else did all the organizing, arguing, and pleading; and when you'd heard enough you rendered judgment and nobody could dispute with you. Plus, since there were so many days on the calendar when official business was forbidden, there was plenty of time to socialize.

And socialize we did. A serving praetor was always in demand as a guest, so we dined out almost every evening. With my lictors clearing the way for our litter, we could negotiate Rome's crowded streets with ease. The prestige of the office was tremendous. A praetor held imperium and was qualified to lead armies in the field, although it had been a few generations since sitting praetors had done so. At last, Julia had the social standing to which she knew she was entitled.

To cap it all, I could look forward to a splendid provincial governorship when my year in office ended. Even an honest man could get rich as propraetor.

Thus, we felt ourselves specially favored by the gods as we made our stately way along the Via Appia, that oldest and most beautiful of the Roman highways, lined with majestic cedars and pines, straight through the richest farmland on the peninsula. Julia shared a litter with two friends, Antonia and Circe. Antonia was a sister of the famous Marcus Antonius, one of Caesar's most loyal supporters. Circe was one of Julia's cousins, also named Julia, but nicknamed Circe because, so my Julia claimed, "she reduces men to quadrupeds."

I rode a splendid chestnut from my new stables. Julia had insisted that my dignity now forbade using hired mounts. Beside me rode my freedman Hermes. Around us was my staff of secretaries, assistants— many of them sons of friends just starting on their careers—and all the general hangers-on needed to support the dignity of a senior magistrate. In the rear of the procession were a couple of wagons full of household slaves, most of them Julia's personal attendants.

We traveled in leisurely fashion. I felt no compulsion to rush, and I was savoring the advantages of my new status. At each town along the road we were banqueted like visiting royalty; and as we passed each grand villa, a slave came running out, bearing his master's invitation to dinner. As often as not, I accepted.

After the previous twenty years of my career, it was a welcome change.

But, eventually, we came in sight of Vesuvius. The beautiful if somewhat ominous mountain raises its conical bulk near Italy's most splendid bay, a faint plume of smoke drifting lazily from its peak, its sides carpeted with green, steep vineyards planted on nearly every accessible patch of its incomparably fertile soil.

"Do you think it could erupt?" Julia said, her lovely patrician head poking out of the litter's expensive hangings, another praetorian extravagance.

"It hasn't in living memory," I assured her.

Southern Campania is home to many delightful towns, such as Cumae, Stabiae, Pompeii, Herculaneum, Baiae, and many others, but I was not just yet ready to visit them. Instead, we took a little road that branched from the Appian and cut through the countryside surrounding the jewellike Bay of Baiae.

Here the serene fields were tended by slaves who were industrious but not overworked, their labors overseen by benign herms that stood at intervals along the road. In time we came to another road, this one little more than a paved path, that led to a splendid villa.

"Here we are, my dear," I said.

"Stop!" Julia ordered the litter slaves: eight matched Libyans who had cost me dearly and ate voraciously whether they were engaged in transportation or not. Julia and the other two emerged from the litter and stood gazing upon the estate, squealing with delight.

And it was worth a squeal or two. There were at least twenty buildings on the place, big and small. The main house was an imposing structure—white walled, roofed with red tiles—that stood atop a low stone platform. Its simple design complemented the far older Greek temple, Doric in style and beautifully maintained, that stood nearby. Everything in sight was laid out and constructed in the most exquisite taste.

"Oh, wonderful!" Julia exclaimed. "And this is truly to be ours?"

"Nothing set in stone so far, my dear, but at least we have the use of it for now."

"It will be ours," she stated with great finality.

The villa belonged to my father's good friend and patron, Quintus Hortensius Hortalus, the great orator, jurist, and scoundrel. The old villain was then on his deathbed, and had summoned me to his side when he learned of my election. I found the once-imposing old man wasted away to almost nothing, his incomparable voice reduced to a whisper. I had fallen afoul of him more than once and had even tried to prosecute him for criminal acts upon occasion, but he had always regarded this as mere politics and never held it against me. Now, seeing him in such a pitiful condition, I could summon up no hostility against him. A whole era of Roman political life would die with him.

"Congratulations, my boy," he croaked out. "Imperium at last, eh?"

"It comes to most of us if we live long enough," I told him. "But thank you anyway."

He managed a croupy laugh. "You haven't changed. And *praetor peregrinus*, at that. That's good. You'll get to travel about, let the people see your face. They'll remember, and that will be of value, when the time comes. Listen, my boy, I wish I had time for chitchat, but I don't. I have a villa in Campania, near Baiae."

"It is famous," I said.

"Yes, well, nobody's in it right now, and you will need a place to live when you're in the district, and accepting the hospitality of a local grandee would be a bad idea. Sure as Jupiter is randy, that man will have a case before your court and he'll expect favorable treatment. Believe me, I know how it works. Why not use my villa?"

"That is most generous," I said fervently. The very thing he had mentioned had been on my mind as well.

"Good, good." He mused for a while. "You know, I've no one worth willing the place to, so—well, just see if you like it."

Now all my old hostilities disappeared completely. At any other time I would have been suspicious, the prospect of an inheritance being a classic means of control. But he was clearly dying and had nothing to gain from me. I babbled my thanks and made my exit. Half the important men of Rome were outside waiting to pay what would almost certainly be their final respects to a man who had been one of the most distinguished senators of the age. But he stopped me before I reached the door.

"Decius."

I turned. "Yes, Quintus Hortensius?"

"Hang on to that wife of yours."

"You mean Julia?" I said, astonished.

"Who else would I mean? Besides being a charming woman, she's a Caesar, and her uncle Julius is the coming man. Forget the rest, no matter what your family says. Being married to his niece could save your neck someday."

"I intend to keep her," I said. Already, he was drowsing. Even dying old men talked of Julius Caesar.

Now we made our way toward the big house and I allowed myself to believe that this could be mine. All along the path fresh garlands had been strung between the herms in honor of our arrival. I had sent a runner ahead to advise the staff of our approach. It is always a bad idea to drop in on such a place unannounced. Then you just get to see what the place really looks like when the master's not around.

There were at least a hundred people awaiting us before the house. At such an establishment, this was a mere skeleton staff. A man as wealthy as Hortalus could easily have five hundred household slaves alone when he was in residence, with several thousand more tending the fields.

"Welcome, welcome, Praetor!" chorused the well-drilled staff. "Most happy and gracious Senator and Lady, thrice welcome to the Villa Hortensia! All honor to the Praetor Decius Caecilius Metellus the Younger! *Evoi! Evoi!*"

"Goodness!" Julia said. "I wasn't expecting this."

"Old Hortalus had the most important men in Rome calling on

him," I told her, "not to mention foreign kings and princes. He probably has a Greek chorus master to drill his slaves in these little ceremonies." Nonetheless, I was flattered.

A tall, dignified man came forward, a staff of authority in his hand. "Praetor, my lady, I am Annius Hortensius, freedman of the great Hortensius Hortalus and steward of the Villa Hortensia. I bid you welcome. Please regard this house as your own and myself as your personal servant. All that may be done to render your stay pleasant will be performed with utmost diligence."

He introduced us to the housekeeper, a formidable woman belted with keys and graced with a face of iron, and the principal servants, most of them freedmen and -women. The rest would be known to us only by their occupations.

While our own slaves and the villa's made our quarters ready, we were given a tour of the place. We Metelli were not exactly paupers, but there were too many of us to concentrate so much wealth in one place. In truth, only a handful of men could match the splendor of Hortalus's properties, of which this was only one. The collection of Greek sculpture was breathtaking, and most of it was displayed in formal gardens landscaped especially to provide a setting for them. He had no fewer than three originals by Praxiteles, including a stunning sculpture of the Graces. You see copies everywhere, but this was the original.

We saw the huge fish ponds that had been Hortalus's passion. He had written long books on the subject and for many years had engaged in a rivalry with his friend Phillipus, who was afflicted with the same mania. The ladies of our party were delighted with the grotesquely fat fish, who gathered at our approach to be fed, mouths agape like baby birds. Urns of fish food stood by for the use of anyone inclined to this activity. Julia and her friends tossed out enough food to founder a pride of lions. Then the tour continued.

"If you would be so good, Praetor," Annius said solemnly, "how did you last find my patron?" We were making our way toward the temple.

"In a very bad way, I fear," I told him. "You and the rest must prepare yourselves for the worst. However," I added with some satisfaction, "I have reason to believe that he has made excellent provision for you all."

"What temple is this?" Julia asked. "It is so lovely!"

"This is the Temple of Campanian Apollo," the steward said proudly. "It is the oldest Greek sacred structure in Italy, founded by colonists more than four hundred years ago. The great Hortensius has made its maintenance and enrichment his dearest project. All the decayed old marble he replaced with the finest Parian. The tile roof he restored with glittering bronze. Where the trees of the sacred grove had died, he brought in and had planted full-grown trees from the holy precincts of other temples."

"He's never been one to do things by halves," I acknowledged.

"Is there still a priest in residence?" Julia wanted to know. "Are ceremonies still performed here?"

"Oh, yes. Southern Campania has a large Greek community, and they have always supported this temple. The priests of Apollo hold a hereditary office, and the current one is a direct descendant of the founding priest, who was a citizen of Athens. His name is Diocles."

At this moment a lovely young woman emerged from the temple accompanied by two slave girls who bore long ivy wreaths. She wore a simple, elegant gown of dazzling white belted with gold. Under her careful direction, the girls began to drape the wreaths around the altar.

"And this is Gorgo, daughter of Diocles," the steward said.

"We must meet her," Julia insisted.

As we crossed the well-kept lawn one of the slave girls caught sight of us and spoke to her mistress. The young woman in white crossed to the top of the stairs and awaited us there, her hands folded modestly before her. When we drew near, she inclined her head gracefully.

"The Temple of Campanian Apollo welcomes the praetor and his lady," she said in beautiful Attic Greek. Julia answered in the same language, which she spoke as perfectly and as naturally as she did Latin. All upper-class Romans learned Greek, but with the Caesars it was something of a mania.

"So you knew we were coming?" I said after the steward formally introduced us.

"The whole district has anticipated the arrival of the distinguished Senator Metellus and Lady Julia."

Meaning that everyone wanted to meet Julius Caesar's niece. One more praetor wasn't likely to cause much of a stir.

"Here comes part of the district now," I noted.

A little party of horsemen was approaching along the paved road leading to the temple, their mounts clopping along on unshod hooves. Hermes gave a low whistle. It was meant for the horses. They were superb, far more splendid than my own. The riders were an exotic lot. Four were tawny-skinned, bearded men with their hair dressed in numerous plaits. They rode bareback, each controlling his mount by a single rope halter looped around the animal's muzzle. Each wore a brief, white tunic and carried a sheaf of javelins in a quiver across his back.

Their leader was an extraordinarily handsome young man who sat a Roman saddle and wore Greek dress, but whose skin was the same desert color as his followers'. His mount was draped with an elaborate caparison that trailed hundreds of tassels of scarlet and gold.

"Numidians," I observed, "horses and men both. What brings them here?"

"That is Gelon, the slaver's boy," the steward informed us. "I will get rid of him."

I cocked an eye toward Julia. She was watching Gorgo, and the priest's daughter was watching the handsome young horseman. Her eyes were bright, her cheeks flushed, her mouth a bit open, as if she were about to speak. Uh-oh, I thought.

"No need, Annius Hortensius," I told the steward. "He may have business with me. I am praetor of the foreigners, after all."

"His sort belongs in court, all right," the man sniffed.

It has always seemed a little odd to me that, while we all make use of slaves and can hardly imagine life—much less civilization—without them, we harbor a great contempt for slavers, as if our own slaves appeared in the house by magic. Of course, the steward had been a slave once and doubtless had little love for the breed.

"I want to meet him," Circe said. She was a brown-haired beauty who had spurned the suits of Marcus Antonius, Gnaeus Pompey the Younger, Catullus the poet, Marcus Brutus, Cassius Longinus, King Phraates of Parthia (really!), and many others less illustrious.

"He's too far beneath you," Antonia told her. "We Antonii, on the other hand, are known for our low tastes."

"Rein yourselves in, ladies," Julia advised. She was eyeing the boy, too. He alit gracefully, kicking one leg over the saddle and sliding down, catching himself with no trace of awkwardness. He strode toward us, smiling. He even had beautiful teeth. However stingily the gods may have dealt with him in the matter of pedigree, they made it up handsomely in physical attributes.

"Praetor! So soon among us! I am Gelon, son of Gaeto, merchant of Baiae. I bid you welcome to our district." Here he performed a courtly bow, a gesture never performed by Romans but somehow dignified and without the groveling implications of the Oriental bow. "And to your lady, the distinguished Julia of the Caesars, and the lovely Lady Antonia, and this other Lady Julia whose name of preference I must learn, and to all your entourage, welcome again!"

The women cooed and fluttered like pet doves. So much for patrician dignity.

"You are uncommonly well-informed," I noted.

"As it happened, a party of my father's agents who returned yesterday from Capua, attended a ceremony at which the Capuans honored you."

"Well, that explains it. We thank you for your very courteous welcome, Gelon, and we look forward to our stay in beautiful southern Campania."

"Should you desire to see the many sights of the neighborhood, Praetor, please allow me to be your guide. It would be both an honor and a pleasure to me."

"I may well take you up on that," I told him. Behind me I heard scandalized little sounds from the stuffier part of my following. He was, after all, a slaver's son and a foreigner to boot. But I didn't care. I was the one with imperium and could do as I pleased. I was going to have to keep an eye on Julia, though.

"What are you doing here?" This indignant shout came from a bald, white-bearded specimen who, to judge by his white robe and laurel chaplet, had to be Diocles, priest of Apollo.

"I'm supposed to be here," I informed him. "I'm the new *praetor peregrinus.*"

"Not you!" he cried, pointing a skinny finger at Gelon. "Him! That African slave seller! He fouls the holy precincts of Apollo!"

I was perfectly aware that he hadn't meant me, but I couldn't help having a little fun. "Oh, he can't be all that bad, surely. His horses are as handsome as Apollo's own. Could such splendid animals be owned by a man unworthy to approach your temple?"

The old boy tried to calm down and regather his dignity. "The honored praetor is pleased to jest. This lowborn foreign scoundrel has been seeking out my daughter at every opportunity." He shot that lovely young woman a venomous glare, and she lowered her eyes, then stole another adoring glance at young Gelon.

"That proves only that he has good taste," I said. Then Julia moved in to smooth things over, a task she undertook on my behalf with some frequency.

"Reverend Diocles," she said, stepping close and laying a soothing hand in his arm, "forgive my husband's levity. He is a very serious man in court but nowhere else. And this young man has acted most courteously. Please do not mar our arrival with rancor."

Actually, I didn't mind a bit of rancor. It livened things up. But the old man acquiesced with a fair degree of grace. "I would do nothing to make your arrival among us any but the most pleasant of experiences. Gorgo!" he snapped. "Go back inside."

The girl turned wordlessly and obeyed, wiggling her bottom rather more than necessary. The display was intended for young Gelon, but I admired it anyway.

"And I, too, will take my leave of you, Senator," said the youth who was the focus of these contending passions. "Perhaps I will have the privilege of seeing you again at the banquet to be held in your honor."

"I shall look forward to it," I assured him, and with that he mounted. It was a performance far removed from the undignified scramble with which I placed myself on a horse's back. He seemed to flow onto the saddle as if lifted there by the hands of an invisible god. The women gasped in admiration.

"He rides pretty well," Hermes said grudgingly, "but I'll wager he's no good with a sword."

"Diocles," my wife said, "please have dinner with us this evening. I would love to meet your wife as well."

"Alas, my wife died many years ago," he told her.

"Then bring your lovely daughter."

"Gorgo? To the house of the praetor? She is not worthy—"

"Nonsense. I would love to become better acquainted with her."

"Then, to please you, my lady—"

"Splendid!" Julia could work people like a politician when she wanted to.

We took our leave of the priest and began to walk back toward the villa. "Looks like it will be lively times in Campania," I observed.

Julia poked me with her fan. "You should not have provoked him. He is a priest, after all."

"Just of Apollo," I said. Perhaps I should explain here that Apollo, though worshipped in Rome, was not in those days highly regarded as a deity. He was brought to Rome from Greece by our last king, Tarquinius Superbus. Four and a half centuries of residency did not make him a Roman, and people still regarded him as a Greek import. It has only been in recent years that the First Citizen raised him to the dignity of a State god and built him the splendid temple on the Palatine. He did this because an ancient temple of Apollo resides on the headland overlooking Actium, and he credits Apollo's favor for his unexpected victory in the naval battle fought there against the fleet of Antonius and Cleopatra. Personally, I think he gives Apollo the credit so that Marcus Agrippa, who really won the battle for him, won't get too much of it.

The grounds and gardens were so splendid that I didn't think the house could possibly match them, but I was wrong. The steward led us through room after room, each of them a jaw-dropper in point of luxury. Every room had exquisitely frescoed walls and ceilings, painted with mythological scenes in the highest degree of artistry. We learned that these were renewed every year, plaster and all, because Hortalus couldn't abide faded colors. There floors consisted of picture mosaics, each room's featuring a different deity and known by that god's name. Since there were so many rooms, there were gods represented I had never heard of.

The library was not a single room but a whole series of them, each packed with books stored in racks of fragrant cedar. One room was devoted entirely to Homer and commentaries upon him, another to the Greek playwrights, another to the philosophers.

His wine cellars contained amphorae of wine from every region of the world, the great jars seeming to stretch on into infinity. Old Hortalus had needed plenty of wine, because not only did he entertain lavishly but also watered the trees in his olive orchard with wine, believing they yielded superior fruit and oil because of this special treatment.

But even these wonders paled when we saw the baths. Even the finest public baths in Rome were not as splendid nor as extensive. You could have rowed a trireme on the larger pools. The hot baths were fed with water piped in from Baiae's famous hot springs by miles of underground aqueducts laid in at enormous expense. Not only were the waters health giving but also the splendid air was not marred by the pall of woodsmoke that hangs over conventional hot baths. Marble was the only stone used in these baths, unless you counted the jewels and coral with which the bottoms of the pools were decorated. And all of them were surrounded by more of the fabulous statues Hortalus had collected so single-mindedly.

It was not exactly the most luxurious dwelling I had ever seen. I had, after all, lived for months in Ptolemy's palace in Alexandria. But for a private citizen's house it was pretty comfortable. Lucullus and Philippus and a few others owned properties even more lavish, but Quintus Hortensius Hortalus owned several more like this one. And this was a man who, by his own choice, never accepted the offices of propraetor or proconsul and thus never had a province to loot. It just goes to show you what a successful career in the law can get you.

"I just know I'm going to love it here!" Julia proclaimed when the tour was over.

I was having second thoughts about the whole matter. "You understand, my dear, that these are the fruits of a lifetime of conniving, political corruption, bribery—I could go on for hours. I have a feeling that, lacking Hortalus's stupendous income, this place might get rather expensive to support."

"Nonsense. Just stick with Caesar and we will never have money problems." She said this with great finality, as she said most things.

Later on that evening I discussed the same misgivings with Hermes.

"Sell off some of the statuary," he advised. "The price of just one or two of those pieces would keep this place running for years."

"It's a thought," I admitted, "though I would hate to lose them. Originals by Praxiteles!"

"The wine, then. Even you can't drink your way through that much. Not if you live to be a hundred."

"Even worse!" I groaned.

2

I HELD MY FIRST ASSIZES IN CUMAE, A TOWN
I had never visited previously. Cumae is believed to be the oldest Greek
colony in Italy, perhaps a thousand years old at this time. It was once the
capital city of Campania, but that was long ago. As all the world knows, it
is the home of the Cumaean Sibyl, the hereditary prophetess of Apollo
and, after the Delphic, the most widely consulted of the sibyls. Cumae is
always full of people from all over the world who have come to seek her
counsel and so, as praetor of the foreigners, there was business there for
me to attend to.

Besides the foreigners, the resident Greeks, the Romans, and the
Campanians, the other major population group was the Samnites. These
people, who spoke the Oscan dialect, had for many years been firm allies
of Rome. But within living memory, they had been our implacable enemies, contending for control of central and southern Italy. When my father
was a young man, the word "Samnite" was used interchangeably with

"gladiator," since most of our Samnite prisoners of war were assigned to that exciting if rather demanding profession.

While Julia and her ladies went to tour the sights of the town, I and my staff held court. The basilica was a fine one, an imposing structure built in the years since Cumae became a Roman colony. Although not as lofty as the vast new Basilica Aemilia in Rome, recently rebuilt by a member of the Aemilian family (using Caesar's money, of course), it had beautiful proportions and tasteful decoration.

Since the weather was splendid, a dais had been set up on the steps of the basilica, shaded by an elaborate awning and facing the town's forum. When I arrived, preceded by my lictors and surrounded by my staff, the bustle and hubbub of the forum stilled, the lounging idlers rose to their feet (save a few crippled beggars), and everyone faced the dais as a gesture of respect. This I took as a good sign. It meant that the people here were content, glowers and rude noises being the rule when they were not.

And why should they not be content? They were members in good standing of the greatest empire the world had ever seen, enjoying all its advantages without being involved with the political infighting of the capital; and Roman justice was always an improvement over whatever system had been in place previously.

A man in the striped robe and bearing the crook-topped staff of an augur solemnly proclaimed that the omens were propitious for official business. A priest performed the required sacrifice, and we were ready to proceed.

A young relative of mine named Marcus Caecilius Metellus stepped forward and proclaimed: "People of Cumae, attend! On behalf of the Senate and People of Rome, the distinguished *Praetor Peregrinus* Decius Caecilius Metellus the Younger has come from Rome to hear your cases concerning foreigners and render judgment. Hail the Senate and People of Rome!" The crowd returned the salute fervently. Marcus had a fine, trained orator's voice. He was about eighteen at the time, just beginning his public career and soon to serve as military tribune.

A gaggle of local officials joined us on the dais. Like so many Italian towns, Cumae was governed by annually elected *duumviri*: two local magnates who kept close watch on each other, each determined that his colleague not steal more than himself. The holders of lesser offices—three praetors, a couple of aediles, and so forth—were mostly men who had held the duumvirate themselves, and they took the office in rotation. All these men were members of three or four prominent families who regarded office holding as an ancestral privilege. The same was true of the Senate at Rome, only the pool of families there was somewhat larger.

"Have we sufficient *equites* present to empanel a jury, should we need one?" I asked a *duumvir*.

"Easily," he answered. "This isn't Rome. We seldom use more than twenty or thirty jurors."

Roman juries often numbered in the hundreds. Even the richest men found that many difficult to bribe. Not that some didn't try, and successfully at that.

"It's a bad law, anyway," I said. "Any free citizen should be eligible for jury duty."

"That would lead to anarchy!" said an indignant official. "Only men of property are competent to make legal judgments." The rest made sounds of agreement. They were all *equites*, of course.

"We used to say that only men of property could serve in the legions," I observed. "How many of you have ever shouldered a spear?" They bristled, and Hermes gave me a nudge. I was starting things badly. "Oh, well, what's up first?"

Most of the cases that morning involved suits brought against foreign businessmen. By law, such men had to have a citizen partner. Usually, it was this partner, or his advocate, who argued on the foreigner's behalf. Except for an occasional question I had very little part in the proceedings except to listen. I was no legal scholar myself, but on my staff I had several men who were, and these could provide me with any necessary precedents.

Swift justice is the best justice, and I had all but cleared the docket before noon. The last item was the only criminal case of the day: a Greek sailor accused of killing a citizen in a tavern brawl. The man hauled before me in chains was a tough-looking specimen, his dark-tanned skin very little paled by his months in the town's lockup.

"Name?" I demanded.

"Parmenio," he said.

"Would you prefer to be tried in Greek?" I asked him in that language.

He seemed surprised at such consideration. "I would."

One of my lictors smacked him across the back with his fasces. "'I would, *sir!*'" he barked.

"I would, sir. That is very kind of you, sir."

"Do you have an advocate?"

"Not even a friend, sir."

"Then will you speak on your own behalf?"

"I will, sir."

"Very well. Lictor, call up the witnesses."

A half score of men who had the look of professional idlers came forward and they all told substantially the same story. Upon a particular date they had been carousing in a particular tavern when an argument broke out between this foreign sailor and a citizen. Flying fists had escalated to flying furniture and the citizen had ended up dead on the floor, brained by a weighty, three-legged stool.

"What have you to say for yourself?" I asked the defendant.

"Not much, Praetor. We were playing at knucklebones and I won most of his money. The last roll, he said I threw the Little Dog when anyone could see that I threw Venus. I called him a liar and he called me a boy-humping Greekling. We fought. I did not intend to kill him, but I did not want him to kill me, either. Also, we were both drunk."

"Admirably succinct," I told him. "Would that all our lawyers appreciated brevity. This is my decision. The fact that you were drunk is neither here nor there. A self-induced incapacity does not constitute a defense. You have killed a citizen, but you did not lurk in ambush or provide yourself with a weapon in advance, and these facts are in your favor. Also, you have not wasted this court's time with a windy self-justification and made us all late for lunch and the baths.

"So I will not sentence you to the cross or the arena. I declare this killing to be death by misadventure in a common brawl. For shedding the blood, not to mention the brains, of a citizen and disturbing the public order, I sentence you to five years as a public slave, your owner to be the town of Cumae. Perhaps five years of cleaning the local sewers and gutters will lead you to a more sober, thoughtful life."

The relief that rolled off the man was all but palpable. The crowd applauded and declared that this was a sterling example of Roman justice at its best. The truth was, homicide was not regarded as a particularly serious crime, as long as poison or magic were not involved, and a killing in a fair fight hardly qualified as murder at all. It was this man's misfortune that the dead man was a citizen and he was not. No doubt he was already plotting his escape.

I declared the court adjourned and was looking forward to a pleasant afternoon of eating, bathing, and socializing when I noticed a striking man who had stood among the onlookers and now wore an expression of disappointment. He was very tall, with a dark, hawk-featured face and dense, square-cut black beard. He was dressed in a long robe of splendid material, worked with a great deal of gold thread. I sent a lictor to summon him.

He approached, smiling. "Praetor, your notice does me honor." He glanced toward the local officials who, noses high, affected not to notice him and added wryly, "More honor than some think I deserve."

"That's all right. I'm the one with imperium here, so I can do as I like. You're Gaeto the Numidian, I presume?"

"I am he."

"I met your son recently. The resemblance is not difficult to spot. Do you attend courts often?"

"At every opportunity. I like to get the first look at those who are condemned to slavery. If you had not given that man to the city, I would have bid on him."

"I would think your business would be depressed of late, with all the Gallic captives flooding Italy."

"Most of them are unskilled and useful only for farm labor gangs. I buy for quality, not quantity. And expert seaman are in high demand."

"How would a captain prevent a slave sailor from escaping?" I asked him.

"Where would such a one go? The sea is a Roman lake. To sail beyond the Pillars of Hercules or to the eastern end of the Pontus Euxinus means living among savages. No, he would stay on his ship and follow his calling. After all, the work would be the same, the food the same, the dangers and the obedience to his captain the same as when he was free. Only the pay would be different, and what sensible man would trade living in civilization for life among barbarians over a handful of denarii?"

"When you put it that way, it makes sense," I admitted. Then I remembered why I had summoned him. "Gaeto, I realize that this does not come under my official purview, but I fear that your son may be heading for trouble."

The man frowned, a formidable expression on his powerful face. "Trouble, how so? If he has offended you in any way, I shall thrash him immediately."

"Nothing like that," I assured him. "But there seems to be something going on between the boy and the daughter of Apollo's priest on the estate I am inheri—where I now reside."

The frown was replaced with a smile. "Carefree, affluent young men pay court to beautiful young women. What could be more natural?"

"Naturalness does not come into it. You are a foreigner here and the people of this district are citizens, even the Greeks and Samnites among them. The priest is an aristocrat of ancient family, while your profession is, shall we say, held in low esteem. Your son could find himself the target of resentment. People would dredge up old stories about Jugurtha and the Numidian war and, next thing you know, a mob of local drunks would set fire to your house and stone you to death when you came running out with your clothes on fire and that would be a pity because, as the man on the scene with imperium, I am empowered to call in soldiers to put down civil unrest and I would indeed do so and then *I* would be the one everyone would hate and them my family would be very unhappy with me for alienating a whole pack of voters." I said that last sentence in a single breath, a tribute to my oratorical training.

His smile turned grim. "I see. I will talk to my son about this." Then he brightened. "In three days, Baiae will give a banquet in your honor. I will be there."

"I look forward to it."

"I think you may find it an illuminating experience."

And with that enigmatic utterance, he took his leave gracefully.

I THINK I CAN SAY WITHOUT RESERVATION that Baiae is the most beautiful place in Italy. It is situated on a jewellike little bay about eight miles from Cumae and about an equal distance from my new (and, I hoped, soon to be permanent) abode. It had been a part of Cumaean territory when that city was independent and served as its port. Because of its superb setting, salubrious climate, and hot springs, it had for centuries been a favorite spot for the great and wealthy to build their villas and it was the favorite resort for Romans during the hot months.

Also, its reputation for luxury and immorality were legendary, and that was the part that appealed to me. Since the destruction of Sybaris, Baiae has reigned supreme as the home of libertines, rakes, and voluptuaries. Its scandalous life goes on day and night, made possible by that marvel unknown in Rome, effective street lighting. Lamps, cressets, and torches are kept alight during the dark hours by a crew of diligent public slaves. Cato, upon seeing Baiae thus illuminated, was scandalized. "People should *sleep* at night!" he cried.

A town more different from Rome is hard to imagine. Its streets are broad and never steep. Lest the populace be troubled by the scorching sun, all the streets and plazas are covered by awnings of costly cloth. The streets themselves are paved with colorful tiles, swept and scoured clean by another gang of slaves. All the streets are lined with planting boxes and giant vases carved from tufa in which grow flowers and fragrant bushes in incredible profusion, so that the air always smells sweet, no matter which way the wind is blowing. Fine trees grow before the spacious porticos. There are many tiny parks and gardens scattered throughout the town, where exotic songbirds sing in cages hung from all the trees. Should the birds tire the ear, each park has its own consort of musicians and singers, also owned by the town.

The boating parties of Baiae are legendary, and the bay's wharfs are lined with pleasure craft, from small gondolas suitable for four or five inebriated carousers to covered barges that would carry several hundred guests. For really splendid occasions, a great number of these barges could be yoked together in the center of the bay with the whole free population of the town aboard, along with enough slaves to keep them entertained.

Baiae has no penniless rabble like Rome's. The greater part of the permanent population are *equites*, and even the shopkeepers enjoy a property assessment only slightly lower. Even the slaves are the envy of slaves in other parts of Italy. The very street cleaners live in barracks much finer than the tenements of Rome's free poor.

Cato's final word on Baiae was characteristic: "What a waste of fine farmland." That alone was enough to make me fall in love with the place.

The delegation that greeted us when we were within a mile of the city was decked out in snowy togas, flower chaplets, and the insignia of many offices and priesthoods. Images of the gods were borne on litters, and musicians tootled while temple slaves in white tunics swung elaborate golden censers on chains, perfuming the air with fragrant smoke. A civic chorus (that old Greek specialty) sang songs of welcome.

"Not bad for a man who never even conquered a single nation of barbarians," I said with some satisfaction. "I wonder if every praetor gets this treatment or just the ones married to a Caesar."

"I'm sure your own dignity is quite impressive enough, dear," Julia said.

We were carried in her elaborate litter, rather crowded now, what with Circe and Antonia making a pair of sweet-smelling cushions behind us. I had wanted to ride, but Julia had vetoed that. It is all but impossible to wear a toga on horseback, and Julia declared that I must enter the town in my purple-bordered *toga praetexta*. An old-fashioned Roman would have walked, but there were limits to my respect for tradition.

"Noble Praetor," cried the leader of this delegation, "all Baiae welcomes you! I am Lucius Lucillius Norbanus, *duumvir* of Baiae and master of the vintner's guild."

"And I," said the man next to him, "am Manius Silva, *duumvir* of Baiae and master of the perfumer's guild."

In order of precedence, the others were introduced, officials and priests, distinguished foreign visitors including a couple of princes, a vacationing Parthian ambassador, and a deposed king of some country in the general vicinity of India.

"And now, Praetor," Norbanus said, "allow us to bear you into the city in a manner befitting your rank."

Whereupon I was led to another litter, this one open and furnished with a curule chair grandly draped with leopard skin. It was hoisted to the shoulders of ten stalwart, yellow-haired Gauls, and in this state I was carried to the city while beautiful young girls strewed flowers before me. What a pity, I thought, that such an office is held for only a single year.

The road to Baiae, like those to most Italian municipalities, was lined with tombs, and just outside the gate of the city we paused at the most imposing of these, a great marble confection that had the appearance of being layered atop a much older, simpler one.

"This," Norbanus announced, "is the tomb of Baios, helmsman of the ship of Ulysses. When the wanderings of that angry man were at an end, Baios settled here and founded our city."

No matter where I go, every city claims a Trojan War veteran as its founder. I don't even have to go anywhere, since Rome makes the same claim. Doubtless there is some reason for this but I can't imagine what it is.

From the tomb, our little procession passed through the gate, which was little more than an ornamental arch, since this town was never meant to be defended, and into the city proper, where I was showered with enough flowers to glut the floral lust of a triumphing general. Somehow, I didn't allow this to go to my head. I could tell that these people didn't care a peach pit for another visiting Roman official. I was just one more excuse for a party. Well, that was fine with me. I liked parties as much as anyone. Maybe more than most.

We wended our way through the city to the bay, and there I was carried onto a bridge laid atop a line of boats; and this was not a simple boat bridge of the sort used by the legions to cross rivers and straits but an elaborate construction, painted and gilded, its roadbed covered with turf, its railings sporting statues of Triton and Nereids and other fabulous sea deities and covered by the inevitable awning, lest anyone get sunburned while getting to the festivities.

The banquet was held on one of those artificial islands I mentioned earlier. This one consisted of a central barge you could have raced chariots on for size, surrounded by two-story barges, so that the whole thing was surrounded by a gallery and topped by an immense canopy held up by poles twice the height of ship's masts and dyed, unbelievably, purple.

"There can't be that much purple dye in the world," I muttered. That dye is the most expensive substance known to man. The purple border of my *toga praetexta* had cost enough to buy an excellent farm complete with staff. I had nearly had a seizure when presented with the bill. Oh, well, the expenses of office were intended to keep the riffraff out.

A herald of thunderous voice announced us, naming the most distinguished members of my party. Then we got to meet all the local grandees, most of them wealthy *equites* like the *duumviri*. These were mostly heads of various guilds and syndicates. I quickly discerned that few of these were involved in the actual manufacture of their products. Rather, they were importers, distributors, and speculators in goods, mainly high-priced luxury items but also staple products like wine, grain, oil, and garum.

The men for the most part observed the sumptuary laws, their clothing, while of the highest quality, consisting of the usual white tunic and toga and no more than a few gold rings by way of jewelry. Their wives, however, provided a sharp contrast. Each sought to outdo the others in showy finery or shocking immodesty. All were draped with jewels and pearls; their hair was dressed into towering, complicated styles, adorned with more jewels and pearls and powdered with gold dust. And then there were the gowns.

In Rome, the infamous, all-but-transparent Coan cloth was worn by a few rich, scandalous women but only at private parties attended by the fashionable set. Here in Baiae, women wore it at public banquets. It was frequently forbidden by the censors, who, it seemed, failed to impress the women of Baiae.

"This is shocking!" Julia said in a strangled voice as these women lined up to be presented.

"I'm getting to like this place better by the minute," I told her.

"You would."

"Look," I said. "There's a woman wearing a dress you can't see through." I inclined my head toward a tall lady with flaming hair whose gown was a startling emerald green.

"That gown is pure silk!" Julia hissed. "She just wants to show that she can afford such a thing. Who can afford pure silk? I've only seen such dress at Ptolemy's court."

We were conversing in the subdued tones one uses at such occasions, smiling and nodding as we did. Catilina's wife and daughter had owned silk gowns, but I didn't want to call Julia's attention to my relationship with the latter lady.

First to be presented was the wife of Norbanus, one Rutilia, who wore an astounding wig made entirely of hair-fine gold wire. Her close-pleated gown of pale saffron Coan cloth displayed a more than ample body and that her use of cosmetics did not end at her throat.

"You honor us with your presence," Rutilia said. "The two of you really must be our guests at a little evening entertainment Norbanus and I are hosting in a week's time."

"It would be our honor," Julia answered. "Is it a special occasion?"

"Of course. It is in honor of your arrival. I can promise that all the most fashionable society of Baiae will be there without all this—" she waved gilded fingernails toward the glittering throng "—vulgar crowding."

"Well," I said, "we wouldn't want *too* many millionaires treading on our toes, would we?" Julia nudged me in the ribs.

"We shall be anticipating the event eagerly," Julia assured her.

"Wonderful." She beamed. "Well, I mustn't monopolize you. So many boring people to meet, eh?" She bowed slightly and made her way off, swaying and jiggling fetchingly.

And so we went through the greeting line. Last of all was the tall, red-haired lady in the emerald silk gown. Apparently she thought the extravagant dress was display enough, for her gold, jewels, and pearls were relatively restrained.

"And you would be?" I asked.

"Jocasta, Praetor," she said, "wife of Gaeto the Numidian." She had a furry voice, very pleasing to the ear.

"Then you would be the mother of that charming young man we met, Gelon. He does you great credit." Apparently, Julia did not find her voice or perhaps other attributes as pleasing as I.

"I wish I could claim him, but Gelon is the son of Gaeto's eldest wife, Riamo. She has never left Numidia and rules over the household there."

"And is your husband here?" Julia asked, looking out over the multitude. "My husband has met him, but I have not had the pleasure."

"Oh, he is certainly here," the woman said, smiling. "There are very few gatherings in Baiae to which Gaeto is not invited."

"How—" Julia searched for a word, a rare practice for her, "—how enlightened."

And then we were swept off to be greeted by another pack of notables, after which it was time for the banquet proper to begin. We were led to an empty couch on a dais, where the magnates of the district reclined on couches at a long table. Other tables and couches stretched in long rows down the full length of the great central barge, and soon the servers were bringing in the first courses.

In traditional fashion they first brought out eggs prepared in every imaginable fashion, some of them from birds I had never heard of. This being a coastal town—and the banquet held on the water to boot—it was fitting the most abundant and imaginative part of the feast were the fish courses. There were great varieties of shellfish along with the finned variety and great concoctions of lampreys, eels, octopi, squid, dolphin, and even skewered whale flesh. All this was accompanied by splendid wines, and soon the occasion was most convivial.

The talk was light and frivolous, which was not unusual. After all, this was not a pack of dry old philosophers debating the merits of Pythagoras's harmonic theories. But there seemed something strange about all the talk, and eventually I realized what it was.

"Julia," I said in a low voice, "do you realize that nobody has mentioned Julius Caesar once? Or Pompey or the eternal struggle between the *populares* and the *optimates*?"

"Odd, isn't it?" she said. "These people aren't interested in senatorial politics. They gauge status by wealth, not breeding. They compete through display and by outentertaining their peers, not by currying favor with the masses."

"I find it a great relief. In Rome, I always find myself sprawled next to some old patrician who thinks he's my better because his ancestors settled in Rome fifty years before mine, around a thousand years ago."

"Well," Julia said, "in Rome you certainly wouldn't see *their* sort at the same table as the city's elite." She nodded toward the end of our table, where Gaeto and his flame-haired wife reclined between a shipping contractor and a priest of Mars, with their wives, and all of them getting along as convivially as any born peers.

"You're letting your patrician snobbery show, my dear," I chided her.

"But the man's a slaver!" she protested.

"Your uncle Julius just made slaves of a whole nation."

"Conquest is honorable," she pointed out, "and degradation is the price of defying Rome. It's not the same as making a living buying and selling human beings."

That was it, of course: the buying and selling part. Just slaughtering a pack of barbarians and selling off the survivors was not the same thing at all. Patricians weren't supposed to engage in trade. I wondered what she would think had she been present to see Uncle Julius auctioning off thousands of prisoners at a time, wheedling up the price with the touch of an expert. The slavers used to follow the legions like vultures, and Caesar knew exactly what he could get from them. I suppose Julia thought it was all right for him to sell them, since he hadn't exactly bought them.

The servers brought out a specialty of the region: a fish stew containing a great variety of shellfish in a savory broth tinged with aromatic saffron. This is one of my favorite dishes, and I forgot all about slavers and Caesar while I dug into the scallops and oysters, cracked crab claws, and, at intervals, dipped bread into the broth.

"I see we've found your weakness," said a woman named Quadrilla. She was the wife of the *duumvir* Manius Silva. She was a small, dark woman and her Coan-cloth gown rested on her like a shadow. On her head she wore a silver diadem set with black pearls. Her vulpine little face was engagingly acerbic.

"Keep me supplied with this," I told her, "and you'll have nothing but favorable judgments from me. This must be what the gods eat on their better days."

"My husband exaggerates," Julia assured her. "Much as he loves good food, he is boringly conventional in his public duties. I wish I could say the same for his off-duty activities."

While these women discussed my shortcomings, I let my gaze roam over the crowd. Everyone seemed extraordinarily happy, except those who were too inebriated to feel much of anything. In true Baiean fashion, there were specially trained slaves to carry these off to their litters before anything unpleasant happened. I saw my freedman, Hermes, arm wrestling with a man who, from his short, two-striped tunic and small topknot, I took to be a charioteer, the two of them surrounded by attractive young women. Hermes was strong, but men who have spent years holding and controlling the reins of a quadriga have hands and arms like iron. Hermes lost the contest and his wager, but he seemed to care little for his defeat. He smiled blissfully as the girl next to him, her hair dyed a startling purple, massaged his sore arm.

A short distance from us, Circe and Antonia had planted themselves at either side of young Gelon. The lad seemed quite accustomed to such feminine attention and was regaling them with something that made them rock with immoderate laughter. I looked all over but did not see Gorgo, the priest's daughter. The priest himself was at our table, but was not looking as merry as the rest, perhaps because he was sharing the table with Gaeto.

By late evening the party began to break up. It might have gone on all night, but a stiff breeze sprang up off the sea and the boatmen advised that the great raft be taken apart and towed ashore. Before leaving, I got up and addressed the community.

"People of Baiae, at last I have found the one place in Italy where people truly know how to live!" This brought vigorous applause and shouts of agreement. "Now that I've seen Baiae, I may not even bother going to Pompeii and Puteoli. What would be the point?" At this, the crowd roared with approval. "In fact, I may just settle here permanently!" Raucous clapping and pledge making ensued.

On that note, the wind redoubled and everyone hastened to get ashore. Our litter was brought over the boat bridge from shore, and we crawled in. I was replete with the all the delicacies I had taken aboard and my head was only lightly buzzing from the wine. The bridge rocked with the growing waves, but our lurching steadied as the bearers took us ashore.

"I am going to have to get one of those Coan-cloth gowns," Circe said.

"I already have one," Antonia informed her. "I'd have worn it tonight if I'd known it was the fashion."

"Not in my party, you wouldn't," Julia said. "The dignity of the praetor has to be upheld, and it wouldn't look good if the women in his entourage dress like trans-Tiber prostitutes." She affected to ignore their laughter. "I suppose there's something to be said for transparent gowns. How else would we know that Rutilia, the wife of Norbanus, gilds her nipples or that Quadrilla, the wife of Silva, has a navel stretched three times its natural size to accommodate that huge sapphire?"

"How did she do that? I wonder," Circe mused.

"Started with a small, navel-sized sapphire," Antonia said, "and replaced it with a larger one and then a larger, until she could accommodate that stone."

"The concubine of the marble merchant has Scythian tattoos all over her thighs and buttocks," Circe remarked.

"They were Thracian, not Scythian," I told her. "I've seen those designs before."

"I can see where your attention was all evening," Julia said. Then she grew thoughtful. "They are a strange lot of people. With all that wealth and dazzle I expected them to behave like rich, jumped-up Roman freedmen, all vulgarity to go along with their ostentation. But they are as suave and cultured as any of the better class of Romans, considering how many of them are tradesmen."

"A little light on the gravitas, though," Antonia said. "And that suits me just as well. I'll take frivolity over heavy political talk any day. Or night."

I was wondering about Gaeto's words to me. He'd said that I might find the banquet "illuminating." Had he meant this social leveling? Certainly, I would never have expected to see a slaver at the table of honor at a banquet in Rome. Or anywhere else.

3

THE NEXT FEW DAYS, I TRAVELED AMONG the towns of the district, holding court, being feted and entertained, and generally enjoying life.

One day I went to the lovely little town of Pompeii. Actually, all the towns of this district are beautiful. Pompeii showed off its greatest adornment by entertaining me with an afternoon in the amphitheater. This splendid structure is made of stone, taking advantage of a natural depression in the ground. The depression was improved by digging, forming a perfect oval that was lined with stone seats. The outer, aboveground wall is a complete circle of graceful arches, decorated with fine carvings. One enters this imposing structure by ascending a double stair built against the outer wall, then taking one of the inner stairs that descend among the seats.

This clever building seats no fewer than twenty thousand people.

That is not a great number compared to Rome's Circus Maximus, which can accommodate one hundred thousand, but it is huge for a town the size of Pompeii, which lacks sufficient free population to fill half these seats. At festival time, people from all the surrounding countryside and nearby towns flock to Pompeii to attend the spectacles.

On that afternoon the gladiators from the local school came out to entertain us. Since the occasion was not a *munera*, the fights were not to the death but only to first blood or a declared decision. We lounged at our ease in the *editor*'s box as they marched out in their finery, colored plumes nodding from helmets, the sun flashing on polished armor, blades and spearpoints glittering.

Campania is the homeland of this dangerous sport. The funeral combats are enormously popular in Rome, but in Campania they form a veritable cult. These men were as fine and skillful as any I had ever seen, fearless and tireless as they fought in pairs, matching a man from one style with another of contrasting weapons: large shield against small shield; sword and shield against net and trident; spear against sword; curved sword against straight; even a man who fought with a sword in each hand against a heavily armored man with a small shield and a spear. Two teams of horsemen pelted one another with javelins.

Hermes and I, and the other men of my following, enjoyed all this immensely. Julia had chosen not to attend and forbade the women of our party to go. She said that, since women were forbidden by law to attend the *munera*, there was no reason why they should go to the sham fights. Of course, women went to the fights anyway and nobody stopped them, but Julia was a great stickler for the proprieties during those years. (In more recent years, the First Citizen has reinstituted the adult-male-citizen-only rule for the *munera*. It has not improved his popularity. Half the fun was seeing how excited the women got.)

In the box with us that day was a man whose dress and beard were Greek, and everything about him reeked of wealth. He took a keen interest in the fights and seemed knowledgeable about the fighters, for he knew each man by name, his style, and the number of his victories. When the two-sword man and his opponent came out, he leaned toward me and said, "Praetor, which of these two do you fancy?"

I could not imagine how a man bearing two offensive weapons could defend himself properly. "I favor the spearman. He has good armor and a shield. He can attack and defend himself at the same time. The other man can only attack."

"That is the conventional interpretation, but there is nothing conventional about such a fight." He smiled in that superior Greek way. "I think that, should you bet on the two-sword man, you will leave this place richer than when you arrived."

"Who would take such a bet?"

The Greek looked around, then said, "Since no one else seems inclined, I will bet on the spearman myself. One thousand sesterces, five-to-one odds."

"Five-to-one in whose favor?" Hermes wanted to know.

"In the praetor's of course. If my man wins, he pays me a thousand. If his wins, I pay him five thousand."

"Why would you bet at five to one on a man you think will lose?" I asked him.

He smiled again. "I am a sportsman. I like long odds."

"Very well, then," I said, curious to see where this would lead. "Done."

We settled down to watch the match. The men saluted and then squared off under the sharp eye of a trainer. Other trainers armed with staves stood by, ready to separate the combatants should they get carried away and actually try to kill each other, a not uncommon occurrence among these spirited men.

The spearman wore a leather sleeve covered with metal plates on his weapon arm and high greaves strapped to both legs. His helmet had wide cheek plates with throat protectors. To defend his body he had a round, deeply convex shield. To supplement his spear he carried a straight, slender sword behind his shield. This was a type of fighter rarely seen in Rome but popular in the south.

By contrast, the other man was all but unprotected. He wore a light helmet and had studded leather guards on both forearms, and that was the extent of his protective gear. His swords were legionary type: twenty inches long, straight, broad and double-edged.

They looked to me for the signal, and at my nod the trainer shouted, "Begin!"

The two went at it immediately, with the two-sword man pressing in aggressively, forcing the other man back several steps and seeming, to me, to expose himself recklessly.

"A pair of double-edged *gladii*," said the Greek, "means about eighty inches of razor edge. That is a formidable thing to face."

I'd thought of that myself, but I was more interested to see how my man was going to defend himself from that spear, which had reach. This became quickly apparent. When the spearman thrust, my fighter used his left-hand sword to block while simultaneously aiming a thrust at the other's face. And so it went through several exchanges; each time the spearman attacked, the swordsman used one weapon to defend, immediately counterattacking with the other.

This was what I had not anticipated. A soldier uses his sword to block only as a desperate measure. Clanging sword against sword damages both weapons. Swords are expensive, and you want to keep yours in good condition for the rest of the battle. Thus, soldiers depend on their shields and armor for defense, reserving the sword for attack against an enemy's vulnerable areas. Swords are intended to cut flesh, not wood or metal.

But, I now saw, if you had two swords, and were paying for neither of them, you could afford to let them get notched, blocking and parrying your enemy's weapons. You'd get new swords for the next fight. Plus, you could keep your enemy guessing which sword was going to be used for what.

Both men fought with exceptional spirit and skill, and we were all jumping to our feet and shouting like boys attending their first *munera*. The spearman crouched behind his shield and tried to keep the other at a distance with short thrusts, first toward the face, then at the body and legs. The swordsman danced out of the way, sprang forward and back, and kept drawing the other's shield up and down by attacking from different directions. He hoped to tire his opponent's shield arm and create an opening that would let him attack the unprotected torso.

Finally, the spearman overextended on a thrust, and the left-hand sword came down, shearing away the iron point. Immediately, the man dropped the useless shaft and snatched the reserve sword from behind his shield. But in that instant the right-hand sword darted in over the shield and scored a cut on the man's shoulder.

Immediately the men with staves jumped in and separated the two fighters while we cheered and applauded. The loser's wound bled freely but it was only a superficial cut, the best sort of wound for a gladiator: a real crowd-pleaser that doesn't incapacitate the man.

"It seems that you won, Praetor," said the Greek. He reached into his robe and drew out a well-stuffed sack, which he handed to Hermes. "Sport doesn't get better than that. I am Diogenes, perfume importer and partner of Manius Silva. Please accept these gifts for your esteemed lady." He reached behind him and a slave placed a small wooden box in his hands. The Greek worked the latch and raised its lid. Within, nestled in fine wool felt, were perhaps twenty exquisite little glass vials filled with clear liquid, some colorless, others amber tinted. "These are a modest sampling of the perfumes I import. I hope she will find them pleasing."

I accepted the gift. "You are a generous man and a good loser, Diogenes."

He smiled again. "I am a Greek. We are good at losing."

He took his leave, and when he was gone Hermes said, "He arrived with his losses already counted out and bagged. Decius Caecilius, I believe you've just been bribed."

"No, I've just won five thousand sesterces. That Greek may think he's bribed me, but he's wrong."

"Bribed to do what?" Hermes wondered.

"Doubtless we'll know soon enough," I assured him.

That evening, Julia and the other women had a sniffing party. They made admiring sounds over the fine cedar box and the beautiful glass vials, and then they unstoppered them and began to dab scent on themselves, on each other, and on their slave girls. Each new perfume brought a babble of excitement. When all had been tried, the women gazed at the vials in wonder.

"Decius," Julia said, "these are some of the costliest scents in the world. This collection is worth far more than you won with your foolish bet."

"No bet is foolish if it wins," I told her. "Maybe it was you the Greek wanted to bribe."

"The vials are Babylonian glass, the very finest," Antonia reported. "Any time that Greek wants to bribe me, I'll be glad to accept."

"I'm not certain it's the Greek doing the bribing," I said.

"Manius Silva?" Julia said.

"He and Diogenes are partners," I said. "It would make sense if Silva wanted to bribe me, to send his foreign lackey and keep his own hands clean."

"I notice," Circe said, "that no one thinks the Greek is just a foolish gambler who is princely about gift giving."

When the laughter died down, Hermes enlightened her. "I've been asking around. He's not just Greek, he's from Crete. Everyone knows that the Cretans are born liars and connivers. They couldn't be truthful under torture."

"I've never liked them," Antonia said. She had good reason. Her father was known as Antonius Creticus. But the Creticus was not an honorific voted by the Senate. It was bestowed in derision by the populace when he was defeated by the Cretans. In my opinion, any Roman who could get himself whipped by Cretans deserved worse than a funny name.

"What else did you learn?" Julia asked Hermes.

"Just that he's recently back from a purchasing expedition. It seems each year he makes a circuit of the big markets: Alexandria, Antioch, Cyprus, Berytus, and so forth. He spends about half the year at this, then he returns and spends the balance of the year here in Baiae."

"And what did you learn about Silva?" I asked him. "Presumably you didn't just snoop around about the Greek." Hermes was my freedman and client. He also considered himself my protector. Like my family, he thought I was incompetent to protect myself, so he compulsively investigated anything he thought might be a threat to me, such as this Greek with his enigmatic bribe.

"Manius Silva is the son of a freedman. His wife comes from a highly placed local family, although rumor has it she became a prostitute after her father was ruined during Sulla's proscriptions."

"I knew that belly button was too big for a respectable woman," Circe said.

"What else?" I asked Hermes.

"Silva owns a big perfumery down by the shore on the edge of town. Besides the perfumes he buys, Diogenes also brings back a lot of ingredients and materials from his trips. The perfumery does a lot of mixing, blending, refining, and so forth."

"That must be the building we passed after we visited Neptune's temple two days ago," Julia said. "Remember the smell?"

Circe sighed. "Like all the flowers in the world, and musk and ambergris—"

"Musk and what?" I asked her.

"Ambergris," Julia told me. "It's a mysterious, waxy substance found floating in the sea. A naturalist at the museum in Alexandria told me that it is thought to be secreted in the stomachs of whales and vomited up when they are sick."

I was not sure I had heard her correctly. "You are telling me that perfumes are made with whale puke?"

"You'd be surprised at what goes into perfume," Antonia said. "The placentas of some animals, the anal glands of certain—"

"Tell me no more," I pleaded, shutting my eyes. "There are some things we men should never know!"

THE EVENING CAME FOR OUR DINNER with Norbanus and his gilded wife. Their home was not a town house in Baiae but rather a villa just off the road connecting Cumae and Baiae, and only about five miles from where we were staying. The connecting road was made brilliant with torches and lanterns and melodious with singers and musicians. Lest anyone get bored along the quarter mile to the house, men dressed as satyrs chased women dressed (or, rather, undressed) as nymphs through the copses by the road.

"Oh!" Antonia said, pointing to one especially impressive satyr, "I hope he catches a nymph! I'd like to see that in action."

Julia squinted toward the hairy, horned Dionysian. "Surely it's not real."

We had no chance to find out, as we arrived at the villa a few minutes later, the satyr having had no success in his pursuit of the fleet-footed nymphs.

Norbanus and Rutilia greeted us, the lady dressed this time in another Coan-cloth gown, this one not merely transparent but practically invisible. Their welcomes were effusive and rich with false humility. Slaves brought us garlands and the huge flower wreaths that were the custom of the district. Perfumed water was sprinkled on our hands and hair, and we were given large bowls of watered wine. To my astonishment, there were lumps of ice floating in the wine.

"Where do you get ice at this time of year?" I asked.

"It's brought down in winter from the mountains," Norbanus explained. "There are lakes up there that freeze, and the ice is sawn into blocks. These are packed in straw and carried down in wagons. We store the blocks in caves dug into the hillsides, packed with more straw. Stored this way, it melts very slowly and will last until the end of summer. Most of the larger villas here have ice caves."

"There is always some new decadence to be found in Campania," I said. "I may never recover from this stay."

Rutilia smiled. "Let us hope not. Rome could stand a little sophistication. Especially when this year is over." She meant that this was a censorship year, the one year in five when a pair of beady-eyed old senators whipped the public morals into shape. This year, one of them, Appius Claudius, made it his special mission to purge the Senate of unworthy members, taking special aim at men who had squandered their patrimonies and gone deeply into debt. He considered the chronic indebtedness of the governing class to be the greatest evil of the age. He cracked down on violators of the sumptuary laws; those who wore silk in public or more rings per finger than the law allowed, or who spent too much on weddings or funerals, and other threats to the Republic.

There has always been a faction among us who attribute the virtue and success of our ancestors to the great simplicity in which they lived. They think that we've been corrupted by things like soft beds and hot baths and Greek plays and decent food. If we'd just go back to living in huts, they say, sleeping on the ground, eating coarse barley and hard cheese, we could regain our ancestral virtue. These men are deeply insane. Our ancestors lived simply because they were poor. I, personally, do not want to be poor.

"Come meet our other guests," Rutilia said. "I believe you already know some of them."

And indeed we did. There were Publilius the jewel merchant and Mopsus the silk importer and a dyestuff tycoon and several others we'd met, plus an Alexandrian banker and a Greek shipbuilder who were new to us. Then I spotted Gaeto across the triclinium, conversing with Manius Silva. Rutilia followed my gaze.

"My apologies for having *him* here. He has—business dealings with a number of the more important people here. It doesn't do to snub him, much as one might wish to. I hope you don't mind."

"Not a bit," I assured her. "I've found him to be good company. But then, I've gotten on well with Gauls and pirates and senators, so I've no reason to fear the company of a slaver."

She smiled. "A broad-minded Roman. We meet so few of those."

"Just one of my husband's singular traits," Julia told her.

As guests of honor, we were placed at the main couch in the triclinium, one wall of which was open to a large, fountain-centered courtyard. Everyone had brought friends, so couches and tables had been set for them in this courtyard so that we were all, in effect, at the same banquet.

Above the courtyard wall to the southeast the graceful cone of Vesuvius rose in green-clad majesty. As we took our couches a great cloud of dark-gray smoke shot from its crest. From the cloud a rain of something fell, trailing smoke in long streamers. I presumed these to be red-hot rocks.

"It it erupting?" Antonia asked, her face pale.

"Not at all," Norbanus assured her. "It does this every few months, done it for years. Hasn't erupted in living memory."

"That's what my husband said when we arrived," Julia said. "Is it what you people keep telling yourselves?"

"Perhaps it is better to live near a well-behaved volcano," Gaeto said, "than in the lethal political atmosphere of Rome." It was a valid point, but the guests laughed harder than the witticism deserved.

"Point well taken," I admitted. "But in Rome, all the lava and ash fall on the senatorial class. Under a volcano, everyone suffers. I've seen Aetna in eruption. The destruction was truly comprehensive."

"When was that, Praetor?" Rutilia asked.

"During the first consulship of Pompey and Crassus. I was sent to help the grain quaestor, a cousin of mine. We heard about the eruption and went to see."

"That was brave," Circe said.

"Not at all. We watched from the sea, in a fast trireme. Even then, some big rocks landed near us. They were glowing red and smoking, and when they hit the water they exploded in a huge cloud of steam. The noise was quite indescribable."

This led to a discussion of whether volcanoes were really the fires from Vulcan's forge or some sort of natural phenomenon, like storms and floods. I was of the latter opinion, because Vulcan is reputed to be the greatest of smiths and I doubt he would let his fires get out of control.

The food was, as might be expected, superb, but I will not waste words on a description of every extravagant dish, even if I could remember them all. Because the most memorable thing about that dinner was what happened just as it was ending.

It was several hours past sunset. The slaves were bringing out silver trays of fruits and nuts, the usual final course of every dinner, whether a modest meal at home or a splendid public banquet. In keeping with the place and company, these were not simple items, fresh from the tree and vine, but elaborately preserved, honeyed, salted, or otherwise enhanced. Even though more food was the last thing I needed, I gave them a try.

We were complimenting our hosts on their splendid layout when we were distracted by the sound of pounding hoofs.

"That beast is being ridden hard," Silva commented.

"Someone with an urgent message," I said with a sense of dread, knowing that this sojourn in southern Campania had been entirely too pleasant. Knowing that this message had to be for me and that it wouldn't be good, I hoped that it wasn't word from Rome that civil war had broken out.

But when the man came into the courtyard I recognized him as one of the messengers belonging to Hortalus's villa.

"Oh, I hope there hasn't been a fire," Julia said.

"Praetor," the messenger said, "you must come at once to the Villa Hortensia. There has been a murder."

This set up a babble all over the courtyard. Murder was a common thing in Rome, but in these easy environs it was a great rarity.

"Murder? Who?" I demanded.

"Gorgo, daughter of Diocles the priest."

At this there was uproar and shouts of outrage. The murder of a slave would have caused comment. That of any freed or freeborn person would have been cause for excitement. The murder of the beautiful young daughter of a prominent man was sure to cause a sensation. I sensed that things could get quickly out of hand, so I took immediate action.

"I must return to the villa at once," I said. "This thing has occurred at my residence. Norbanus, Silva, as *duumviri*, you should come with me."

"Certainly," said Norbanus. "Litters will be too slow. Everyone take horses from my stable." He began to bark orders to his stable master.

"Excellent," I said. "All here who are magistrates come with us."

Silva turned to the messenger. "How did this happen?"

I held up a hand. "Let's have no secondhand information. It just leads to rumor and confusion. We will go view the body and question any witnesses there may be. Until we have done so and prepared a report for the municipal authorities, I abjure all here to refrain from idle speculation and from spreading tales that at this moment must be baseless."

"Very wise, Praetor," Norbanus said. "I, for one, fully support your actions."

"That poor girl!" Julia said. "What could have happened?"

"I don't know yet," I told her. "But I intend to find out."

As was my usual practice in such situations, I was watching those present. Everywhere I saw shock, outrage, at least a thrilled titillation. No help there. Gaeto's swarthy face had gone ashen. The slaver came to me and spoke in a low, urgent voice.

"Praetor, I wish to come with you."

"Gaeto, you are not a magistrate. You are not even a citizen."

"Nonetheless, I would esteem it a great favor if you would allow me to accompany you. I would be in your debt. In this district, that is not a small thing."

I was pretty sure what he was thinking, and I could not help but sympathize. "Very well, but do keep to the side and do not interrupt while we transact official business."

He bowed. "I am most grateful."

There were some odd looks when he rode out with us, but nobody said anything. The night was fine, but the cloud still rose from Vesuvius, and now its underside was stained a lurid orange. If this was not a true eruption, I hoped never to see one.

It was nearing dawn by the time we returned to the villa. Julia and the other women were following by litter. I had sent Hermes and some of the younger men of my party ahead on the fastest horses, to secure the murder scene and separate witnesses. These were precautionary measures I had devised in my career of investigating crimes. Much can be learned at a crime site, as long as it remains in the condition it enjoyed while the crime was being committed. I had little hope of this being the case when I arrived on the scene, but it was worth a try.

How futile had been my wish became clear as we entered the villa grounds. We rode straight to the precincts of Apollo's temple, and there I found a great crowd gathered. Most were slaves and freedmen of the villa, many of them bearing torches. The cluster was densest a little to one side of the temple, by the olive grove.

We dismounted outside the grove and I called for the steward. The man appeared, looking harried and drawn. "Praetor Metellus! This is a terrible thing! Nothing like this has ever—"

"Annius," I said, "I want you to clear this rabble out of here and back to their quarters. They are not helping and they could be doing a great deal of harm. Is there anything resembling a witness around here?"

"Sir, I have found nobody who—"

"Then get these people away from here."

"At once, Praetor!" He clapped his hands, waved his staff, and began to herd everyone back up to the main house. Everyone, that is, except the temple staff. I saw the girls who had been assisting Gorgo the day we arrived, along with some men who had the look of sweepers and haulers, groundsmen and such. I approached the girls, who were weeping copiously.

"What has happened here?" I demanded.

"Sir," began one, "the god must be angry with us! We were awakened by—"

"What is your name, child?"

She snuffled loudly. "Leto, sir." She was a honey-haired beauty, locally born from the sound of her voice, a bit older than the other two.

"Then calm yourself, Leto. I am not angry with you and I doubt Apollo is, either. Are you slave or free?"

Either my voice or my assurances seemed to calm her. "I am a slave, sir. We all are. Slaves of the temple." She indicated the other two girls. "These are Charmian and Gaia." The girls bowed. Charmian had a look more bold than demure. She had dark hair and classically Greek features. Gaia, despite her name, was clearly a German, strong and big boned.

"Praetor," said Charmian, "you and Apollo may not be displeased with us, but the master is sure to be. We are—were—his daughter's attendants, and she was murdered while we slept. He may flog us or sell us or put us to death."

"Then I will speak to the priest. He will do nothing to you, so long as you tell me exactly what happened. Withold nothing and add nothing to your account, do you understand?"

They nodded. "Yes, sir."

"Then tell me what you know." By this time the *duumviri* and other dignitaries had gathered around. Gaeto, true to his word, stood to one side.

"We were awakened—" Leto began.

"No, start with when you last saw your mistress alive."

She took a deep breath. "We had just finished the sundown service. We put away the sacred implements and extinguished the fire. Our mistress told us to go to bed, that she was going to the spring to bathe and would join us later."

"Did she usually bathe in the evenings?" I asked her.

She frowned, thinking. "Not often but sometimes. Especially when the weather has been hot."

"Where was Diocles, the priest?"

"Yesterday he went to Cumae for a yearly ceremony at the sibyl's enclosure. We did not expect him until tomorrow or the day after. He has been sent for."

"So you went to bed. What then?"

"A scream awakened us. It was horrible! At first, I didn't even think it was a human sound. It woke the whole household. It was then we realized that the mistress wasn't there. We searched the house and temple, and the groundsmen searched the fields and orchards. Astyanax found her."

"Which of you is Astyanax?" I demanded.

A young man in a dark tunic came forward. "I am, sir. I tend the olive grove. That is where I searched." He was visibly shaken, almost trembling, his voice weak. Slaves are always uneasy when there has been a murder in the house, and with good reason. If the victim is discovered to have been killed by one of them, every slave in the household is crucified.

"Let's go view the body," I said. With the slave named Astyanax in the lead, we entered Apollo's sacred grove. There we found Hermes. Marcus and a couple of my other young men stood by with torches. Hermes was crouched by a still, white form and he straightened at our approach.

"We got here too late," he reported. "The whole household of the temple and most of the villa's were down here gawking. We ran them out of the grove, but it looks as if people have been racing chariots here."

Indeed, the ground was heavily trampled and fouled with sooty oil dripped from torches. Whatever evidence I might have found there was assuredly lost.

"Well," I said, "let's have a look at her."

The body was covered with a white cloak and Hermes drew it back. Gorgo was still beautiful, but she had the pathetic look the dead always seem to have. She wore only jewelry: a fine Egyptian necklace, golden bracelets on her wrists, fine serpent armlets around her upper arms. She was stretched out with her legs together, her hands folded just below her breasts.

"Surely she wasn't found this way?" I said.

"The girls straightened her out and covered her," Hermes said. "They were about to carry her inside the temple when I stopped them."

I beckoned and the girls came forward. "Was she found on this spot?"

"Yes," Leto said. "We couldn't bear to leave her like—"

"It speaks well of your devotion that you were willing to touch her before the rites of purification were performed. But I need to know what she looked like when she was found."

"She was sort of twisted up on the ground," Leto said.

"I will show you," said Charmian. She dropped to the ground and twisted her body, limbs scattered in a haphazard posture as if death came in mid-struggle. "Like this." She stood and brushed herself off.

"Marcus," I said, "lower your torch beside her head. Be careful not to singe her hair." I bent close and examined her neck. There was a ligature mark, not as deep and livid as many I'd seen, but clear indication that she'd been throttled. Her eyes were not swollen and red as so often in strangulations, but her lips were bluish.

"Did you arrange her face as well as her body?" I asked the girls.

"We closed her eyes and shut her mouth," Leto said in a tiny voice. "It was just too ghastly."

From somewhere I heard the sound of running water. I straightened and followed the sound. About twenty paces away a spring bubbled from an abrupt outcropping of rock. Here an artificial pool had been excavated and lined with marble, watched over by a pair of protective herms. Light steam rose from the water, along with the faintest whiff of sulfur. I stooped and dipped my fingers into the water, which was warm. It was an offshoot of the hot springs that had made Baiae such a popular resort. Next to the pool was a small, white heap: a woman's dress, neatly folded.

"Is this where she came to bathe?" I asked.

"Yes," Leto answered.

"Did you touch these clothes?"

"No, Praetor. Well, her cloak lay beside the dress. We used it to cover her."

"Was it folded?"

"Yes, sir."

I could see the local dignitaries and even some of my own party were mystified by my questions. They probably would have hauled all the slaves down to the local lockup and questioned them under torture. Well, I had my own methods.

Then I saw a small cedar box on the marble flags at the edge of the pool. It was open, its contents a bronze scraper, a sponge, and a small flask. I picked up the flask and unstoppered it. It was scented bathing oil. I had just replaced the flask when a tormented wail came from the edge of the grove.

"Uh-oh," Hermes said. "Sounds like Papa's back."

"Gorgo!" the old man screeched. "Where is my daughter?" Then he broke into deep sobs.

"Well," I said, straightening beside the pool, "we might as well go talk to him." We found the old priest weeping beside his daughter's body. "Diocles, please accept my condolences. We are conducting an investigation and I am certain that we shall soon—"

Diocles wasn't having any of it. He looked up, his expression of grief replaced by one of fury. "Investigation? Why in the name of all the gods is an investigation necessary?"

"Diocles, I—"

He shut me off again, pointing a trembling finger at Gaeto. "We all know what happened here! That slaver's boy has been trying to force himself on my daughter for months! He tried again this night, and she fought him off and he killed her! I want him on the cross for this!"

"Diocles," said Manius Silva, "let's not jump to conclusions. Let us and the praetor do our duty. Gorgo may have surprised a runaway slave hiding in the grove and he slew her to prevent her raising a cry. There are still bandits in the hills; there are robbers."

"Would robbers and bandits have left her jewels?" Diocles demanded scornfully. "It was Gelon! This is what happens when we allow slavers—"

"Enough, Diocles!" Norbanus said. "We share your grief, but this is an official matter now."

"We'll know soon enough," I said. "Hermes?"

"Praetor?"

"Go rouse my lictors. Get them mounted, with their full regalia. Then you and Marcus take fresh horses and ride with the lictors and arrest Gelon, under my authority. Bring him back here."

"Praetor!" Gaeto cried. "This is not just. You have no cause to do—"

I took him aside and said quietly, "I have plenty of cause, and justice has nothing to do with it. I'm arresting the boy for his own protection. Those people back at Norbanus's house have spread word of this already. Everyone in the district will think Gelon is the murderer because he's a slaver's son and a foreigner, and he lives and acts like a visiting prince. There may be a mob assembling at your house right now. If my men can get there in time, I'll keep him safe here, at the villa. You must not resist me in this."

He nodded. "Of course, you are right. I will find the best lawyer in Campania."

"With luck he may not need one, but if I were you, I'd look for one now."

Something occurred to me. "Annius!" I shouted.

The steward scurried over. "Praetor?"

"Send me the villa's horse master. Not the stable master but the riding master."

"At once, Praetor." He did not bother to express astonishment at this request. Things were happening too fast for poor Annius.

"As for you, Gaeto," I went on, "I think you should lie low. At the very least, people are going to be hissing and throwing things at you. Keep your boy's Numidian escort reined in. If one of them so much as points a javelin at a citizen, I'll have the lot of them on the cross. Do you understand?"

He bowed. "It shall be as you say, Praetor. And, sir, whatever you can do—"

"Yes, yes, I'll do what I can for the boy. For what it's worth, I doubt that he did this, but my opinion isn't what counts."

I went back to the gathering by the grove. "Listen to me, everyone! General opinion seems to be that Gelon, son of Gaeto the Numidian, is the culprit here. That being the case, I am taking control of this matter as *praetor peregrinus*. I will hold the suspect under arrest while a trial is scheduled and his defense is prepared."

"No need for that," Norbanus said. "We have a perfectly good municipal lockup for felons."

"I don't want to throw him into some flea-ridden pit with runaway slaves and bandits. He'll stay here. As for the rest of you—" I gazed around at the assembled notables "—I want you to return to your homes and duties. I am holding you responsible for the behavior of your fellow citizens. I want no mobs, no rioting, no rabble-rousers talking up wars two generations past. If there is disorder, I will not hesitate to call in soldiers to reestablish order. Am I understood?"

"Praetor," Silva protested, "this is not Gaul or Sicily. We have a peaceful, well-ordered society. All shall be according to Roman law."

"See to it," I said. I knew it is always best to assert one's authority at once, especially since my only authority here was that a foreigner was suspect. Still, I had expected more protest from these men. Clearly, none of them wanted any part of this case. That would bear thinking about.

4

IN THE GRAY DAWN I TRUDGED BACK toward the villa. Halfway there I was met by the horse master. He was a tall man, a Spaniard by the look of him, who walked with a pronounced limp. I read the marks of the cavalry on him.

"The praetor sent for me?"

"Yes. You've ridden with the *alae*, haven't you?"

He looked pleased. "Fifth *cohors equitata*, attached to the Fourth Legion in the Sertorian War, first under General Metellus, then under General Pompey. I am Regilius."

"Well, Regilius, General Metellus was my uncle. General Pompey, I am happy to say, is no relation at all."

He grinned. "Wasn't much of a general, either, at least not in that war. At least your uncle fought Sertorius. Pompey bribed the traitor's friends to kill him."

"Very true. Regilius, I have a task for you. It is almost light. I want you to go all around the sacred olive grove and look for hoofprints. If anyone rode there last night, I want to know how many there were and what they were riding."

He grinned again. "Haven't done any scouting or tracking in a good many years, but I haven't forgot how. If there's horse sign out there, you'll know about it within the hour." He threw me a sloppy salute and whirled on his heel, shouting for his grooms. It was good to have someone around who knew his business.

Back at the villa I sat on a terrace and called for some breakfast. Trays of hot bread, sliced fruit, and pots of herbed oil and honey all appeared with magical swiftness, accompanied by heated, heavily watered, and slightly sour wine. This last was a wake-up drink much favored by Hortalus and others of his generation. Ordinarily I did not care for it, but just now it was what I needed. As I ate and pondered, I saw a line of litters coming down the road toward the villa: Julia and the other women, finally making it back from Norbanus's house.

The bearers brought the lead litter onto the terrace and set it down. Moments later Julia emerged. From within came a faint sound of snoring.

"Silly cows," she said, seating herself at the little table while I poured her a cup. "They slept the whole way back. Not even a murder can keep them awake." She took a sip and made a face. "This stuff is awful. Well, tell me."

So I filled her in on the night's doings. She followed me with great concentration. Julia's mind was as fine as any lawyer's, despite her overindulgence in Greek philosophy.

"All this evidence and you still don't think it's Gelon?" she said when I finished.

"Why do you think it was?" I asked her.

She bit into a sliver of melon. "A wellborn lady takes at least one slave girl with her when she goes to bathe. Gorgo dismissed her girls to their beds. Then she put on her best jewelry. A woman doesn't go out to bathe alone, in her best jewels, unless she is meeting a lover. We saw how infatuated she was with the boy, and he was clearly besotted with her."

"Lovers don't kill each other," I said.

"Yes, they do. More often than you'd think."

"But why?"

She shrugged. "You'll have to question him. But don't expect it to be a good reason, or one that would make sense to us. People in love are not sane."

"Profoundly true."

At this moment the horse master walked up to us and saluted again. "One rider, Praetor, on a small mare, Roman shod. It was hitched to a tree for no more than an hour."

"Would a Numidian ride a shod horse?" I asked him.

"We're talking about the slaver's boy, right? If I had beauties like his, I'd never ride anything else. No, Numidians don't ride shod animals and they don't ride mares, even unshod. Unless—"

"Unless what?" Julia demanded.

"Unless they don't want to be recognized as what they are. If I was a Numidian and I didn't want to be noticed around here, I'd put on some Roman clothes and ride a mare. A shod one."

"Thank you, Regilius."

"I'll keep my eyes open, Praetor," he said. "I'm pretty good at this. If I run across that mare's prints anywhere, I'll know them."

"That would be very helpful."

He grinned again. "This is like being in the *cohors equitata* again, chasing after the Lusitani in the hills."

"See that Norbanus's horses are returned to him."

"Already done, Praetor."

When he was gone I said to Julia, "I don't think it makes any sense. She might have angered the boy by obeying her father, telling him not to see her again, but if you are right, she was far from wanting to break it off."

"He may have come to confront her over another lover. It needn't have been anything serious. A jealous lover can see betrayal where there is none. Pass me the honey."

51

I picked up the pot. "It seems a little extreme——" She grabbed my wrist.

"What have you been up to? Have you been in my perfume box?"

It was as if she were speaking another language entirely. "Whatever are you talking about?"

"I can smell it on you. Have you been fondling another woman? It's on your hands."

"Just a dead one." I sniffed my fingers. Sure enough, they smelled faintly of perfume. Then I remembered. "Oh, it was Gorgo's bath kit. I took out a flask and unstoppered it. It was just scented oil."

She looked at me in exasperation, a familiar thing. "Did you think that it was just common oil steeped with rose petals? This is the scent called Zoroaster's Rapture. It is an incredibly costly perfume. It comes out of Persia in tiny amounts and nobody knows how it is made."

"Well, this is educational. How would a priest's daughter have come by such a scent?"

"At a guess, it was a gift, probably from Gelon."

"Is this one of the perfumes I was bribed with?"

"It was one of them. So we know the local source for it."

"Yes, I'll have to have a talk with Silva and his partner, Diogenes. See if they sold any to Gelon."

"And if they didn't?"

"Then we have a problem. Of course, they may lie about it. People often lie to investigators. It's almost reflexive."

"People are usually guilty of something, even if it's not what you are asking about. It makes them shifty and evasive."

"Too true. Well, I've gotten pretty good at ferreting out the truth. I'll take them one at a time and——"

"You'll do no such thing," Julia said firmly. "You are a praetor now, not an investigator for one of your high-placed relatives. Send Hermes. You've trained him and he's very expert. Besides, he's younger."

"I'm not exactly doddering," I protested, but I knew she was right. Not that I was too old for it, but it would look bad for me to go personally to question suspects and witnesses. It would lower my dignity in the community, and I couldn't afford that.

"You haven't slept," she said unnecessarily. "What you need is a nap."

"Oh, a night or two without sleep shouldn't trouble a Roman magistrate. Why, in Gaul—"

"Go to bed!" she commanded.

"All right."

A FEW HOURS REST DID ME A WORLD OF good. I awoke in midafternoon, strode out into the courtyard, and splashed water on my face. A slave was there instantly with a towel.

"Has Hermes brought in the Numidian yet?" I asked the girl.

"They arrived not an hour ago, Praetor," she said chirpily. Like most of the slaves in this house, she seemed happy and content. I suppose if all you have to do is carry a towel around waiting for someone to splash water on his face, you certainly can't complain of overwork.

"Where?"

"The orchard-viewing wing, Praetor."

Old Hortalus was as dotty about his prize trees as he was about his fish. He watered some of his prize olive and apple trees with undiluted wine with his own hands, not trusting a slave to do it. It should come as no surprise that he built a special wing onto his villa to look at them.

There was a terrace outside the large dining room. Here Hortalus and his friends could eat and drink at their ease while they admired his trees. On the terrace my lictors lounged, keeping a wary eye on a sullen little group of Numidian bodyguards.

"Any trouble out of them?" I asked the chief lictor.

"No, Praetor. They wanted to resist, but the young man ordered them to lay down their arms."

I went inside. Gelon sat, dejected to the point of distraction, watched over by Hermes and several others of my following, all of them armed. The boy sprang to his feet and was about to say something, but Hermes shoved him back down.

"I shall speak to you presently," I told him. "Hermes, come outside with me."

We went out onto the terrace. "Where was he?"

"Not at his father's estate. He was in the family's town house in Baiae. Seemed to be still in bed when we arrived."

"What was the mood in the town?" I asked.

"Word was just beginning to spread when we got there, about two hours after daybreak. Things were getting ugly among the forum idlers and amateur orators. Someone was haranguing the crowd to go burn Gaeto's house down and lynch the boy, but it was still too early to whip up any real mob rage."

"Afternoon and evening are the times for mob violence," I said, having long experience with the phenomenon.

"Anyway, most of the indignation was from the Greek community. The Romans and others didn't seem all that enraged. If it had been a priest of Jupiter involved, it might be different."

"That's a relief. The best thing about a town like Baiae is there is no huge crowd of idlers with nothing to do except cause trouble. There's not much poverty or popular discontent. Perhaps we can handle this without too much unpleasantness. Now, we are going in there to talk to Gelon. After that, I have some tasks for you."

"Snooping?" he asked with a smile.

"Don't get ahead of yourself. If the boy comes right out and confesses, there will be nothing to investigate. But first, what is your impression? When you told him he was under arrest for killing Gorgo, how did he act?"

"At first he seemed numb, as if he were half-asleep when we called on him. Then he was like a bull hit between the eyes by the flamen's hammer. Too shocked at learning the girl was dead to put up much resistance when the lictors laid hands on him. At least, that was the impression he gave. Whether it was false—" he shrugged "—I'd have a better idea if he was a Roman. With foreigners it's different."

I knew what he meant. People of different nations express the same thing in different ways. Gauls are happy in battle and hilarious at funerals. Egyptians shake their heads to say yes and nod to say no. Persians are solemn when making love, and Greeks weep at the death of their enemy. How could we know if a Numidian was really grief stricken or enraged?

We went back inside. "Gelon," I began, "I don't suppose I need to tell you in what an incredible heap of trouble you've landed?"

Again he jumped to his feet and this time Hermes didn't restrain him. "Praetor! You cannot believe that I would kill a woman I loved!"

"Actually, I can believe it quite easily, and that is giving you all the benefit of doubt. Others less favorably inclined than I are deeply convinced of your guilt. If you are truly innocent, you had better be able to prove it. I can promise you a fair, impartial trial, a Roman trial. Even now, your father is combing the district for the best lawyer to be found. There are some good ones living here."

"What advocate of repute would defend a slaver's son?" he asked bitterly.

"That would depend on how much money the slaver has. It is my impression that your father is not yet ready to apply for the dole. He'll get you a good one and you'll be well defended. It would help if you could provide evidence in your favor." Actually, it was forbidden for Roman lawyers to accept fees. It was quite all right, however, for them to accept *presents*. Hortalus had acquired his opulent villas and other properties through a long and successful career at the bar. He never accepted a fee, but few people had friends as grateful and generous as Quintus Hortensius Hortalus.

"I swear I am innocent! By Tanit and Apollo, by Jupiter—"

I held up a hand for silence. "You'll do plenty of swearing and invoking at your trial, for whatever good it will do you. What I need to know, right now, is where you were last night."

"Why, I was at home."

I sighed. "I was afraid you were going to say that. You're quite sure you were not out carousing with your cronies? Sacrificing at the Temple of Pluto, perhaps? At least whoring in one of the more reputable lupanars?"

"I was at home," he said stubbornly.

"You will need witnesses to that effect. And they had better be free. I don't know about Numidia, but under Roman law, slaves can testify in court only under torture, and then nobody believes them anyway."

"My guards are free men, but they were off duty for the evening, in a tavern somewhere." He thought about it. "Jocasta was there."

"Jocasta? Your— Would the term be stepmother?" Now that I thought of it, she hadn't been at Norbanus's banquet.

"There is a Numidian word for the relationship between a son and a junior wife. I don't think it translates."

"Probably not. Can she testify that you were at home all night?"

"I—I think so."

The boy's ordinarily handsome face was contorted with his conflicting emotions: grief, rage, bewilderment, fear. I tried to discern guilt among them but I could not. This, as Hermes had indicated, meant little.

"I will speak to her. Anyone else?"

He shook his head. "No. Father was away, as you know. The rest of our family are in Numidia. The guards are men of our tribe. The rest of the household are slaves."

"And you had no assignation with Gorgo last night?"

"Assignation? What do you mean?"

I described the circumstances under which we had found the unfortunate girl. Now a new anguish came over his face: on top of everything else, betrayal.

"If she didn't go out to meet you," I said, "then who?"

"It—it can't be! She would not have—"

"For your sake," I told him, "you had better hope she would. Whoever was waiting for her in the olive grove, she went to meet him more than willingly." I let that sink in for a minute, softening him, then, "Young men courting women send them gifts. What did you send her?"

He stammered for a moment. "Gifts? Just small things: a silk scarf, a book of poetry by Catullus, a ring set with a carnelian."

"Small things," I said, "small but costly. The sort of things she could hide from her father. How did you get them to her?"

"We met in public places on festival days—there was never a secret meeting. Other times, I would meet one of her girls in the market and send things that way."

"Which girl was the go-between?" I asked, making a bet with myself.

"The Greek girl."

I'd won my bet. It was bold-eyed Charmian. "Nothing else? No costly perfumes, for instance?"

"Perfume? No, I thought of it, but the Greek girl warned me not to. She said the old priest might notice such a thing, since Gorgo used only rose water."

"I see." I arranged my toga in an imposing manner and gave him a brimming measure of Roman gravitas. "Gelon, I am giving you an unusual measure of attention because I think this is a very unusual case. Hear me now: I am giving you freedom of this villa, although you will be watched at all times. If you try to run, that will be construed as an admission of guilt. You will be tried in public, prosecuted by one advocate, defended by another, and your guilt or innocence decided by a jury. As praetor, I merely preside over the court and pronounce sentence should the jury return a verdict of guilty."

"But I did not—"

"Should the verdict be guilty," I went on, "there will be calls for your crucifixion. Roman citizens may not be crucified, but slaves and foreigners may. I can promise you only this: If you are found guilty, I will not condemn you to the cross nor to the arena nor any other degrading death. A quick beheading will suffice. Do you understand?"

He swallowed hard. "Yes. Thank you, Praetor."

"Very well, then. I will go now and try to set this district in order. Rome is a riotous city, but we don't like to see disorder in the municipalities and provinces."

I left him in a miserable heap and went outside. Julia was waiting.

"I thought you were supposed to be a praetor," she said. "Why are you behaving like a defense attorney?"

"I find it difficult to believe that boy murdered the girl."

"It's not your job. You are to preside over the trial."

"But I always like to know when I'm being lied to," I pointed out. "The more I investigate, the better I am able to determine that."

"You just like to snoop. So do I. I was listening while you questioned the boy. Did you notice that he said 'you cannot believe I would kill *a* woman I loved,' not *the* woman."

"The distinction did not escape me. It needn't mean too much. His father has at least two wives we know of. The boy may not consider his affections to be exclusive to any one woman."

"That is an attitude he shares with the entire male species. What do you plan to do now?"

"Would you like to pay a visit to the Temple of Apollo?"

"Not to sacrifice, surely?"

"No. I want to search the girl's quarters before anyone thinks to hide evidence."

She smiled. "That is exactly what I would like to do."

So, arm in arm, we walked down the pleasant garden paths to the beautiful little temple. When we arrived, the temple slaves were draping it in dark wreaths to signify mourning. The remains of a sizable fire smoldered on the altar, small tongues of flame leaping from time to time amid the crackling of resinous wood. It formed a miniature of smoldering Vesuvius, visible in the distance behind the temple.

We climbed the steps and a slave rushed into the temple. Moments later Diocles the priest emerged. He looked drawn but dignified. "Praetor, my lady, welcome to Apollo's temple."

"We've come to pay our respects, Diocles," I told him.

He bowed. "I am honored. My daughter is honored."

So we tossed a handful of incense on the fire and passed within. Gorgo lay on a simple couch, covered with a thin shroud, at the base of the statue of Apollo. At her feet two of her slave girls, red eyed and still weeping, sat on the marble floor, their garments torn in token of mourning. They were fair-haired Leto and German Gaia.

"Her pyre is being prepared before the family tomb," the priest said. "Her ashes will be interred with those of her ancestors."

"We shall attend, of course," Julia said.

"And now, Diocles," I said, "I would like a look at Gorgo's quarters."

His bowed head snapped up. "What?"

I placed a hand on his shoulder. "Just a little formality, in preparation for the trial. I know you would prefer that I do this personally, rather than some appointed *iudex*."

"I— yes, of course, Praetor. I appreciate your, ah, delicacy in this matter."

We followed him through a door behind the statue of Apollo and into a fine garden, beyond which lay a modest house built in the austere Greek fashion. Inside, the priest led us to a room opening off the courtyard. It was no more than a cubicle, with a narrow bed, a clothes chest, a chair, and a small vanity table. While Julia examined the vanity, I felt the thin pallet. I looked over the sill of the small window but found no loose bricks or any other sort of hiding place.

I would have liked to ask Diocles to step outside, but I had no decent way to do so. He watched without expression as Julia opened the lid of the chest and went through its contents. She looked at me and shook her head.

"Is all satisfactory?" the priest said formally.

"Yes," I told him. "Now, where do her slave girls sleep?"

He seemed astonished. "Why, in the next room. Why do you ask?"

"All part of the investigation. I would like to see it."

"Very well."

We went into another small room, this one crowded with three sleeping pallets and a single large clothes chest. We repeated the earlier search.

"Where is Charmian?" I asked as I checked the pallets.

"That one is being disciplined," Diocles said.

I felt a stab of guilt. I should have spoken to him sooner. "Last night, I told the girls you would not punish them so long as they told me exactly what happened. It is not my practice to tell a man how to discipline his own household, but this is a criminal investigation."

"No, Praetor, it is not about— what happened last night. It concerned another matter entirely."

"I see. Well, I think we are done here. Diocles, I apologize and I thank you for your forbearance. This had to be done."

He inclined his head gracefully. "You need not apologize for performing your duty, Praetor, and, again, I thank you for your discretion."

We took our leave of him. On our way back to the villa, we compared notes.

"What did you find?" I asked.

Julia took out a small scroll tied with ribbon. "Just this. It was in the bottom of the slave girls' chest, tucked into an old purse. I stuck it beneath my stola while you distracted the priest. You?"

"There was a hard lump in Gorgo's pallet. I'll send Hermes to find out what it is this evening. He's an accomplished burglar, and the household will all be at the funeral."

"You noticed the altar?" she said.

"Oh, yes. There was a big fire burning on it just an hour or two ago, and it's past midafternoon. Apollo's sacrifices are performed just at sunrise and just at sunset."

"Exactly. Afternoon sacrifices to Apollo occur only during an eclipse and I don't recall one today. So what was being burned with such haste?"

"I'll have Hermes go through the ashes. Maybe something will be left. Now, let's have a look at that scroll."

We sat on the parapet of one of the smaller fish pools. The fat inhabitants swam up in hopes of food and then, disappointed, resumed their endless circling around a statue of Neptune in the pool's center.

Julia untied the ribbon and unrolled the scroll. It was made of the finest Egyptian papyrus, the writing done with a reed pen using red ink of excellent quality. It was in Greek, the writing precise, arranged in short lines. I read a few verses aloud and glanced at Julia to see if her face had reddened, but she was too sophisticated for that.

"This," she commented, "is some of the most heated erotic verse since Sappho."

I frowned in fake puzzlement. "So it seems, but why would one want to lick a doe's hoof?"

"As you know perfectly well," she said, "in erotic verse, the doe's hoof is a traditional symbol for the female genitals. All these other symbols are similarly inclined. Rather too many of them for good taste, but the verse is excellent."

"Do you think it's original or a copy of some poet's work?"

"I don't recognize the poem, but the style resembles the Corinthian."

"It's addressed to one Chryseis," I said.

"Of course. It's traditional to give your lover a pseudonym in such poetry. Everyone knows that Catullus's Lesbia was really Clodia."

"It was in the slave girls' room," I pointed out. "Do you suppose it might have been meant for one of them? They're all attractive girls, and some local swain might be paying court to one of them."

"Don't be dense, dear. Don't you remember who Briseis was?"

"Oh. Right." In the *Iliad*, of course, Briseis was the captive girl seized from Achilles by Agamemnon, setting off the chain of events that ended with the funeral of Hector.

Chryseis was the daughter of Apollo's priest.

5

In the evening, with the cool offshore breeze making the flames of the new-lit torches flutter, we attended the funeral of Gorgo, daughter of Diocles. The family tomb was located beside the road to Baiae, about a mile from the temple. A large contingent of the local Greek community had turned out, along with all the usual notables.

It is not Greek custom (or Roman, for that matter) to give women elaborate funerals, especially if they are not married and mothers. Still, it was a simple, dignified ceremony and I found it more congenial than the elaborate sort. The quietly sobbing slaves were infinitely preferable to the wailings of hired professional mourners. Their grief seemed to be genuine.

Diocles gave the eulogy, speaking of Gorgo as a virtuous, blameless girl, one who had never caused gossip or given her father (the mother, apparently being long dead) any cause for displeasure, worthy to bear the name of the famous Spartan queen, and so on in this vein. It was a conventional oration, but most funeral eulogies are.

When the final words were pronounced, Diocles took a torch from an attendant and touched it to the pyre. This, too, was modest, merely enough wood to cremate the body decently, not an ostentatious construction of logs stacked twenty feet high. But the wood had been soaked in cedar oil, and the slaves threw frankincense onto the flames by the double handful from bags donated, along with the soaked wood, by Manius Silva.

When the ceremonies were over, I invited the attendees to partake of some refreshment. Earlier in the day I had had slaves from the villa set up tables near the tomb, beneath an awning in case of rain. There we served sweet cakes and honeyed wine, traditional Roman funeral fare at least since the obsequies of Scipio Africanus, more than 130 years before. (In Scipio's day, these sweets were esteemed great luxuries.)

"It's good to have the facilities of the villa," Julia said. "We've never before been able to afford this sort of liberality." She wore a dark stola, with her palla covering her head. Most of the ladies present were thus attired. Even the usually flamboyant Quadrilla, Jocasta, and Rutilia dressed somberly.

"I can't argue with that," I agreed. Being able to live and act like a grandee has its attractions, and I warned myself not to grow too fond of its seductions. Once accustomed to such a life, one begins to make excuses to prolong it. It becomes easy to overlook ethical lapses and to seek the favor of unworthy persons. It is, in short, deeply corrupting.

Of course, some men were not at all disturbed by the allure of corruption, as witness my benefactor, Quintus Hortensius Hortalus. He'd made a career of corruption and done very well out of it.

Mopsus, the silk importer, came forward to thank us for our generosity. "Praetor, I know this raises your credit with the populace, and it was already high. Tell me, has the slaver's son confessed yet?"

"He maintains his innocence firmly," I told him.

"Well, I guess we could expect that. I suppose there must be a trial."

"All will be done according to law," I assured him.

"Naturally, naturally. Still, the sooner the wretch is condemned and executed, the sooner the place will return to normal."

He was the first. One notable after another came up, took me by the hand, and informed me that a trial was scarcely necessary, the boy was guilty, why waste everybody's time?

"There seems to be a strange unanimity of opinion," I told Julia when the funeral guests were making their way back toward Baiae and the other towns.

"The slaver is a despised figure," she said. "It's natural that people would suspect the worst of his son."

"Yet there seems to be little real malice. It's as if—as if people just want it to be over."

"Why?" she asked. "It isn't causing all that much unrest; the tenor of life here hasn't altered a great deal."

"As you said earlier, most people are guilty of something; they all have something to hide. Maybe they are uneasy at the prospect of an investigation."

A shift in the wind brought us the smell of fragrant smoke, only faintly tinged with the smell of incinerating flesh. "I wonder why Silva donated all that expensive wood and incense. As far as I know, he's not related to the priest and they don't seem to be particularly close friends."

"Maybe for the same reason you laid on these funeral refreshments: It is traditional for office holders and those standing for high honors to give ostentatiously. He's a *duumvir* of Baiae, he's very rich, and he's competing with the others for public esteem. He may have done it as a *euergesia*."

She used the Greek word for the obligation laid upon the wealthy to provide public works and entertainment for the people. It is the same custom that drives Roman candidates to bankrupt themselves building temples, bridges, basilicas, and porticoes, giving lavish entertainments and banquets and *munera*, all to win the favor of the populace and, more important, to outdo all the other great men in so providing. In Greek communities, there is no greater honor than to be known as a *euergetes*.

"Maybe you are right," I said to Julia, "but I am beginning to suspect everybody now."

She gave my arm a squeeze. "Isn't that always the best policy?"

That evening I visited Gelon in the villa's palaestra. This gymnasium was as large as any such public facility in Rome, and a great deal more luxurious. The sand in the wrestling pit and on the running track had been imported from the Arabian desert, all the stonework was of the finest marble, the statuary were all portrait figures set up at Olympia to celebrate champion athletes of centuries past.

Here my lictors and the young men of my party exercised and practiced when I had no need of them. I had enjoined my crew very strictly that all were to be fit and any who grew too slack would be sent home. As a holder of imperium, I could at any moment receive orders from Rome to take command of an army, and they would be obliged to follow me to war.

When I arrived at the palaestra I found Gelon and his guards in a sand pit, under the watchful eyes of my lictors, engaged in spirited sparring with six-foot staffs, apparently a Numidian combat sport. Gauls and Spaniards and Judaeans are also fond of this weapon, but this Numidian play seemed more subtle than that practiced by the others. I enjoyed this exhibition for a few minutes, then beckoned my chief lictor.

"Praetor?" he said, jogging up to me.

"How has the prisoner comported himself?"

"Quite well. He frets at confinement, but there's plenty to amuse oneself with in this place. The stables are double guarded."

"Have you locked away all the practice swords and javelins? At this juncture I'm more concerned about suicide than escape."

"We have, but I think you needn't worry. It did him a world of good when you assured him he didn't face the cross or the beasts. No real man fears a quick beheading. He seems content to wait out events."

"Good, but keep a close watch on him anyway." I dismissed the man and walked over to the sand pit. Gelon saw me and lowered his staff. "Praetor. You've returned from the funeral?"

"Yes. It was a good service and she's on her way now with all the proper rites observed."

He lowered his eyes. "I am sorry that I could not attend. When I am out of this, I'll sacrifice at her tomb."

"Commendable, but don't buy any black ewes just yet. First, we have to get you acquitted and I've yet to see any way to do that. Have any significant facts occurred to you? A man in your situation usually receives a flood of exculpatory memories."

"Just that I did not kill Gorgo, that I was at home when it happened."

"I haven't spoken with Jocasta yet. I will call on her tomorrow, after court. Are you sure there is no one else to vouch for your whereabouts?"

He shrugged. "I am sorry. There is none."

I left him, feeling unsettled. For a man facing death, he was not terribly desperate to demonstrate his innocence. Perhaps, I thought, I was too hasty in ruling out crucifixion.

I rejoined Julia in the triclinium where a late supper had been laid out, just our own party attending, no guests for once. I lay on the couch with a sigh of relief and picked up a hard-boiled egg. A slave filled my cup and I sampled the superb vintage. I was getting too used to this.

"What a strange visit this has turned out to be," Circe said. "Murder, erupting volcanoes—what next?"

"It isn't erupting," said young Marcus. "I spoke with a local naturalist today. He calls this a 'venting.' He said every few years Vesuvius lets off a bit of smoke and ash, maybe emits a little lava, then it will go back to just smoking for several years."

"It makes me nervous," Circe said.

"Thank you, Decius Caecilius," said Antonia.

"For what?" I asked.

"For making Gelon our houseguest. Now that he is no longer connected with the priest's daughter, I'll have to work on him."

"I hear there are good armorers over in Pompeii," said Marcus. "You might want to get yourself a throat protector."

"You will leave that young man strictly alone," Julia ordered. "He is a suspect in a case the praetor is trying. He is a prisoner, not a guest."

Antonia shrugged. "Prisoners, hostages—what's the difference? Two years ago my brother had that Gallic prince Vercingetorix in the house. He was a prisoner, but do you think I let that stop me?"

"A barbarian prince, even an enemy prince," Circe said, "is a far cry from the son of a Numidian slaver."

"I'm always amazed at the ability you ladies have to draw distinctions," I said.

"This is your fault," said Julia. "You never should have brought him into this house. The local lockup would have been quite good enough for him, even if he is innocent. It might have taught him a little humility."

"Lectures on humility from a Caesar!" Antonia cried, laughing. "I like them arrogant, even the wicked ones."

Julia gave up and applied herself to dinner. It seemed that patrician propriety was not to be a feature of our household for the duration.

When dinner was done, Julia and I stayed behind in the triclinium, and I called for Hermes to report. He seemed uncommonly somber when he came in, not at all his usual mischievous self.

"The altar was clean swept," he reported, "and I couldn't find where they dumped the ashes, so I went straight to the house."

"You got in and out undetected, I trust?" I asked.

"Naturally."

"Pride in burglar skills is not becoming in a free man, Hermes," Julia chided him.

"Says the poem thief," I commented. "What have you found?"

"First, this." He tossed me a little bundle of something hard that gave beneath my fingers when I caught it. It was a small bag of purple silk. Whatever was inside, the bag itself was a minor extravagance. I released the drawstrings and withdrew the contents. Julia gasped and snatched it from my fingers.

It was a necklace formed of some twenty lozenges of gold, each the size of Julia's thumb, each set with an emerald as big as the nail of that digit and carved with the image of a deity.

"This is fabulous!" Julia exclaimed. "You've never given me anything this fine."

"I've never been that rich," I reminded her. "Still, we've seen ladies around here wearing jewelry as expensive. But if Gelon gave her that, Papa must be giving him a more generous allowance than my father gave me."

"There was more going on in that girl's life than keeping the temple tidy," Julia commented, unable to stop fondling the necklace. Just what I needed. Now she would want one like it.

"All right," I said to Hermes. "This bauble didn't put that wan look on your face. What else did you find?"

"As I was leaving I thought I was alone in the place. But I heard someone crying. It didn't sound like grief for the dead woman. I traced the sound and found a lockup next to the pen for sacrificial animals."

"I suppose you just had to look," Julia said.

"There's a little window in the door. It was dim inside, so it took a while for me to make anything out, but I saw that it was the slave girl Charmian. She had good reason to cry. She'd been severely beaten. From her neck to her heels she's striped like a zebra. And it wasn't done with rods or a *flagellum* either, it was laid on with a *flagrum*." He referred to the fearsome whip with multiple thongs studded with bone or bronze.

"Well," Julia said, "from your description she's rather a bold creature, and such women easily fall afoul of their masters. Besides, the priest had good reason to be displeased with her. He may hold her responsible for letting Gorgo stray out that night."

"But why just Charmian?" I asked. "Why not the other two, Leto and Gaia? Go on, Hermes."

"I called her name. After a while she looked up. Her face was so swollen and bruised she was barely recognizable. I asked her why she'd been punished so, but for a long time she couldn't talk at all. Finally she said, 'I'll talk to the praetor, no one else.' Then she lowered her head and I think she passed out. I couldn't linger."

This was the reason for his grimness. Hermes had been a slave and could sympathize with the unfortunate girl, even though he had given his own masters far more grief than they ever gave him.

"I have to do something about this," I said.

"What?" Julia demanded. "You have no right to interfere with a citizen disciplining his own slave. He can kill her if he likes and you have no say in the matter. That's the law."

"I know it is, but I don't like it."

"Anyway, he may have good reason to beat her." But she said it without conviction, for the sake of form. She knew perfectly well that the girl could hardly have earned so savage a beating.

But I had to wonder. Just what did that girl know that she would tell only me? Somehow, I had to find out.

THE NEXT DAY I HELD COURT IN BAIAE. The cases were all the same: some disgruntled businessman of the city bringing suit against a foreign competitor. The boredom induced by such cases is difficult to describe, but it works like the face of Medusa in turning a man to stone. I am afraid that I rendered judgments based on whether I found one plaintiff or defendant more congenial. Anyway, it served them right for wasting my time so.

About midday a slave came to my curule chair and handed me a message. Eager for anything to break the monotony of my day I unrolled it and read: *Please come to my house as soon as you dismiss the court.* It was signed *Jocasta.* I tucked it away with some satisfaction. I had intended to seek her out and she was relieving me of the trouble.

I rushed the court through the final cases and pronounced adjournment. There was some muttering at my haste, but I've had worse than mutters thrown at me in my day. Hermes came up to me. He had been away all day investigating.

"No luck finding the merchant who sold it," he said, referring to the fabulous necklace. "But it's Phrygian in origin."

"That's not much help," I said. "Keep looking. And don't assume that any merchant is telling the truth."

"Do you think I'm a beginner at this?"

"Go. I'm headed for the house of Gaeto to talk with his wife Jocasta. She may be the boy's only alibi."

"Don't assume she'll tell you the truth," he said, grinning.

"Get out of here."

I saw the messenger slave and beckoned him to me. "Take me to your mistress," I told him. Silently he turned and I followed him from the forum, bidding my entourage to meet me in the evening at the villa. They were mystified. Ordinarily, one as august as a praetor goes nowhere alone, without even his lictors. But I wanted to question the woman by myself, and witnesses are the same thing as spies.

The boy led me to a house of modest size, by the standards of Baiae. It lay on one of the broader streets, near the edge of town by the city wall. I placed a hand on my guide's shoulder. "Is this the house of Gaeto?" It seemed entirely too small and was nowhere near the slave market.

"This is my mistress's town house," he explained. "My master's house is on the bay, outside the city wall."

"I see." He would not be the first husband to indulge his wife in this lavish fashion. Nor the first to regret it, either. Wives with their own houses have been the subject of scabrous comedies since the days of Aristophanes.

We entered the courtyard, and moments later the woman appeared, this time wearing a dress no more extravagant than was common for the wealthy women of Baiae. Apparently, she reserved silk for special occasions.

"You honor my house, Praetor," she said. "And you must have hurried right over from court. You must be hungry."

"Famished," I agreed.

She led me to a table in the impluvium next to the pool with its fountain playing around a figure of a dancing faun. There a table had been laid out lavishly.

"This," I said, eyeing the superb viands, "could be construed by some to be a bribe."

"I won't tell anybody," she said. "Besides, it rates far below the standards of Baiae bribery."

"Senators and magistrates come cheaper in Rome," I told her, reclining on the couch. Instantly, a slave removed my sandals and another pair commenced washing my feet. Others filled my cup, arranged my cushions, and fanned me, all unnecessarily, but then that is what luxury is all about.

Jocasta took a couch opposite me, artfully allowing her peplos to gape slightly. Well, more than slightly. Clearly, the garment had been designed to gape and she had a good deal to display thus. Women have frequently practiced these wiles upon me, almost always with success.

"Try some of the honeyed pheasant breast," she suggested, serving me a plate of it with her own hands. I took it and tried a slice. It was superb, but I had by this time come to expect no less. I took a good swallow of the wine, which I recognized to my surprise as Gaulish. I had always thought that benighted province would never produce drinkable wine, but a few years before some vineyards there had begun producing a rather decent vintage, and this was far more than decent. I refer of course to our old, southern province of Gaul, where the people were respectably clad in togas, not to the trousers-wearing part.

"Gelon tells me," I began, "that he spent the night of the murder at his father's house and that you were there."

"Yes, I was there." She popped a ripe strawberry into her mouth.

"Why weren't you at the dinner given by Norbanus? Your husband was there."

"I don't like being snubbed by all those grand ladies. My husband enjoys flaunting his wealth and influence at such events, but I can do without them. The civic banquet where you were honored was quite another sort of thing."

"I see. Will you be able to testify that Gelon was in that house for the entire night?"

"Yes—that is, I believe he was."

"Your memory seems to be less than certain on this point," I noted.

"Gelon was in the house in the early evening, after his father had departed for the house of Norbanus. We had dinner together. Afterward, I retired to my bedroom. I never heard anyone leave during the night, and he was there the next morning, when your men came to arrest him."

I washed down a fig with the excellent wine. "Forgive me, Jocasta, but that is thin."

"Does it matter? I am just the slaver's wife and everyone will think I am covering up for the slaver's son."

"You would have to come up with a much better lie than that to rouse such suspicion."

"I fear it is the best I can do. My husband may forbid me to testify, anyway."

"I will speak to him on the matter. You requested my presence here," I reminded her. "Surely it wasn't just to tell me that you have no compelling reason to believe that Gelon killed the girl."

"No, I had a different but connected reason to ask you here."

"This sounds devious. Please continue."

"I believe you should be looking into the activities of the priest Diocles."

My cup hand paused halfway between table and mouth. "Why?" The cup resumed its progress.

She grew oblique. "Tell me, have Norbanus and Silva approached you, urging you to execute Gelon and be done with it?"

I was no slouch at obliquity myself. "And if they have?"

"Ask yourself why."

I had been asking myself exactly that, but I would have been foolish to reveal this to her. "Come to the point, Jocasta. What are the priest and the *duumviri* up to?"

"By now you've seen that Baiae and much of southern Campania are fat on the luxury trade. Landowners control things up in Rome, but down here the likes of Silva and Norbanus and all the rest are cocks of the dunghill. Silk, perfume, incense, dyestuffs, gems, gold, extraordinary slaves—if it is precious, expensive, rare, those men control it and they make millions from it. Where there is so much wealth, there is corruption. I doubt I am telling you anything terribly surprising."

"I am aware of the connection between money and political influence. I fail to see what this has to do with the case at hand."

"Where there are luxuries, there are sumptuary laws, import duties, trade restrictions, and many other inconveniences to the pursuit of further wealth. Even in a common year there is a great deal of bribery, coercion, and influence buying to be done. In a censorship year like this one, the problem increases tenfold."

"I can see that this might be of concern to men like the *duumviri* and their colleagues including, I am sorry to say, your husband. How might the priest be involved? He seems an austere man. His house is modest, as are his clothes, his household, and his late daughter."

"That girl was not the modest, blameless idol the old man described in her eulogy." What she felt delivering these words was difficult to read, but I sensed deep emotion there.

"What mortal has ever matched up to his or her eulogy? The form is stylized and consists almost entirely of conventional phrases. I myself have delivered eulogies for utterly wretched human beings and made them sound like fit companions for the gods."

She laughed, and she had a good laugh, one that made all the flesh she was displaying jiggle. "Well, be that as it may, the girl was—I don't want to speak ill of the dead and attract her vengeful spirit—" she spilled a few drops of wine onto the pavement in propitiation "—but that young woman was spreading herself pretty thin."

"And if she was promiscuous, what of it? That's the stuff of family scandal, not the concern of a senior magistrate."

"It is if her activities involve treason."

"Treason?" I said, intrigued. In those days treason was an exceedingly slippery concept. With so many men and factions vying for supreme power, each tended to define the concept his own way. These days, it just means anything the First Citizen doesn't like.

"Treason," she reaffirmed. "We don't engage in Roman-style power politics down here, but we aren't entirely unaware of how it's played. Campania and points south are old Pompeian territory, full of his *clientela*."

"I can hardly be unaware of that."

"Before much longer, it's going to come to a showdown between Caesar and Pompey."

I closed my eyes. Finally, those two names. I had thought I was away from it all, but no chance of that. "The names are not unfamiliar to me. But activity on behalf of one or the other scarcely merits the onus of treason."

"It does when dealings with foreign powers are involved."

Perhaps I should clarify something here. Clientage—that interlocking series of relationships that so closely binds men not necessarily of the same family—has always been a bedrock of Roman society and remains so even now. But in my younger days it carried even greater import. Citizen clients were obliged to vote for you, and noncitizen clients owed you all the accustomed duties. Hence, politically ambitious men took every pain to expand their *clientela*. Great men had millions of clients, encompassing whole districts. In Italy, this meant a great well of loyal manpower when raising legions. The greatest men, like Caesar and Pompey, had foreign kings and by extension their kingdoms, among their *clientela*. Needless to say, the First Citizen put an end to that upon assuming dictatorial power.

Once again, my cup paused in its ascent.

"Before we proceed further," I said, "I should very much like to know how it happens that you know what these men have been up to." Men in my experience generally did not make their women a part of their political lives. There were exceptions, of course. Clodia, for instance. Or, for that matter, my wife, Julia.

"My husband's business subjects him to long absences from Italy. During those times, I conduct his affairs here. Whether they like it or not, those men have to deal with me frequently."

This did not satisfy me, but I let her go on.

"I am quite aware when one or more of those men are in financial difficulties, and when one is, they all are. They try to conceal this from me and everybody else. The pattern of their dealings changes and they begin to meet in secret. Their meeting place is always the same: the Temple of Apollo."

"Mere changes in commercial habits should not reveal such a thing to you. How did you come by this knowledge?"

"The usual way. I employ spies in their households."

Immediately, I thought of the unfortunate Charmian, now languishing in the ergastulum with her back cut to pieces. I would have liked to surprise Jocasta with this knowledge, but it's always good to keep something in reserve.

"What did your spies report?"

"That the *duumviri* and certain others met with the priest and discussed the secession of the former Greek colonies of southern Italy, Baiae, Cumae, Stabiae, Tarentum, and Messana, and several others. Soon after these meetings their pecuniary problems cleared up as if by magic."

"Whose money?" I demanded.

"Who wants to see Rome brought low? There is no shortage of candidates, but the remaining free Greek states seem the likeliest, don't you think? Macedonia is always fretful and in a state of rebellion."

"Macedonia is poor."

"Rhodes is not. Rhodes is rich and powerful and still, just barely, independent. Ptolemy chafes under the Roman heel and might like to be truly independent instead of a Roman puppet. And Alexandria is a Greek city. They might all see a coming civil war as their last chance. If all of them subscribed to a bribe fund, it would scarcely dent their resources to buy powerful sympathizers in all the humiliated towns."

"With the priest as go-between?"

She said nothing, merely selected an especially fat cherry and dipped it in honey. There was a great fad for cherries back then. A few years previously Lucullus had brought the first cherry trees to Italy as part of the loot from his eastern campaign. He had planted a vast orchard and made seedlings and cuttings available to Italian farmers at only a nominal cost—one of those acts of *euergesia* Julia had spoken of. The new trees were just beginning to bear and everyone was eating cherries.

"What is the girl's part in all this?"

"As I said, she was spreading herself thin among the local male population, and it seems she had a habit of babbling in the throes of passion. I don't think the priest would have killed his own daughter for it, but any of the others would have."

I set down my cup. "These are no longer the days of Sulla. It is not sufficient to bring charges against a prominent citizen to see him executed and claim a part of his wealth."

"You wrong me, Praetor!" she said, smiling. "I am merely zealous in my devotion to the Senate and People of Rome."

"I daresay. And what is your husband's part in all this?"

"None at all. He is Numidian, not Greek."

"But you are Greek," I pointed out.

She shrugged. "I am a woman. I can't vote in anyone's elections or hold office or even express myself publicly on any matter of importance. Greek, Roman, Numidian—what's the difference to me?"

"I can't bring charges against anyone on a basis of what you've told me."

"Who said anything about bringing charges?" she said, popping another honeyed cherry into her mouth. "I believe it simply bears thinking about. Don't you agree?"

6

H̲ERMES AND MARCUS WERE WAITING FOR
me when I left Jocasta's town house.

"Julia's furious," Marcus informed me cheerfully. "She says you've
already demeaned yourself by, first, doing your own interviewing instead
of sending one of us; second, going to that woman's house alone; third—"

"Enough," I told them. "I'll hear all about it when I get back to the
villa, never fear."

"You'll never guess who's in town," Marcus said.

"Come along to the baths," Hermes advised.

Intrigued, I walked along with them, my lictors clearing the way before us. The town baths were, predictably, lavish, located just off the forum. There was a small crowd gathered on its steps, surrounding three
men, two of them wearing purple-bordered togas like mine. These two
weren't serving magistrates that year, though. There was no mistaking who

they were. I had my lictors push through the crowd and threw my arms wide.

"Marcus Tullius!" I cried. "Quintus! Tiro!"

The oldest of them grinned. "Decius Caecilius! Praetor Metellus, I should say. Congratulations!"

It was, indeed, Marcus Tullius Cicero; his brother, Quintus; and his former slave, now freedman, Tiro.

"I thought you would never get back from Syria," I told Cicero, taking all their hands in turn. "And I never expected to see you here! I would have thought you'd be in Rome, where all the political action is going on."

"I've petitioned the Senate to celebrate a triumph, so I can't go into the City until I get permission. I'd rather spend the hot months down here than hang about outside the walls, missing everything." Cicero had been one of the first prominent Romans to build a vacation villa near Baiae. The whole district adored him as if he'd been a native, instead of from Arpinum. That was probably one reason why he loved the place. In Rome, the aristocrats never let him forget that he was a New Man from a small town, not one of their own.

I grasped Tiro's hands warmly. "Tiro, my heartiest congratulations. I hear you are a country squire now."

Quintus Cicero grinned. "He's a landowner and a gentleman now, and increasing his holdings all the time. He'll be looking down on us all soon."

Tiro smiled modestly. "I hope not. Praetor, I see that your Hermes has also donned the toga." He took Hermes' hands.

"Now that I'm free," Hermes said, "he feels entitled to work me harder."

"I understand you've had some work to occupy you here," Cicero said. "Do tell me all about it, Decius." He turned to the surrounding people. "My good friends, please give me leave. I have dealings with the praetor. We shall have a fine banquet in a few days. My brother and I will be here all summer."

Amid effusive greetings and farewells, we retired to one of the baths' small meeting rooms. These were chambers of modest size furnished with chairs and long tables, usually employed by local business associations, fraternal organizations, funeral clubs, and so forth. It had a permanent staff of slaves to serve wine and light refreshments. We arranged ourselves around the central table and accepted the proffered cups of watered wine. A slave set a tray of salted, dried, and smoked snacks on the table and withdrew discreetly. We each took a ceremonial sip and bite and got down to business.

"I hear tales of a rather bizarre murder case in your jurisdiction, Decius," Cicero began.

"It is a—strange case," I said.

"For you to admit that," Quintus Cicero said, "proclaims volumes."

"Let me enlighten you," I said. I told them of the progress of the case thus far, leaving out only my recent interview with Jocasta. I was not yet satisfied that this was not merely a tissue of lies to distract my investigation. Experienced investigators and judges that they all were, they followed my words closely and I knew that they would render no judgment that was not cogent and to the point.

"What a strange matter," Cicero said when I was finished. "The low status of the suspect of course works in his disfavor, but the great amount of wealth to be found in all directions confuses things. Quintus?"

His brother thought for a moment. "Much seems obvious and is all too obvious. The passion of young love, jealousy—these things provide sufficient motive for the act but not for the subsequent pressure brought to bear by the moneyed class of Baiae. There is something far more compelling at work in this."

"I agree," Cicero said. "Tiro?"

The freedman had his answer ready. "I think Hermes is right. The slave girl Charmian has the answer. She must have been present when the most important events of this business took place. The only difficulty is getting access to the girl. Apparently, she is willing to speak to the praetor."

"Exactly," Cicero said. "And herein lies the difficulty: How are we to compel a citizen to surrender one of his slaves and make her talk?"

This may seem strange to many who are not conversant with Roman law and practice as they were in those days. Here we were, a little group of some of Rome's more powerful men, unable to figure out how we could get a Greek priest to allow us access to one of his slaves to ask her some questions.

But one of the most important observances in Roman life was the acknowledgment of the absolute power of a citizen over his own property, and that property included his slaves. In the past, people of our class had been destroyed when their own slaves had denounced them to tyrants like Marius and Sulla. And then there had been the rebellion of Spartacus.

The result had been some draconian laws concerning the rights of citizens to control their own slaves. Even the highest magistrates had no power to compel the testimony of slaves without the cooperation of their masters. At this time, it was political death to accept slave testimony save under the most stringent conditions.

"Marcus Tullius," I said, "the boy's father, the Numidian Gaeto, is looking for an advocate. Might you be interested in taking the case?"

Quintus nudged him. "Why not? It's been a while since you've argued in court, big brother. This would be an exercise of some long-disused muscles."

But Cicero shook his head. "No, it is unthinkable. Oppressed provincials are one thing, but for Cicero to defend a slaver's son? I am sorry, Decius, but it would be unseemly. The boy may be innocent, as you believe, but I could not take a hand in this."

I was disappointed, and I could see that Quintus and Tiro felt the same. This was another example of the self-importance that Cicero suffered from in his later days. The Cicero I had known in his younger days would have taken the case on just for fun.

He correctly interpreted our expressions. "Of course, I shall be more than happy to consult with his defense attorney. I am certain that a properly eloquent defense will persuade the jury to acquit."

"Even if he's guilty," Quintus muttered.

"I'm afraid," I said, "that a jury here is likely to be heavily weighted with Greeks, and the priest has great prestige in the Greek community. Also, I think many of the local men had a more than moderate fondness for the girl."

"Nothing a rousing speech can't fix," Cicero assured me. "Any idea who this man Gaeto has hired?"

"Is old Aulus Galba still around?" Quintus asked. "He's said to have the best legal mind south of Rome."

"As I understand it," I said, "he was one of last year's *duumviri*, so he's probably tight with that lot. There are about ten families in these parts who take the duumvirate in rotation."

"I suppose he's out, then," said Cicero. "Well, there must be somebody suitable."

"I'm sure there must be," I told him. "So you've petitioned for a triumph?" Behind Cicero, Quintus rolled his eyes while Tiro made a careful study of his fingers, folded on the table before him. Clearly, this was another of Cicero's late-life eccentricities. He had been sent out to Syria as governor with the task of repelling a Parthian incursion. Cicero was a lawyer and pure politician, the unlikeliest soldier Rome could have sent. He detested military life as much as I did, yet here he was, trying to vie with the likes of Caesar in celebrating a triumph. This for some doubtful successes after young Cassius had already taken care of the serious fighting.

"Exactly," Cicero said with his customary certitude. "All the prerequisites have been accomplished, all the legalities observed; the Senate has no just cause to deny me a triumph."

"I am sure," I told him. I revered Cicero, and was willing to overlook his sometimes startling character flaws. I, for one, was certain that the man who could decisively whip the Parthians had not yet been born in Rome. If the Senate granted him a triumph, it would be an indication that their standards had fallen considerably.

With promises of future visits, reciprocal dinner parties, and legal consultations in the forum, our meeting broke up. With my little following I set out for the villa.

"You could have hoped for more help from Cicero," Marcus said as he walked along beside my litter.

"I could have, but times have changed."

"You've done him plenty of favors in the past," Hermes grumped. "I could see that Quintus and Tiro wanted to help out."

"I'm not sure they or anyone else could have," I mused, my mind wandering.

"What's that?" Marcus asked.

"He's going into one of his moods again," Hermes informed him. "No use talking to him now."

I had a great deal on my mind, and my ruminations weren't improved when we reached the villa and Julia got her claws into me.

"You just had to get together with that slaver's slut, didn't you?" she began while I was still halfway in my litter.

"Slut? She may be a perfectly virtuous wife, for all we know."

"Spare me. We'll have this out later. For now, we're about to have dinner with the dictator of Stabiae and his wife and some other dignitaries of that town. Do gather up your gravitas and try to be both presentable and coherent." She did me an injustice. Since donning the purple-bordered toga I had made a special effort to moderate my drinking and avoid loose speech. It was no use pointing this out to Julia.

In the event, the dinner was a success. For the record, in towns like Stabiae, Lanuvium, and some others the dictator was simply the senior magistrate. He had nothing like the powers of a true Roman dictator. Despite all the problems occupying my thoughts, I made sure to be witty and charming, things that have usually come easily to me.

When the last healths had been drunk and the guests helped into their litters and sent on their way with presents and good wishes, Julia resumed her interrogation, but she was somewhat mollified by my excellent behavior.

"All right," she said as we relaxed in one of the villa's imposing impluvia, "what did you learn from her?"

"I'm not sure I learned anything, but I heard a lot. Let me tell you

and see what you think." I gave her the story Jocasta had told me and Julia's expression was more than skeptical.

"This makes no sense," she said when my recitation was done. "These are people with everything to lose. Why would they participate in some crackbrained conspiracy against Rome?"

"My own thought," I told her. "And while the Greeks are well-known political morons, I doubt that even Greeks could seriously entertain the idea that some old colonies might gain permanent independence from Rome and that this could be a desirable thing. So what is really going on?"

"I have no idea, but I am cheered to learn that you weren't utterly besotted by the woman's immodest dress and more than abundant flesh. I've known you to be distracted by these things before."

"I won't deny it. But I'm a serious man these days. I am a Roman praetor and such men as I do not succumb to the temptations of loose women."

"Hah! If that's true, you are unique among Roman magistrates of our generation." She rolled close and wrapped an arm around my waist. "And if you are suddenly so dignified, why are you going around questioning suspects? That's a freedman's job."

"Do you think Jocasta would have spoken to Hermes as she spoke to me?"

"Probably not. But only because you are the one she wants to deceive. The questions are: Why the deception and what is the real story? What is she covering?"

"And for whom?" I said.

"The obvious answer is her husband," Julia speculated. "It is probably he who is up to something, not the others."

"How does this help Gelon?" I demanded.

"Perhaps she doesn't want to help Gelon," Julia said.

This brought me up short. "She doesn't want to help him?"

"Why should she? She isn't his mother. She may have children of her own she wants Gaeto to favor. She may be pregnant. It's not unknown

for a subsequent wife to edge other wive's children out in favor of her own."

"I hadn't thought of that," I admitted. "I've been going on the assumption that she wants to protect her husband and his son."

Julia gave my waist a little squeeze. "This is why you married me," she said, "to think of these things that tend to escape you."

I pondered for a while. "That necklace."

"What about it?" Julia asked.

"It bothers me. The girl went out in her best jewelry. Why didn't she wear that necklace?"

"You see? My subtlety has rubbed off on you. My guess is that the necklace was the gift of a different lover. She wouldn't have worn it to meet the one who hadn't given it."

"So which lover was the poet?"

"Need it have been one of them? Why not a third?"

"Why must things be so complicated? And just how many affairs could that girl have concealed from her father?"

"Men can be selectively blind," she pointed out. "Women rarely are. I've been studying the poems. I am all but convinced that the writer is Greek, not a Roman writing in Greek. There are giveaways in the use of the two languages."

"I'll defer to you in this. Your command of Greek is far better than mine."

"And there's something else about it—I can't quite put my finger on it, but I think it will reveal itself with further study."

For Julia to express herself with less than full certitude was unusual, so I did not press her over this tantalizing hint.

THE NEXT MORNING I MADE IT MY business to locate Gaeto. As I sat through another morning of desultory cases in court, Hermes was away, in search of the Numidian slaver.

The last case of the morning involved my companion of the Pompei-

ian amphitheater, Diogenes. Standing as his citizen patron was Manius Silva. I had a feeling that I was soon to learn what I had been bribed for.

The bailiff announced, "Suit is brought against Diogenes the Cretan by the perfumer Lucius Celsius. The charge is fraud and unfair business practices."

A dispute between scent peddlers was not quite on a level with struggles for world dominion in the Senate, but I seemed to have a personal stake in this matter, so I bade them continue. The men involved took the usual oaths.

"Celsius," I said when the formalities were done, "what is the nature of the charge you bring against Diogenes?"

"This Greekling," Celsius said, pointing a skinny finger at the man, "this perfidious Cretan, has been counterfeiting some of the costliest scents in the world, concocting them from cheap ingredients and selling them at the highest price!" The man shook with indignation, probably for the benefit of the jury. He was a painfully thin, balding man of about forty years, and from the smell of him he dipped his toga in his own wares.

"Diogenes, what have you to say?" I asked.

Manius Silva stepped forward. "As the citizen patron of Diogenes, I will answer these charges, noble Praetor. The splendid Diogenes is honest and blameless, as all citizens of Baiae are quite aware, and he speaks only the truth."

Here there was muffled laughter from the many bystanders. To hear a Cretan described as honest, blameless, and truthful was a rare joke.

"Order, there," shouted my chief lictor. The mirth subsided and Roman justice resumed its progress.

"Each of you will have his say," I proclaimed. "But I don't intend to waste the rest of the day hearing a wrangle over perfume. This trade, I remind you, is strictly regulated by the sumptuary laws, which are being rigorously enforced this year. Each of you has until the fall of a single ball to state his case."

I nodded to the court timekeeper, and the old slave pulled the plug on his water clock. This clever device released water at a measured rate and, by a subtle mechanism, dropped steel balls at regular intervals. These fell into a brazen dish, making a loud clatter.

"Celsius," I said, "you may begin."

The man cleared his throat ostentatiously and withdrew a roll of papyrus from the folds of his toga and opened it. "The lying, counterfeiting Cretan rogue Diogenes, in violation of the most sacred rules of the Brotherhood of Narcissus, the ancient guild of perfumers, has brazenly concocted a number of the costliest scents, using cheap and inferior ingredients, and passing off these noisome substances as genuine, sells them at the full price, as regulated by the—" he made a half turn and bowed in my direction "—sumptuary laws." This raised a laugh.

"The scents thus falsified include those known as Pharaoh's Delight, Babylonian Lilac, Tears of the Moon, Zoroaster's Rapture, Milk from Aphrodite's Breast, Gardens of Ninevah, Illyrian Blossom,—"

"Enough," I told him. "We don't need a whole roster of the smells that drive us poor husbands to bankruptcy. Why do you believe that Diogenes has been counterfeiting these fragrances, which, I hear, are largely made of things like whale vomit and afterbirths and anal glands and other revolting substances."

He rerolled his papyrus with a frown. "Sir, that is base calumny. Ambergris, for instance, has almost no scent of its own. It merely stabilizes—"

"I don't want to hear perfumer's shoptalk!" I barked. "I want to hear evidence!"

"Well, then. Certain persons in my employ have told me that, secretly, Diogenes buys up great loads of flower petals, lemon peel, cedar oil, and other fragrant but common substances and in a kitchen of his manufactory blends them with distilled wine and pure oil until he achieves an approximation of the great perfumes, at least close enough to deceive the nose of one unskilled in perfumery."

"And who told you this?" I demanded.

"Certain persons employed in this nefarious process."

Silva leapt to his feet. "Praetor, I object! The word of suborned slaves is worthless!"

"Sit down," I said. "You shall have your turn presently. Celsius, the word of suborned slaves is worthless. You'll have to do better than that."

He sputtered. "What sort of evidence would satisfy you, Praetor?"

"You don't have to satisfy me," I told him, "but you must satisfy this jury." I waved a hand toward the eighty or ninety men who sat on benches looking bored. Under the Sullan constitution these were all *equites* with a minimum property assessment of four hundred thousand sesterces. In reality, I suspected that they would rather see a bribe than evidence, but I wasn't going to let it be that way.

"Perhaps," I said, "you might produce some of this fake perfume and explain to us how it differs from the real thing."

"I—I did not come prepared for this!"

"That was thoughtless of you."

"Besides, Praetor, you are not a perfumer. How would you know the difference?"

"If it takes a professional to tell the difference between real and fake," I demanded, "why are we paying so much money for this stuff?"

He almost yelled an answer, caught himself, then went on in a reasonable tone. "Praetor, we have wandered rather far from the matter of this lawsuit."

"I suppose so," I admitted. "I could bring my wife. She has an infallible nose for perfume."

"Praetor—" Just then the ball fell into the dish with a resounding clang. "This is not just!" he squawked. "I did not get to present my case!"

"We'll let Diogenes have his say anyway," I said. "If you're in luck, he'll bungle it worse than you did. Silva, have you engaged an advocate?"

He stood and adjusted his toga grandly. "Hardly necessary, Praetor. If it meets with your approval, I shall speak on behalf of my friend Diogenes."

"You don't need my approval. If you are prepared, speak up." I nodded to the timekeeper and he restarted the water clock.

"First, Praetor, judges of Baiae, and good men of the jury, allow me to point out that this man Celsius is a jealous business rival of Diogenes, so his testimony is suspect from the first word. Why would he bring suit against Diogenes unless he was losing business to my friend?

"The truth is that Diogenes offers these famous perfumes to the public not at an inflated price but rather at a *lower* price than other perfumers can profitably accept. They imagine that he can do this only by counterfeiting, but in fact it is because he is a far better businessman than they."

He made an expansive gesture toward the audience. "While these men sit here in Baiae, overseeing their slaves and enjoying the comforts of our lovely city, Diogenes spends a full half of every year in perilous travel, braving the wine-dark sea, the wind-driven sands of Ethiopia and Arabia, the savage inhabitants of far-flung lands, all to seek out the best purveyors of rare and costly perfumes and those obscure ingredients that go into the scents we blend, quite openly and honestly, for our domestic production.

"By thus taking the dangers, privations, and hardships upon himself, by not trusting middlemen and not paying their exorbitant fees, he is able to effect a considerable saving in each year's outlay, savings he is able to express in lower prices for his wares. Is this dishonest? No, the dishonesty is in the envy and resentment of his rivals and these, Romans all, hope to sway the jury by attacking his Cretan origins. But I know that my fellow citizens are not persuaded by this calumnious slander.

"And as for those 'persons in his employ,' as he so delicately puts it, will a slave not lie for a few coins? Will a slave not sell out his master if offered the chance? Does the old saying not warn us, 'You have as many enemies as you have slaves'? That Celsius even stoops to such a practice is proof of his villainy!"

With the last word the ball clanged into the dish and the audience applauded, jury included. He'd done extremely well. I might have been persuaded myself, had they not already tried to bribe me.

"There we have it," I announced. "There is no solid evidence in this case, just the arguments of two business rivals. Diogenes may be guilty of counterfeiting, but to this I say, what of it? As far as I am concerned, if you can't tell the difference between one scent and another, and you pay an exorbitant price just for its name, then you're an idiot and deserve to be fleeced.

"As for Celsius, any Roman citizen who can't outwit a Cretan is a poor credit to the descendants of Romulus. All in all, this whole case is an unworthy waste of time. That's just my opinion, though. The decision rests with you worthy *equites* of Baiae, who, I am certain, will render judgment in the highest traditions of Roman justice. Do keep in mind that, if Diogenes has tried to bribe you with samples of his perfume, he may have used counterfeit."

With this I sat back in my curule chair while everyone gaped, then chattered in low voices. Apparently I had satisfied nobody, and that suited me perfectly. I affected nonchalance while the local magistrates coached the jury and all the rest babbled among themselves. I wondered whether the scents I had been given were real or fake. If fake, Julia was going to be infuriated. The five thousand sesterces had been real, though. I suspected that Diogenes and Silva were wondering whether it had been well spent.

The jury retired into the basilica to debate and, no doubt, to compare bribes. I passed the time in idle conversation with the city magistrates and my own legal experts. My stomach was grumbling, but it would have created a public scandal for a praetor sitting on his curule chair to have lunch right in front of everybody. Sometimes, I think, we carry gravitas too far.

Where, I wondered, had Hermes got to? He shouldn't have trouble finding one of the district's most prominent, if somewhat notorious, inhabitants.

In time, the jury returned and the bailiff recited a few of the hallowed judicial formulae concerning justice and truthfulness before the gods, then the eldest juror handed him the ballot jar. The bailiff dumped the marked tesserae on his table, and he and his assistants counted them out, ballots for innocent to go in one pile, guilty in another. At the end of it, all the ballots were in a single pile.

"The jury finds unanimously for the defendant," he announced. "Diogenes of Crete is innocent." The audience cheered or made rude noises as their sympathies lay.

"So much for that, then," I said. "This court is adjourned. Let's get some lunch."

Manius Silva came up to me, fury in his face. "The verdict was just, but it came no thanks to you, Praetor!"

"What of it? Is it my task to guarantee a favorable verdict here?"

"It is when you've accepted—" I gave him a stern look and he paused. The men of my party gave him stern looks. My lictors gave him stern looks, fingering the edges of their axe heads.

"You were saying, Manius Silva?" I asked.

"Nothing, Praetor. Thank you for conducting so fair a court." He whirled and stalked off.

In truth, I was happy that Diogenes had been found innocent. I didn't care about his business practices, and the man had been good company. As far as I was concerned, a fine judge of fighting men was far preferable to some disgruntled scent merchant.

There came a clatter of hoofs and I saw Hermes and a couple of the young bloods of my party ride into the forum. Indignant looks went their way, for mounted and wheeled traffic were forbidden during the daylight hours, but as special assistants to the praetor they had a dispensation. Hermes slid off his mount and strode to the judicial platform.

"Have you found him?" I demanded.

"I did. He's dead, Praetor. Murdered."

7

MY LITTER CARRIED ME TO THE EDGE OF the town, where my horse was waiting, saddled. I got out of the litter, tossed my toga into it, and ordered the bearers to return to the villa. Mounted and free of the cumbersome garment, I felt invigorated, even younger. Boredom and the trappings of power can be a deadly combination. I was eager for some excitement and I was getting it.

"How?" I demanded as we rode.

"You'll have to see for yourself," Hermes shouted above the clatter of our horses. The splendid road was smoothly paved, lined with imposing tombs and stately shade trees. It led along the shore and featured frequent rest areas where travelers could picnic. Each of these featured a fine view of the picturesque bay and had its own bubbling fountain and marble latrine. They left nothing to chance in Baiae.

Hermes led us onto a side road that descended a gentle bluff to the shore. At the end of it was an extensive villa that included many large outbuildings, almost a small village in itself. From the house stretched a stone jetty. It extended into water deep enough to anchor a sizable ship. There were some small boats tied up to it, and nets hung drying from racks along its sides.

We'd picked up an escort of town guardsmen. These were men in whom I reposed no confidence. They wore gilded armor that looked like something an actor would wear onstage, they were in poor physical condition, and their officer was a wellborn young lout who avoided service in the legions by performing this "essential" civic duty.

I dismounted at the entrance to the compound and began to bark orders. "You lot," I shouted to the guards, "secure all the approaches to this place. Let no one enter or leave!" They saluted and bustled to obey me. That disposed of them. I was perfectly confident that they would accomplish nothing.

For a moment I stood surveying the place. It entirely lacked the stench that so often hangs over a slave compound like a noxious fog. This place was well run, at least. "Marcus," I said, "get me the steward. He should be here to meet us. If he's fled, I'll have him hunted down and killed."

"He's here," Hermes said, nodding toward the barred gate. A man with a pale, worried face was hustling from the main house with a ring of massive keys in one hand. He was accompanied by a pair of guards who wore leather harness and were armed with whips and bronze-studded clubs of olive wood. Not Numidians this time. These looked like Sicilians.

The man unlocked the gate with shaky, sweating hands. The guards tugged it open, and we passed inside.

"What kept you?" I said.

"Your pardon, Praetor. We have been making an inventory of the staff and the sale slaves to make sure that all were accounted for. Your man ordered this."

"I did," Hermes affirmed. "Is the count complete?"

"Yes. All are here save the young master and his tribal guards. We have not seen them since the—the arrest."

"What about the lady of the house?" I asked.

"The master's junior wife and her girls have been resident in the town house for several days, sir."

"And who might you be?" I demanded.

"Oh. Sorry, Praetor. I am Archias, steward to Gaeto. I trust you will pardon my distress. First the young master arrested for murder, now the master—"

"Perhaps it is time that I see your late employer. You are to stay close. I will wish to have a tour of the establishment when I have viewed the body."

"Of course, Praetor. Please come with me." We followed him to the main house. It looked much like any fine country house in this district except for the activities. In the distance I could hear a Greek palaestra master calling out exercise commands. Occasionally the crack of a whip sounded above the mutter of the several hundred inhabitants.

"How did you discover him?" I asked as we passed inside the house. The atrium was spacious and blessedly without the pretentious portrait busts with which so many social climbers seek to ape the ancestry of the nobility. The impluvium was splendid and decorated in fine taste, but once again without pretension.

"I must confess it, sir," said Archias, "I went to seek him when your man came this morning to demand an audience."

"He was summoning your master to me," I told the man. "Kings have audiences, not slave merchants."

"Of course, sir," he said stiffly. I was being deliberately rude. You often get a better degree of truth from people who are upset and off guard. "In any case," he went on, "it was far later than he usually rises, and I got no answer to my knock. He was in here."

He had stopped before a door that opened off the impluvium, the most common location for bedrooms in Roman houses—and Gaeto seemed to have gone entirely Roman in his domestic habits, save his supernumerary spouse. Beside the door were two Egyptian slaves dressed in stiff, white linen kilts and formal wigs. They didn't look like guards.

The steward swung the door open. I saw that it was fitted with a heavy bolt that could be fastened from the inside. One rarely sees lockable doors within a house, except on storerooms and wine cellars. But this was a sensible precaution for a man who dealt in human livestock and dwelled in the midst of his merchandise.

Gaeto lay on the floor beside his bed, fully clothed. His eyes were open, his head drawn back as if he had been observing the heavens for omens when he died. There was no blood staining his clothing nor on the floor.

"How did he die?" I asked. I scanned the room. There were no displaced or broken furnishings, no sign of a struggle.

The steward summoned the two Egyptians and they entered. At his direction they lifted the body gently and turned it over. "These men are undertakers, Praetor," said Archias. "Skilled Egyptians are much in demand in Italian funeral establishments."

No wonder these two had no qualms about handling the dead. Unlike Roman *libitinarii* they did not wear masks or gloves, but men raised in an Egyptian House of the Dead are not likely to be squeamish. Their craft involves handling the internal organs as well.

"Ah, now I understand," I said.

Protruding from the back of Gaeto's neck, driven upward into the base of the skull, was a small dagger, buried hilt deep. It was an extremely clever method of assassination. Paralysis would have been instant, death following in mere seconds. The man would have been unable to cry out and no blood escaped.

"His hands show no sign that he tried to defend himself," Hermes noted. "He must have been taken completely unawares."

"So it would seem," I agreed. "Archias, who was in here with your master last night?"

"Sir, last night, just after dinner, I was dismissed with the rest of the staff. We live in other houses within the compound. Only the immediate family and their personal body servants live in the great house."

"Then who was with him last night?" I asked him.

"Nobody. The gate was secured and there were no callers until your man arrived this morning."

"Then he was killed by someone already here," I said, "and that could prove very bad for all of you."

He went even paler. "Praetor, that could not have happened!"

"Then what did happen?" I demanded, indicating the corpse. "Does this look like suicide to you?"

He stammered, then said, "Someone must have come in over the wall."

"I'll want to talk to whoever guarded the gate last night," I told him. I looked around the room and saw that there was nothing to be learned from it or from the body. I had rarely seen a murder site so devoid of usable evidence. Only inference was of any use. "Now give me a tour of the establishment."

We followed the steward outside, and I drew young Marcus near me. "Marcus, ride back to the villa and find Regilius, the horse master. Tell him to ride here immediately and scout the ground around this estate, paying particular attention to the part of the outer wall nearest the main house. He'll know what I want." The boy was clearly mystified, but he did not waste my time with questions; he merely said, "At once, Praetor," and ran for his horse. That boy had a promising future.

"From the wharf"—Archias indicated the jetty visible through the main gate—"the merchandise is brought within the walls and taken to the great compound. Please come this way." He was talking like a tour guide, probably to help get over his jitters. I could sympathize. I had the feeling that he gave this tour often, probably to prospective investors and big-scale buyers. We went into a large courtyard faced by a quadrangle of two-story barracks. The severity of the design was relieved by bright paint, a shady portico, and many fine trees and shrubs planted in huge jars around the perimeter. Lest anyone be too allayed by the pleasant prospect, in the center was a frame to which a number of slaves could be triced for whipping.

Next to the main entrance was a huge signboard of white-painted wood. On it in large, black letters were written the rules of the establishment and a list of punishments for infractions. On the left it was written in Latin, then repeated in Greek, Punic, Aramaic, Syrian, and demotic Egyptian.

"Here," Archias went on, "the new stock are separated by categories. Those destined for domestic service are assigned quarters in the north building, skilled craftsmen to the west building. Entertainers, masseurs, bath attendants, and so forth are housed in the south building; and the most highly skilled—architects, physicians, teachers, and such—live in the east building."

"Where do you keep the dangerous ones?" I wanted to know.

"Oh, sir, the house of Gaeto does not handle dangerous stock. No gladiators, new-caught barbarians, or incorrigibles sold off cheap. Only quality slaves are sold here."

"Your men have clubs and whips," Hermes said.

"That is traditional. It is what all slaves understand. Why, the whipping frame here practically rots from disuse. The rare times it is employed, it is usually because of petty jealousies and fights among the slaves themselves."

"I see. I want to inspect the quarters. And the slaves."

"As the praetor wishes."

"Do they know yet?" I asked.

"No, Praetor. Even the staff have not yet been informed of the master's death."

"Good," I said. "I'll be able to learn a good deal more without a great uproar of false mourning and lamentation. Don't parade them. I want to see them in their natural state."

"Then, please come this way."

The tour was fairly lengthy and educational. The domestic servants had that demure, eyes-lowered appearance that all such slaves cultivate. Doubtless they thought I was some rich buyer come to look them over and they might well end up in my household. My own family rarely bought slaves, preferring to employ only those born within the household, although we sometimes traded them around among ourselves. That was how I acquired Hermes, after he'd worn out his welcome in my uncle's house.

The craftsmen's quarters featured small shops where carpenters, smiths, potters, weavers, and such could keep gainfully employed while awaiting sale, as well as having an opportunity to demonstrate their skills to prospective buyers. I wasn't sure what the Egyptian undertakers did in their leisure time. They didn't seem to be provided with corpses to practice on.

The professionals had more spacious quarters, as befitted their superior rank in slave society. The scribes, bookkeepers, and secretaries were held in least esteem, physicians and architects at the top. At that time, great men were expected to exercise *euergesia* by donating great building projects to their client towns and to the capital. Some simply bought a permanent staff of architects for this very purpose. Even when you weren't having anything built, it enhanced your social status to let everyone know you could afford to own your personal architects, then support them in idleness.

The entertainers' quarters were the most enjoyable part of the tour. Gaeto had bought Spanish and African dancers, Egyptian magicians, and Greek singers and reciters of poetry—men who could recite the entirety of Homer from memory and women who could play every conceivable musical instrument. It is possible that I lingered in this wing longer than was strictly necessary for the purposes of the investigation, but you never know what sort of information might turn out to be of use.

Reluctantly, we went back outside and took a tour of the outer wall. It was about ten feet high, without battlements or a sentry walk. It was no more formidable than the sort of wall that often surrounds a great house in the country, and had probably been built during the Social War or the rebellion of Spartacus or some other time of unrest. Such walls were often demolished in peaceful times to clear the view, but Gaeto had cause to maintain this one.

We went to the main gate and found a pair of nervous-looking guards within and a mob of officials milling about outside.

"You two were on guard here last night?" I said.

"Yes, Praetor," one said. "Nobody came in through this gate and nobody went out. We—"

"Answer the Praetor's questions and say nothing else!" Hermes barked.

"Yes, sir!" The man's accent was pure Sicilian.

"What hours did you stand watch?" I asked.

"Sunset to sunrise, Praetor."

"No reliefs?"

"None, Praetor." He had learned brevity.

"You saw and heard no one approach this wall?"

They looked at each other uneasily. "Actually, Praetor," said the spokesman, "our duties are mainly to keep the slaves from going *out* and to open the gate for anyone arriving after dark with a legitimate reason to come in."

"You don't patrol the perimeter?"

"No, sir. The master never—"

"Just answer what you're asked," I reminded him. "Now, tell me this: Were either or both of you asleep at any time last night?"

"Never!" they shouted as one. This meant nothing, of course. Guards never admit dereliction of duty, even if you catch them snoring.

"Dismiss these men," I told the steward. "Now, I'll talk to that mob outside. When Gaeto is prepared for burial, I want that dagger."

"I shall have it sent to you," he assured me.

Outside the gate was convoked a crowd of Baiae's officials and magistrates and other important people, including wives and all the rabble that usually assembles at the site of scandalous doings.

"Is it true, Praetor?" demanded Manius Silva. "Has Gaeto been done away with?" He still looked peeved at the way I had conducted the morning's trial.

"Dead as Achilles," I confirmed. I watched their faces closely. Some affected philosophic impassivity; others looked relieved, Silva and Norbanus among them. Rutilia looked delighted, but then some people just love murders. She turned to her friend Quadrilla and said something behind a masking hand. Quadrilla's face was grim and her expression did not change at whatever Rutilia said. I thought this odd, but then she might have stuck an even larger sapphire in her navel and it was causing her discomfort.

"Listen to me, all of you," I said. "Things are getting out of hand here. Just because murders happen all the time in Rome is no reason to think you people have some sort of license to imitate us."

"The slaver was probably killed by his own livestock," said Publilius the jewel merchant.

"Let's have no loose talk," I commanded. "I will investigate and the killer will be brought to justice."

"At least we know it wasn't parricide," Rutilia remarked. "That would have brought the wrath of the gods." This brought an appreciative chuckle. Ordinarily I admire sophisticated wit, but at this moment I was in no mood for it.

"Here comes the grieving widow," Quadrilla said.

A litter carried by hard-pressed bearers was descending the bluff. Minutes later it was set before me and flame-haired Jocasta emerged, her clothes in disarray, her bright hair unbound and streaming. She looked around wildly, then at me.

"I see it must be true." Her eyes were dry but furious. "My husband is dead. Murdered."

"I am afraid so," I told her.

"You know it was that priest!" she said through clenched teeth. "He couldn't reach the son, so he killed the father. Have him arrested!"

"I know no such thing. You have my condolences, Jocasta, but your husband had many enemies. Several hundred of them reside in that compound." I jerked a thumb over my shoulder at the wall of the estate. "I will find out who killed Gaeto—slave, freed, or freeborn—and I will render justice."

She hissed, then took a deep breath and gathered her dignity. Greek women have extravagant ways of mourning, but she did not wish to put on such a display for Romans. "I want to see him."

"You don't need my permission," I told her. She strode past me and disappeared within the gate.

"Everyone here," I said, "disperse to your homes and your business. This is just another sensation and it needn't be made worse by a lot of idle speculation."

They did not look pleased with my high-handed methods, but they knew better than to argue. I was the man with the lictors and the imperium. By this time the older men of my staff had caught up, and I beckoned them to me.

"Publius Severus," I said, addressing an elderly freedman who for fifty years had been secretary to some of Rome's greatest jurists, "I need you and your colleagues to search the law books. This man may have been killed by one of his slaves. I need to know if the old law that condemns all his slaves to crucifixion in such a case is valid only if the victim was a citizen. This man was a resident alien."

"I can tell you right now, Praetor," said Severus. "The matter was addressed during the consulship of Clodianus and Gellius, when slaves were murdering their masters right and left. The ultimate punishment was inflicted only in the case of a citizen murder. The status of foreigners is little higher than that of slaves, and the matter is to be treated as an ordinary homicide. Only the murderer and his direct accomplices are subject to crucifixion."

"Excellent," I said, greatly relieved. The last thing I wanted to do was order several hundred crucifixions of people who were in no way responsible for their master's death. We have some truly monstrous, archaic punishments on our law books.

Regilius the horse master arrived and I dispatched him to scout for signs of an intruder. He began to ride slowly along the estate wall, his eyes on the ground.

I ordered everyone back to the villa and we mounted. Riding, this time at a leisurely pace, I discussed the latest murder with Hermes.

"It was someone he knew," Hermes said.

"Clearly. Someone he had in his bedroom after dark, when the estate was closed up. That doesn't let the slaves off. He might have sent up one of the girls. He certainly had some fine stock."

Hermes shook his head. "He was a big, powerful man. No girl did that."

"Why not?" I said. "A moment's inattention, he turns his back, and in goes the knife."

"That stroke was delivered with great power and accuracy," Hermes protested, "right into the base of the skull where the spinal cord joins. It's a job for a trained swordsman."

I nodded, musing. "It's hard to imagine how a woman could have done it. I've known some dangerous women in my time, though. I know better than to rule them out."

Before we reached the villa, Regilius caught up with us.

"That was quick," I said. "What did you find?"

"It was the same Roman-shod mare," he said.

I thumped a fist on my saddle. "The same murderer! I knew it!" Actually, I had known nothing of the sort, but it is always good to appear wise before subordinates. "How did the killer tether the horse?" I asked. "There are no trees between the walls and the bluff. Did you find sign of a picket pin?"

"No, the mare was held."

"Held? There was an accomplice?" This I had not expected.

"Two horses rode up to the wall, both mares, both Roman shod," he reported. "From what I could make out, your killer went over the wall. Probably just stood in the saddle to do it. No problem with a wall that high. The other then rode off, leading the unridden horse, and waited about two hundred yards away. The first did the deed, then came back over the wall and the two of them rode away. Clever bit of planning, too."

"How is that?"

"When I saw where the killer went over, I stood in my own saddle and pulled myself on top of the wall for a look. There's a stable on the other side. You can just step onto the stable roof, then down to the fence, then to the ground and make no noise. If anyone heard those horses, they'd just think they were hearing noises from the stable."

"You're right," I told him. "Now you have two horses to watch for."

"If I see sign of them," he said, "I'll let you know."

When we reached my villa, Julia had to know what had been going on and I gave her a quick rendition.

"We have to inform Gelon," she said.

"I'll tell him," I said, "but not just yet."

"What are you going to do?" she asked, alarmed at my tone or my appearance.

"What I should have done sooner," I told her. "I'm going to the temple to get that poor girl. At least I have legal cause now."

She nodded and Hermes grinned. "Lictors!" he bellowed. Julia draped me in my formidable toga and we trooped off to the beautiful temple of Apollo. A hundred yards from the temple we could hear a woman screaming.

Julia grabbed my arm. "Don't run. It's undignified. That woman is being beaten and she won't die of it before we get there." I was not so certain. After the thrashing Hermes had described, could Charmian survive another as savage? In the courtyard behind the temple we found them.

Diocles the priest looked on coldly while a big slave wielded a whip on a young woman tied to a post. Her back and buttocks were crisscrossed with ugly stripes, and blood ran to her heels and formed a spreading puddle beneath her feet. But the screaming victim wasn't Charmian. It was the big German girl, Gaia.

"Stop this at once!" I yelled. One of my lictors knocked the whip wielder sprawling with his fasces.

Diocles turned to look at me, seeming almost dazed by this turn of events. "Praetor? By what authority do you interfere with my conduct of my own household?"

"By my authority as *praetor peregrinus* of Rome. Diocles, you are a suspect in the murder of Gaeto of Numidia. I demand that you surrender to me certain slaves of your household for questioning in this case and in the matter of your daughter's death. You will turn over to me the girl Charmian and this girl Gaia, and while you're at it, give me the other one, Leto, before you whip them all to death."

The old man turned paler than he already was, and his head began to tremble. "Gaeto? Dead? Well, what is that to me? So the Numidian swine is dead. How dare you accuse me of murdering him, if the killing of such a man can be considered murder?"

"You had the greatest motive to kill him, since you believe his son murdered your daughter. As a resident alien he was under the protection of Roman law and I administer that law. Now fetch Charmian!" I was out of patience and the defiance went out of him.

"I can't," he admitted, seeming to shrink.

"Are you saying she's dead?"

"No, she escaped from the ergastulum. And that German slut—" he jabbed a finger toward the suffering girl "—let her out! That is why she is being punished. And you have no right to interfere." He seemed to regain a bit of his defiance.

"For the moment," I told him, "my power here is absolute. You may bring suit against me after I leave office in the fall. Of course, I may already have had you beheaded by then, so don't count on it."

I walked to the post. Under Julia's solicitous direction, Hermes and the lictors had unbound the girl and lowered her to the ground. Her screams had subsided to a continuous moan.

"She won't be talking for a while," Julia said. "I'll have her carried to the villa and looked after." She snapped her fingers and pointed. A lictor rushed back to the villa for help. They never stepped that lively for me.

"When did Charmian escape?" I asked the priest.

"The night before last, but I only learned of it this afternoon. Gaia had been taking her meals to her and concealed the fact that she had let the bitch out. When I sent for Charmian—"

"Why did you send for her?"

"I had some questions to put to her."

And a whip ready, no doubt, I thought. "Where is the other one? Leto?"

He summoned a slave and sent him to fetch the girl. "Are you really serious about regarding me as a suspect?"

"Serious as Jupiter's thunderbolt," I assured him. "Something very unpleasant is going on here in southern Campania. I came here expecting a pleasant, unexciting stay and you people have disappointed me sorely. This puts me in a vengeful mood, and I am ready to inflict as many executions and exiles as it will take to set things back in order."

"You make much over the death of a nobody," he almost whispered.

"He was somebody," I assured him. "He was a resident alien under my protection. His death and your daughter's were connected and I will have the truth. Should I decide that you are that connection, my lictors will be calling on you."

"Surely you cannot think that I was involved in my own daughter's murder?" His indignation sounded genuine, but some people are experts at faking such things.

"Should I decide so, you will be in need of an inordinately sympathetic jury."

Leto appeared, trembling and almost faint with apprehension. She stared at poor, bloodied Gaia with huge eyes and would have collapsed had Hermes not caught her.

Julia took her hand. "Be calm, girl. You are coming to our house and no one will harm you."

By this time I was beginning to wonder about my ability to protect anyone from harm.

8

I T DIDN'T LOOK LIKE MUCH OF A WEAPON, lying on the table in the impluvium. A messenger had delivered it while we were occupied at the temple. Julia had taken the German girl and Leto to quarters where they could be cared for. I wasn't going to be questioning Gaia for a while, but I hoped to get something coherent from Leto, if she could just overcome her terror.

Antonia picked up the sticker and examined it. The Egyptians had cleaned it before it was sent to me. It was made of a single piece of steel, the handle shaped like that of a miniature dagger. The blade part was triangular in cross section, tapering to a needle point and no more than five inches long. It resembled a writing stylus more than a weapon.

"He was killed with this little thing?" she said.

"It was sufficient," I told her. "It's all in the placement. As any legionary sword master will tell you, a puncture an inch deep in a man's jugular will kill him just as dead as hacking him clean in two. Same thing with this. Put it in the right place, and death is all but instantaneous."

She twirled it in her fingers, fascinated. "I could use something like this. Most often, I strap a dagger inside my thigh when I go out, but it chafes after a while."

"You do?" Circe said. "I usually carry mine down here." She poked a finger into her own ample cleavage. As usual, every new thing I learned about Roman women alarmed me.

"It weighs practically nothing," Antonia observed, tossing it high, end over end, catching it adroitly by the handle on the fall. "You could hide it in your hair. That way, it would still be handy when you're wearing nothing at all."

"Enough of that, ladies," Julia said, entering the room.

"Actually," I pointed out, "little daggers similar to this are sometimes carried by prostitutes, hidden in their hair, as Antonia suggests. They carry them to protect themselves from cruel or violent customers. Assassination is not the point. Such women know how to, ah, distract a man by stabbing him in an intimate spot."

"You two are having a bad influence on my husband," Julia said. "But if it's a prostitute's trick, doubtless Gaeto had a number of them in his slave barracks."

"The murderer came from outside—we've established that," I told her.

"If you can rely on the word of an old cavalryman," she said. "If he made up some details to make himself seem more important, he wouldn't be the first."

"I trust him," I said. "Now what have you learned from the girls?"

"Leto is shattered and not a hand has been laid on her. Gaia is made of stronger stuff and that girl Charmian must have been made of iron to escape after the beating she took. I've dosed both the girls in our custody with poppy juice. I hope they can talk for a few minutes before they pass out."

"They'd better," I said. "I have to find Charmian. Surely she must have had someplace to run to."

"You should send out word that she is to be brought to you when she's found," Circe advised. "Otherwise she'll be turned over to Diocles for the reward and he'll probably kill her. That old man is entirely too fond of the whip."

"And he has something to hide," Julia said.

"Everyone does," I mused, "but I don't want people combing the whole countryside for her. I need her alive and talking, and it's best if she comes to me freely."

"How is she to know?" Antonia asked.

"Hermes will put out word on the slave grapevine," I said. "He knows how to do it."

"You have a romantic conception of slaves' concern for one another," Julia said. "Her fellow slaves are as likely to sell her to Diocles as guide her to you."

"Nonetheless, that is my decision."

Shortly after this, Hermes came to inform us that the girls were able to talk. I told Antonia and Circe to rein in their unhealthy curiosity and stay where they were. They yielded with poor grace. Julia and I went to the room that had been prepared for our unexpected guests. Gaia lay on her stomach. The cushions beneath her were arranged for the greatest degree of comfort. Her stripes were cleaned and anointed with soothing oil, and she was covered with the lightest, gauziest sheet to be found in the villa. Leto sat beside her, holding her hand. She swayed in her chair, calm but almost numbed by the drug. Julia and I took other chairs, while Hermes and Marcus stood behind us.

"Girls," I said, "I need some information from you. I know you both need sleep but this will not wait. I am not going to threaten you with punishment, but I must have your fullest cooperation. You will be much safer that way. Do you understand?"

Leto nodded dumbly. Gaia managed to say "yes" in a weak voice.

"We won't turn you back over to Diocles," Julia told them firmly. "You have been seized as evidence. My husband will have you remanded to the state, and I can then buy you and give you easy work in our own household. My husband can do this. He is a Roman magistrate. But you must answer him honestly."

This seemed to reassure them. "What do you want to know?" Gaia asked, her voice a little stronger. She must have been captured young or else born in captivity. Her Latin was without discernible accent.

"First off," I said, "what was Charmian's offense?"

"She was helping Mistress Gorgo," Leto said, speaking for the first time, although somewhat listlessly. "When the mistress went out at night, Charmian spied the way for her. Sometimes, I would sleep in Gorgo's bed, so it would look like she was there."

"Charmian would hide the gifts the mistress returned with," Gaia said. "When Gorgo could not get away, Charmian would sneak out and tell the—the visitor."

"Gorgo was seeing a lover?" Julia asked. Both girls nodded. "How often?"

"Almost every night," said Gaia.

"Was there just one lover?" I asked. "Two? Many?"

"They never told us," Gaia said. "She confided fully only in Charmian. They were almost like sisters."

"I think there was more than one," Leto said in a tiny voice.

"Why do you say that?" I asked her.

Even in her benumbed state, the girl's face flushed. "Some nights, when I slept in Gorgo's bed, she would just climb in and tell me to go back to our chamber. On some nights she—she smelled different than others." Her head nodded and in seconds she was asleep, still sitting, holding Gaia's hand.

"She never told me that," Gaia said.

"A few words more and you can sleep, too," I told her. "How did you help Charmian escape?"

"I was caring for her. She begged me to help her. She said one more beating would kill her and I knew it was true. She hadn't told Diocles everything and she swore she would die first. He knew she was withholding something and was just waiting for her to recover enough for the torture to resume.

"The night before last, when she was recovered enough to walk, even run if she should have to, we left the temple, went out through the grove by the spring, and from there she ran."

"Where did she go?" I asked. "Did she tell you her destination, who would hide her?"

"She said she would be safe, that she had a friend in Baiae."

"So you returned to the temple and pretended that she was still in the lockup?"

"Yes. Diocles wasn't fooled for long, but I bought her time to escape."

"Gaia," Julia said, "why didn't Charmian accompany Gorgo on the night she was killed?"

"She went, but Gorgo told her to stay at the edge of the grove, not go with her to the spring."

"Had Gorgo done that before?" Julia asked.

"I don't know. I don't think so . . ." The girl was asleep.

We rose and left them there, under the eye of a slave woman skilled in healing. Back in the colonnaded courtyard, we compared notes.

"She went to Baiae," I said. "Who would she have gone to? Who would hide her?"

"It must have been one of the lovers," Julia said. "What other free 'friend' would she have had?"

"We know it wasn't Gelon," Hermes said.

"It's a long walk to Baiae for a girl in her condition," Marcus noted.

"Desperation drives people to do surprising things," I said.

THE NEXT DAY WAS A DAY WHEN official business was forbidden, for which I was grateful. It gave me a chance to wander about in Baiae, ostensibly just enjoying the sights but in reality snooping. Hermes and I made our way into the goldsmiths' and jewelers' quarter which, this being Baiae, was bigger than Rome's.

"Somewhere here," I said, "there has to be someone who knows who bought that necklace."

"Why?" Hermes asked. "It might have been bought in Alexandria or Athens. Somebody may have found it in a shipwreck and peddled it cheap. The man who gave it to her may have stolen it. Why are you so sure that the man who sold it is here? I looked all over this quarter last time."

"Because this morning I sacrificed a very fine ram to Jupiter and I specifically requested that we find that man today."

"Oh, well, then. Let's go find him."

Amazingly, we found the right man on the third try. The shop was one of the smallest, wedged between a huge cameo display and a place that seemed to specialize in rubies the size of minor Asiatic kingdoms.

"Must've missed this one," Hermes muttered.

We went inside and a man looked up from behind a display case. "Yes, sir? How may I—" he caught sight of my purple stripe and jumped from behind the case "—help you?" He was of that Greek-Asian breed so common in the gem trade, the sort who hails from Antioch or Palmyra or some other Eastern metropolis.

"Hermes," I said. He took the necklace from inside his tunic and held it up for the man to see. "Do you recognize this?"

The man took two or three of the massive links in his fingertips and studied the carved gems. "Why, yes. I sold this piece about a year ago. I am quite certain. This is a very remarkable necklace. It's Phrygian. Is there some problem?"

"I just need to know who you sold it to," I told him.

"Of course. Gaeto the Numidian bought it. I've heard he is dead. Is there a problem with the inheritance?"

"Exactly." I was astounded, but I had a politician's knack for covering such lapses. "Did he indicate when he bought it that he intended it as a gift?"

"No, but I presumed that he did intend it so. A man does not wear such jewelry, after all." He thought about this for a moment. "Well, admittedly there are certain men who——but not Gaeto, certainly. He must have intended it for a woman."

"For his wife?" I asked innocently.

"Well, sir"—he chuckled—"in the first place, I understand that he had more than one. In the second, well, in my experience, which is quite extensive, a man rarely buys such a piece for a woman to whom he is *already* married, if you take my meaning."

"I know what you mean," I told him. "I don't suppose he made any indication of just who the recipient might be?"

"I am afraid not. Gaeto was always the soul of discretion." He sighed. "I am sorry to hear that he is no more. I know he was a slave dealer but really quite a splendid man, extremely rich and a very good customer."

"He bought other items from you?" I asked.

"Oh, yes. He had a taste for these massive, Eastern pieces. They are my specialty, you see. Most of the items I sold him, he bought for himself. Men in Numidia wear heavy gold bracelets, for instance. And he bought heavy signet rings, gifts for Numidian colleagues, I believe. And he did not haggle. He knew what my merchandise is worth."

"I am sorry you have lost a valued customer. I rather liked the man myself, brief though our acquaintance was."

"I take it," he said with a wry expression, "that his widow—the local one, I mean—is disputing possession of that necklace with a favorite? It is a common story."

"Yes, yes, but please keep this to yourself for the time being. Delicate legal matter, you understand."

"Of course, of course."

We went out, walked a few streets, and paused by one of the many fine fountains. A little consort of musicians played harp and flute for our entertainment.

"So it was Gaeto!" Hermes said. "He must have been one of her lovers."

"So it would appear," I said. I stared into the swirling waters of the fountain, musing on this new development.

"She was doing the father and the son at the same time?"

"If Gelon is to be believed, he was courting her, but matters had not yet progressed to physical intimacy. As Julia pointed out, she almost certainly was not going out to meet the giver of the necklace, because she wore all her jewelry except that one piece. Gaeto was not the killer, because he was at the banquet with us at Norbanus's house when it happened."

"Don't let him off that easy," Hermes advised. "Men use hirelings to commit their murders and make sure that important people see them when the crime is committed."

"All too true," I agreed. "But I somehow feel that it isn't what happened here. This thing—" my frustration made me lose my vocabulary, a rare thing for me "—this is so different from the sort of crime we are used to in Rome. There, the motives are relatively simple. Men want supreme power and are willing to do anything to get it. When all the confusing shrubbery is cut away, that is what remains: the lust for power. If jealousy is involved, it is because men envy one another's power."

"That's how it is in Rome," he agreed.

"Here, we have wealth, and status, and jealousy and snobbery and, I suspect, love."

"Love?" Hermes said.

"Our first day here, Gelon rode up to the temple and we saw how he and that girl looked at each other. I am certain that that was real. Whoever else she was seeing, whatever other lovers she had, she loved that boy, and he loved her."

"It's not usually a motive for killing," Hermes said, "except when a man surprises his wife with a lover. Under law, that's justification for homicide."

"That's not about love," I said, frustrated. "That's about *property*. It's about honor, if you can define the concept. Love doesn't come into it."

"Still, jealousy is a powerful thing," Hermes said. "If Gaeto was visiting Gorgo on the sly, giving her rich presents, Jocasta would have a reason to kill them both."

I nodded. "That thought has not escaped me. But you pointed out yourself that the blow that killed Gaeto could not have been delivered by a woman."

"A hireling," he said. "This is Campania, homeland of gladiators."

"And would Gaeto have allowed one such into his bedroom at night? And then turned his back on him?"

"That does present a problem," he admitted.

"I don't think my best with a dry throat," I said. "Let's see what the district has to offer by way of refreshment."

"I thought you'd say that."

We turned our steps toward an entertainment district where there were numerous dining and drinking establishments. Rome is a city of taverns and food stalls and street vendors, but Baiae, as usual, is different. This area featured spacious courtyards filled with tables where elaborate lunches and dinners were served at moderate cost. The main difference between eating in such a place and in a private home is that the diners sit rather than recline at table.

A girl brought us a very superior wine and I ordered big bowls of the savory fish stew. We ate and pondered and discussed and got nowhere. We had a superfluity of circumstance and suspects and yet we were woefully ignorant in a few key areas.

"Praetor Metellus!" This was shouted in that singsong fashion women use when they want your attention from a distance. I looked around and saw Quadrilla, Manius Silva's wife, waving frantically. She rushed over to our table, followed by a slave laden with parcels, the plunder of a triumphant day of shopping, no doubt. "Might I join you?"

"Please do," I said, mystified at this seeming friendliness.

"Cleitus," she said to the slave, "take these things to the house and have the litter sent to me here." Wordlessly the man left. "I was hoping to find you today, Praetor."

"I must wonder at that," I said. "Your husband was most displeased with me."

She laughed gaily. "Oh, he was! Serves him right, too, trying to pass such an obvious bribe. Poor Manius! That sly Cretan gets him into more trouble." She accepted a cup from the serving girl and downed a good portion of it.

"Is Diogenes really counterfeiting perfume?" I asked.

"I have no idea. If he does, it's good enough to fool me. But doubledealing and suborning are reflexive with Cretans, they just can't help themselves. Diogenes has to outmaneuver all his competition, by underhanded means if at all possible."

"You mean it wasn't true, what your husband said about Diogenes being such a hardworking and resourceful businessman?"

"Oh, it's all true. But that is not enough, you see. Diogenes could never be content to know that he excelled through hard work and courage and intelligence. He has to know that he's tricked everybody. It's been that way since Ulysses, you know. Ulysses never opened his mouth except to lie, and Greeks have held to that ideal from that day to this. And the Cretans are the most Greek of the Greeks. Deceiving Romans is child's play to them. Diogenes has to prove that he can outlie, outtrick, and outbribe all the other Greeks in Campania."

"They are a competitive lot," I agreed. "Not as homicidal as they used to be, though."

"Homicidal?"

"Yes, you know: the *Iliad*, the House of Atreus, the tyrannicides, Harmodius and Aristogiton, even Alexander and his friends. They were as bloody handed a pack as you could ask for. But these days they'd rather connive than murder forthrightly."

"I'm not sure I follow you." She hadn't been expecting this.

"Just that I have two murders on my hands and I'd like to eliminate as many suspects as possible."

"Don't you think Gelon killed the girl, and her father killed Gaeto in revenge?"

"Quite possible, of course. Likely, in fact. But I dislike having the obvious thrust before my nose. It makes me suspicious."

"As it should. It's so seldom Rome sends us a man of subtlety. I like you, Decius Caecilius, even if my husband is temporarily indisposed toward you. What has stirred up your suspicions?" She sat back and twirled a blue-painted fingernail in her wine.

"A number of things. For instance, the late Gaeto was a man everyone affected to despise, yet I saw him at formal and private functions, always receiving the deference one expects to be shown a public official or a prominent priest or patrician, not a slaver. Why was that?"

"Ah, poor Gaeto." She stared into the bottom of her cup, which seemed to have grown distant in her sight. "I'll grant you, his profession made him lowly—"

Says the probable ex-prostitute, I thought.

"—but he was a remarkable man. One grows so tired, you know, of effete aristocrats, money-obsessed businessmen and their social-climbing wives. And that is about all we have here in Baiae, as you may have noticed. Gaeto was something very different. As wealthy as any of the local tycoons but not at all softened by riches and luxury. He had a manner that is rare in Romans of this generation. I am not saying that he was just some primitive brute. You can buy as many of those as you want in the market."

"You mean," I said, "that he was like a tribal warrior chieftain but a cultured, sophisticated one?"

She smiled lazily. "Yes, that's it. Women like that, you know: a rough man, dripping masculinity, who's had his roughest edges polished smooth. It made him very popular among the ladies here."

Oho, I thought. Here's a new factor. "You mean other men besides Diocles may have had a reason to kill him?"

She erupted in tinkling laughter. "A jealous husband? Here? Not likely! As long as the wife was discreet, the husband would just try to parlay the affair into a business advantage. This isn't Rome, Praetor."

"As I am being reminded constantly. Did your husband or Diocles have business dealings with Gaeto? Not implying any impropriety on your part, of course."

"Only on the most mundane level, I think. Gaeto dealt in high-quality slaves, so he would want to present them to best advantage. That would mean perfumes and scented oils, especially for the house servants and entertainers. And he was princely in gift giving, especially with his African and Asian contacts. I believe he regularly ordered assortments of the costliest scents for that purpose."

"Do you know of anyone besides Gaeto who might have been involved with Gorgo?"

She pursed her mouth and arched her eyebrows. "As far as I know, she was as blameless as her eulogy would have it."

"Is anyone ever that blameless?" I asked.

"Never. But she lived a rather secluded life out there in the temple. We never mixed much with them except at municipal banquets and that sort of event. They're local aristocracy, or fancy themselves so, too well-bred for the likes of us." She laughed again. "If that's how aristocrats live, you can have it!"

"I couldn't agree more, though I'm something of an aristocrat myself. In Rome we like to affect a taste for the simple, rural life. In truth, we'd all love to live like Lucullus, if only we could afford it."

"You're not doing too badly," she said. "Old Hortalus's villa is said to be the finest in Italy."

"Alas, it's just a loan. Before long, I'll have to go down to Bruttium and you know how miserable that's going to be. It's like Rome two hundred years ago and I'll be surrounded by Bruttians."

"It is a backward place," she agreed. "Actually, you should be grateful these murders have occurred. It gives you an excuse to prolong your stay." She looked up under her thick eyelashes and smiled slyly.

"By Jupiter, you're right. I suppose that makes *me* a suspect."

"I think I would commit murder to stay in Baiae and out of Bruttium!" she said, bursting into laughter again. She had been into the wine before she joined our table.

"I still wonder, though," I went on, "why the *men* deferred to him so. Only a small minority would have found in him the same attractions the women did."

"More than you would think," she said. "But you are right. The fact is, many of Baiae's noblest had business dealings with Gaeto. Very deep, important business dealings. Some of our most impeccably respectable citizens are involved in extremely dirty dealings."

"What sort of dealings?" I asked.

She leaned forward on her elbows in a parody of intimacy. "It's all about using money to get more money, Senator. That's what business is. You Roman aristocrats like to pretend that the only respectable sources of wealth are land and plunder in war. The businessmen here prefer the luxury trades. But you and they know the truth: The greatest source of wealth is human flesh. And the only true power is absolute dominion over human flesh." The worldly cynicism in her eyes was an unsettling thing to behold.

"Go on," I said, through with clever banter.

"Do you know why everyone despises the slaver? Because he reminds us that we are all slavers. Where would our empire be without slaves?"

"We wouldn't have an empire," I answered. "We wouldn't have a civilization."

"Exactly. They grow our food, and then they cook it and serve it to us and clean up afterward. They build our houses and tend our baths. They provide us with fornication and when we tire of them, we can sell them off. They race chariots for our amusement and die in our arenas for the same purpose. They teach our children and tend us in our illnesses."

"It's hard to imagine a decent life without them," I agreed.

She sat back with a depraved smile. "We consume them, Praetor, just as surely as if we were cannibals eating their flesh. We dangle before them the prospect of freedom to keep them pacified and ensure more willing service, but the whip and the cross are always there just in case kind treatment and prospective freedom aren't enough."

"It's the price of losing wars and choosing the wrong parents," I said. "Been that way since Deucalion's Flood. What is your point?"

"That we all know it's true and it shames us. So we've singled out the slaver, the man who buys and sells the flesh, to bear the brunt of social disdain while we all merrily profit from his business. If it came out that some of our most revered public figures were silent partners with our richest but most despised resident, certain reputations would be sullied forever."

This tickled my memory, suggested some question that had eluded me or that I had failed to ask. But she went relentlessly on and the moment passed.

"There are worse things than being a slave, Praetor, and I've been some of them. Luckily, it was only temporary and now I'm a great lady again. Some things can be covered over and forgotten. Others can't. Bear that in mind while you look into these killings."

"I shall do so," I assured her.

Abruptly she dropped the serious discussion and resumed the gossipy banter more suitable to the situation. A few minutes later her litter arrived and she made her good-byes.

"Well," I said to Hermes as we resumed our lunch, "what do you make of that?"

"Another woman muddying the waters. Probably trying to throw you off her husband's scent and onto someone else."

"What she said about slaves—what do you think?"

He shrugged. "She didn't say much I can argue with. But it's the way of the world, isn't it? Short of the gods coming down from Olympus and taking a hand in things, how are you going to change anything?"

"How, indeed?"

9

"WHY CAN'T THINGS EVER BE SIMPLE?" I lamented.

"Because people are involved," Julia informed me. "I think natural phenomena are relatively simple and predictable. When people with their passions and hatreds and ambitions are involved, things get complicated."

We were sitting in one of the lovely outer gardens of the villa. The bees buzzed pleasantly among the blossoms, the fish splashed vigorously in the ponds, the birds sang prettily in the trees, the mountain smoked ominously in the distance.

"I wish *that* was predictable," I said, pointing a finger toward Vesuvius.

"As far as I know, volcanoes are as unpredictable as the whims of the gods," Julia said.

"Do you think all the most prominent people here were in league with the late Gaeto? Have they all been making illicit profits from the slave trade?"

"The day I believe a word one of those women says, you have my permission to bury me alive like a promiscuous Vestal."

"I thought so. At least we know now that Gaeto gave her the necklace."

"We know that Gaeto bought the necklace from the jeweler," she corrected me. "It might have been through other hands in the interim."

"Your logic, as always, is better than mine," I admitted.

"What are we going to do about Gelon?" she asked.

"I have to allow him to see to his father's funeral," I told her. "It would be inhumane to do otherwise."

"I agree, but he will have to be kept under close watch."

"Hermes and Marcus and some of the others can ride escort. I doubt the boy will try to escape. Where can a Numidian hide in Italy? And he couldn't get to a ship in time to elude me."

"I hope that is true. It would be a great embarrassment if he were to get away." She added, "And you are going to have to set a trial date soon. It won't look good if you stall much longer and duty calls you elsewhere."

"Bruttium," I muttered.

Reluctantly, I rose and went to the wing where we were keeping Gelon. He had borne the news of his father's death stoically. Of course, I had no idea what their relationship might have been, except that Gaeto had been generous with his son in terms of money. Not every son is saddened by the passing of a father. He had turned pale when I described the circumstances of his father's murder, but that was to be expected. To be murdered in your own bedroom by someone you trust is always an unsettling prospect.

When I arrived at his quarters, I found Antonia already there. Wanting to console the boy in his grief, no doubt. From the look of things, she was succeeding.

"Gelon," I said, pretending not to notice his guilty expression, "today you may ride to your father's house to see to his obsequies."

"That is very good of you, Praetor," he said.

"Before leaving, you will be required to swear oaths before the gods and witnesses that you will not try to flee custody."

"Certainly."

"You will also be escorted by my men. This is more for your protection than from any concern I might have that you will try to escape. There is probably a good deal of hostility toward you among the local populace, especially the Greeks."

"I have no objection," he said.

"May I come along?" Antonia asked.

"You may not," I said.

Thus it was that, a little past noon, we rode from the villa down the Baiae road. As we passed the temple I saw the last smoke rising from the embers of the morning sacrifice. This caused me to wonder how Diocles was coping with his personnel shortage. As we went on to the main road I chanced to look back and I saw the old man standing before the altar, looking at us. The distance was too great to read his expression.

By the time we approached Gaeto's residence and slave compound, the bright day had turned gloomy, with lowering clouds promising rain. It seemed fitting. Not because of the solemn occasion but because the days had been all too bright and pure since my arrival. When things go too well for too long, the gods have something nasty in store for you, and weather is no exception. A break in the fine weather might be a good thing.

We arrived at Gaeto's compound to find preparations well advanced. Jocasta and the steward had arranged what I was informed was a traditional Numidian chieftain's funeral, with certain Greek and Roman embellishments.

On the beach had been erected an imposing funeral pyre, made of seasoned wood with abundant frankincense stuffed into every available cranny. Gaeto lay atop it on splendid cushions, clothed in equally magnificent raiment. He looked startlingly lifelike, almost as if he would rise from the bier and join the obsequies. This was the advantage of having your own Egyptian undertakers.

The musicians from the compound played harps and sistra, and black Nubians using sticks or their palms beat a hypnotic rhythm on drums made of hollowed logs with skins stretched over the open ends. The drum is an instrument favored by no civilized people, but it creates a stirring rhythm when played by skilled Africans and certain Asians.

The rest of the slaves sent up histrionic lamentations, the Greeks among them being especially skillful in this. Ritual mourning is an ancient tradition, and they wailed lustily, though they could hardly have been deeply moved by Gaeto's death.

Some of the slave women, possibly concubines, stripped naked, smeared themselves with ashes, and flogged one another bloody with bundles of thin rods. Jocasta, who was Greek, took a more decorous course, merely unbinding her hair and letting it fall loose on her shoulders, ripping her gown down the middle and, now bare from the hips upward, drawing a single, symbolic stripe of ash across her brow.

Gelon recited a prayer or eulogy in his native tongue, an eerie, high-pitched chant full of gutturals and vocal clicks, with each sentence or verse seeming to end on a rising inflection. At the end of it he took a torch and set fire to the pyre, and as the flames rose the tribal bodyguard rode around it in an endless circle, whooping and pounding their hide shields with their spears.

All in all, it was a fine send-off. The only thing missing was a delegation of mourners and attendees from the town and surrounding countryside. But there was not a single representative of the local population. Whatever deference Gaeto had received in life, he got none at all in death. Something seemed obscurely wrong about this, but I couldn't put my finger on it.

When the fire had burned to embers, the undertakers went in with rakes and took out the blackened bones and wrapped them in many yards of white linen. This bundle they carefully placed in an elaborate urn and over the bundle poured an aromatic mixture of myrrh and perfume. Then they placed the cover on the urn and sealed it with pitch. This urn, I was informed, would travel by ship to Numidia and be placed in the family tomb.

When all was accomplished, a funeral banquet was held in the courtyard of the villa. It was served in Numidian fashion, with all the feasters seated in a circle on the ground, upon cushions. The centerpiece was the urn containing Gaeto's remains—an interesting variation on the Roman practice of having a skeleton or skull among the decorations of the dining room, to remind diners of the transitory nature of life; that the tomb is never far away; and that food, wine, and good company should be enjoyed while we have the chance.

"What will you do now, Gelon?" I asked.

"You mean, assuming that I'm not found guilty and executed?"

"Naturally. If acquitted, will you continue your father's business?" I picked up a leg of roast pheasant. I had learned that the foods traditional for a Numidian chieftain's funeral—whole roast camel, elephant's feet, baked ostrich, and so forth—had not been available. I was quite satisfied with the fare they had been able to provide.

"I don't think so. Trade has never been to my taste. If I am spared, I will sell out and return to Numidia." Jocasta made a grimace of distaste. I wondered if she were part of his inheritance. Clearly, she had no liking for the idea of forsaking ultracivilized Baiae for barbarous Numidia.

"And what will you do there?"

"Resume the traditional family business," he informed me.

"Which is?"

"Raiding."

"Ah. A gentleman's profession." As indeed it was, among Numidians as among Homer's Achaeans.

"And have you discovered my husband's murderer?" Jocasta asked in an abrupt change of subject. She had changed into an untorn gown but had left her hair unbound and her forehead was still smeared with ash. Her eyes were red but dry, as if from the effects of sleeplessness rather than weeping.

"I expect to have the culprit in custody momentarily," I assured her.

"We've been hearing that a lot from you lately," she said, unmollified.

"Madame," I said, "it is not my business to apprehend felons at all. That is the task of the municipal authorities. I take a hand only in the interests of justice, which I feel are not being served in this district."

She bowed her head. "I stand chastened. My apologies, Praetor."

It was raining the next morning when we mounted and made a bedraggled little procession as we rode up the bluff and onto the road that led toward Baiae. The stretch of road leading to Baiae was lined with fine tombs and shaded by large trees. The heavy mist that accompanied the drizzly rain lent the beautiful road a dreamlike aspect, but there was nothing dreamlike about the ambush.

They came from behind the tombs and trees: men on horseback, others on foot. They attacked with quiet ferocity, but the quiet didn't last long. The Numidian guard raised a wild war cry and began to pelt the attackers with javelins while forming a barrier around Gelon.

Hermes already had his sword out, as did my other young men. All except Marcus had fought in Gaul or Macedonia or Syria. Being a serving magistrate I couldn't go about wearing a sword, but I was no fool, either. My sword hung sheathed from the near-front horn of my saddle and I had it out just in time. My attacker took a swipe at my head, but I ducked low and extended my arm, thrusting beneath his jaw. He went off his horse backward with a spray of blood and a gargling cry. My horse collided with his, and its shod feet went out from under it, scrabbling on the wet pavement.

As it fell I managed to jump clear and keep hold of my sword, a circumstance of which I was absurdly proud. I looked around to see the battle well joined, the quarters so close that I could smell the stench of the attackers' bodies and the garlic on their breath. I saw a Nubian go down with a spear through his chest, and then Hermes lopped the sword arm off a mounted man. The arm chanced to fall at my feet and I took the opportunity to appropriate its weapon—a good legionary *gladius*.

I was unarmored and had no shield, so I felt the need of a spare weapon. Besides, I wanted to try out some moves I'd seen that two-sword gladiator use in the Pompeii amphitheater. In Rome, I'd usually waded into street brawls with a *caestus* on one hand and a dagger in the other. In the legions, I'd fought with the customary sword and shield. I was intrigued by the possibilities of two swords, and I had my opportunity to try them out almost immediately.

A burly fellow wearing a rag of tunic and wool leggings charged me on foot, thrusting a sword at my chest. With my left-hand sword I banged it aside as I stepped in and slashed him across the belly with the other from left to right. He doubled over and I brought the left-hand blade down on the back of his neck, almost beheading him.

Two more closed in on me. The nearer held a club in both hands, presenting an interesting problem even if he'd been alone. As he raised the club for a blow, I sidestepped and brought my left-hand blade across in a backhand cut against his left wrist, severing it even as I brought the right-hand sword down on his skull, splitting it. The other man was on me even as the first fell, but Hermes rode up behind him and spitted him from back to front.

I spun around, looking for more men to fight. The only action was from a half-dozen horsemen who were pounding away into the mist, having had enough. The dead and wounded lay all over, bleeding, gurgling, cursing. The surviving Numidians were ruthlessly impaling anything that twitched.

"Stop them!" I shouted. "I need some who can talk!" But it was no use. The tribesmen were beyond control, furious to avenge their slain comrades.

"Casualties?" I demanded in disgust.

"Four of our party wounded," Hermes said, wiping blood from his sword. "Two Numidians killed."

Marcus walked up, having lost his horse somewhere. He was wrapping a cloth around his bloodied upper arm, but he was grinning. "For such a dignified magistrate," he said, "you seemed to be enjoying yourself, Praetor. Wait until I tell Julia."

"Wait until tonight, when that wound begins to hurt," I told him. "I want to see your face then."

"But the ladies will be fussing over me," he said. "I'm a hero, bloodied in defense of my patron. I'll—"

"Hermes!" I said, cutting him off. "Take the lictors and go into Baiae. Get all those officials out here and tell them the last to arrive gets a flogging." Of course I had no authority to do this to Roman citizens, but anger was getting the best of me. Besides, one of my uncles had once had a Roman senator flogged in public, and everybody knew it.

While we waited I examined the dead attackers. The rain stopped and the mist began to clear, making the task easier. They looked like army deserters, runaway slaves, ruined peasants—the sort of bandits who are never quite eradicated from Italy. Their filth and rags proclaimed that they had been living in the hills for a long time.

Two of the Numidians rode out to round up our scattered horses. By the time they returned with the wandering beasts, the good burghers of Baiae had begun to show up, looking none too pleased with my peremptory summons. Well, I was none too pleased with them. Uninvited gawkers also appeared. Violence and bloodshed attract them like flies.

To my surprise, Cicero was with them. "What's going on here, Decius?" he asked. "This district hasn't seen such a pile of bodies since the funeral games for Pompeius Strabo."

"Listen to me!" I said to the assembled officials. "The situation here is getting entirely out of hand. At first it was just a murder here, a murder there—nothing to get upset about. But today I was attacked by a whole crowd of bandits. They tried to assassinate me, possibly to kill this man in my custody." I pointed at Gelon with a sword and realized that I still held a weapon in each hand. Also, I was liberally bespattered with blood from head to foot. No wonder they were looking at me with such strange expressions. Quite a change from my snowy, purple-bordered toga.

"You people have let the situation here deteriorate into a shocking state," I said. "I am minded to call in the troops to restore order. Pompeius has a training camp at Capua and I'm sure he'll be happy to lend me a cohort or two to establish martial law here."

"Praetor, Praetor, you are making too much of this," said Norbanus. "This is simple banditry. What sort of people usually travel on this road? Wealthy citizens, the caravans of merchants—all ripe pickings for bandits. The day was dark and rainy; there was ground fog. These wretches did not see that this was a well-armed band of military men and warriors until it was too late."

"Yes, Praetor," said Manius Silva. "We always have increased bandit activity whenever the volcano gets frisky."

"The volcano?" I said, not certain I had heard him correctly.

"Oh, yes," Norbanus chimed in. "You see, bandits fort up in the crater of Vesuvius. They've done it for centuries. The local farmers bring them food and wine rather than endure their raids. Most of the time they are content with this. There are only a couple of very narrow passes into the crater, so they are relatively safe there. But when there is a venting, the smoke and ash drive them out and they raid in the lowlands until it clears up." Everyone nodded and agreed that this was so.

"You lot," I said, "have to be the most useless pack of soft-assed degenerates on the whole Italian peninsula! You mean to tell me that you allow a whole colony of bandits to camp on your doorstep! Why don't you go up there and exterminate them?"

"This is Campania, Praetor," Norbanus said stiffly. "It's always been the practice here."

His wife, Rutilia, spoke up. "When some malcontent decides to be an enemy of society, Vesuvius gives him a place to go. We'd rather they do that than hang around here and murder us in our sleep."

I turned to Cicero. "Do you think Cato could be right? Is this what too much good food and soft living does to people?"

"Your troubles this day are not yet over, Decius," said the ex-consul.

I closed my eyes and sighed. "What now?"

"Ah," Silva began hesitantly, "Praetor, you see—well, there's been another killing in town. Discovered just this morning, in fact."

"No one important," Norbanus added hastily. "Just a slave."

"What sort of slave?" I asked bleakly.

"A runaway," he answered. "Someone identified her as a girl from the Temple of Apollo."

I didn't say anything for a while and they, quite wisely, didn't intrude upon my ruminations. Finally, I came to a decision.

"I am coming into town. Make a house available for my use. No craft are to leave the harbor, no one is to pass through the gates without my permission. I am sending for troops to enforce my authority and you may consider yourselves under siege until I find out what is going on here and have taken steps to correct it."

"You can't do that!" Silva cried. "You need a decree of the Senate for such a thing. Besides, it will ruin business."

"He can do it," Cicero informed him. "He has the authority to declare martial law under his own imperium until the Senate has reached a decision. General Pompey will back him up. Pompey wants no disturbances in Campania right now."

Everybody knew what he meant. The Senate was disturbed by Caesar's defiance and was turning to Pompey as a savior. Pompey's greatest strength was in southern Campania and points south on the peninsula, all the way to Messina. Here he would raise his legions if need be. He wanted things orderly here.

The white-robed chief priest of the city came forward. "Praetor, before you can enter the walls, you must be purified of this blood and so must your men."

"Delicate lot, aren't you?" I sneered. "In Rome, we bathe in the stuff."

"Decius," Cicero said in a low, warning voice.

"Very well," I said. "I will not offend your guardian gods."

"I will see to the arrangements," the priest said.

"Then go, all of you," I ordered. The crowd, stunned by the turn of events, began to straggle back to Baiae.

Rutilia, again in her golden wig, did not get back into her litter. Instead, she approached me. "Decius Caecilius," she said when she stood before me, "allow me to tell you that you look very good dressed in blood." Then she turned and went back to her litter.

"Cicero," I said, "do you think Roman women will ever be like that?"

"Decius," he said, "haven't you noticed? They already are."

10

By THE TIME WE REACHED THE CITY GATE
the priest had made his preparations and we went through the ceremony
of being washed in purified water, fumigated with incense, passed between two flames, and dressed in new clothing. Thus cleansed of blood,
we entered the city. A spacious town house owned by a friend of Cicero's
was being prepared for us, and while we waited I demanded to be taken to
view the body.

The *duumviri* conducted us to a long, low building behind the Temple of Venus Libitina. As at Rome, the goddess in this aspect was the pa-
troness of the funeral trade and a conductor of the shades of the dead to
the underworld. Chambers for receiving the dead opened off a portico that
ran the length of the building. We were taken to the last chamber. Inside
were three or four bodies.

"This is where we take the bodies of slaves, paupers, and foreigners
who have no patrons or *hospites*," explained the chief undertaker. "Those

usually are sailors who happen to die while in port. If no one claims the body by the second day, they are taken to the burial pits outside town."

Rome had such a facility, though of course much larger. It was something of a scandal that elderly slaves were often cast out of the house to die in the streets and go unclaimed, so their masters could be spared the trouble and expense of decent burial. At least Baiae had few paupers and, it seemed, few skinflint slave owners.

The body lay on a tablelike stone bier, about waist height to me, covered by a sheet to keep away the flies. At my nod a slave drew back the sheet. Charmian lay stiff and pale, bold-eyed no more. She looked thinner than when I had last seen her, as if she had been drained. There were bruises and weals and whip stripes all over her naked body. Her neck was bruised, but whether from the beating or strangulation I could not tell.

"We wondered about this one," said the undertaker. "As you can see, she had recently been severely beaten. That's probably why she ran."

"I want to see her back," I said. The gloved and masked attendants turned her on her side. In her death rigor she moved like a wooden statue. Her back was savaged worse than her front, but I saw no stab wounds. There had been no crushing blow to the back of the skull. I signaled them to let her rest.

"Have you any idea when she died?" I asked the undertaker.

"I think it must have been yesterday evening sometime. The rigor is consistent with that time. Also, if she'd been dead longer, there would be signs; the beginning of decomposition, bites from scavengers, and so forth."

"Had you any idea who she was?"

"Someone said she looked like a slave from the Temple of Apollo, body servant to the girl who was murdered," the undertaker went on. "I sent a messenger to the priest, but we've received no answer yet."

"I'll be responsible for her," I said. "I will pay for her funeral and burial."

"Funeral?" the man said.

"You heard me. She will receive the rites and be decently cremated and interred."

"As you wish, Praetor."

The officials behind me remained stony faced, undoubtedly convinced that I was mad. But they recoiled in horror when I bent close to the poor girl and sniffed. I have the usual dislike of dead bodies, but some things must be done.

"The praetor is gathering evidence," Hermes told them in a voice that told them to keep quiet.

She smelled very faintly of horse. Had she been hiding in a stable? Yet I saw no bits of straw or hayseed in her hair. There was another smell, even fainter but unmistakable: the fragrance called Zoroaster's Rapture. I straightened.

"Has the body been bathed?" I asked.

"No, this is just how she was found," the undertaker explained. "Since she is to have a funeral, we will of course prepare her properly."

"Do so." I turned to the officials. "I want to know where she was found and the circumstances."

Silva gestured, and a man in gaudy military garb came to the front. I recognized him as the officer of the city guard.

"Just after first light this morning," he reported, "I was notified that a young woman's body had been discovered at the municipal laundry. I—"

"Take me there," I said, cutting him off. I wanted to hear the rest of his tale on the site.

In a mass, we walked from the precincts of the temple and through the city and out one of the side gates. This took no more than a few minutes, Baiae being the small town that it was.

"I must say, Praetor," Norbanus said, "that you are making a great fuss over a dead runaway."

"Is everyone here really as obtuse as they pretend," I asked, "or is this some act put on for my benefit?" I glared around, but nobody said anything. "Gorgo, daughter of Diocles the priest, was murdered. Now her slave girl has likewise been murdered. The two are connected. Investigating this unfortunate slave girl's death is as important as investigating Gorgo's."

I might as well have been speaking to them in Parthian. When people are accustomed to thinking in terms of rank, status, hierarchy, and so forth, it is difficult if not impossible for them to think any other way. I had learned long since that my mental fluidity was a rare thing in a highborn Roman. In any sort of Roman, for that matter.

The municipal laundry lay just outside the gate. Although it was just a place where wives and family servants could come to do the household laundry, like everything else in Baiae it was a thing of beauty. A low hillside had been terraced and a stream diverted to descend what appeared to be a great, marble stairway. Here a number of women were at work, beating the wet clothes and bedding with wooden paddles, laughing and gossiping the whole time. On a sunny slope just downhill, bronze drying racks awaited the clean cloth.

There were many places to sit and rest amid the soothing sound of flowing water. Huge, mature plane trees provided abundant shade. Protective herms lined the watercourse, and at the top of the marble stair a benevolent, reclining water god watched over all. It was the sort of scene pastoral poets like to sing about: nature with all its dangerous aspects banished, nature tamed and made orderly.

"Where was she found?" I asked.

The guard captain strode to a spot next to the watercourse, beneath a plane tree. It was a grassy little nook, the sort of place where a family might come for a picnic. "She was laid out here," he said.

"'Laid out'?"

"Yes, Praetor. She was found exactly as you saw her in the *libitinarium*, arranged just as she would have been if she were on a funeral bier."

"But naked?"

"Yes, sir."

"Who found her?"

"Some slave women from the house of Apronius Viba. His house is just against the city wall by the gate, and they were the first to come here this morning."

I went over the ground, but the springy turf and short-trimmed grass held no prints. I saw nothing that might have been lost or discarded by the killer. At the edge of the little clearing a stone stair led up the slope, away from the watercourse. Curious, I climbed it. Everyone else followed dutifully.

The stair traced a curving path beneath low-hanging branches and ended at a broad pavement flooring on a notch cut into the hillside. A retaining wall perhaps ten feet high covered the vertical face of the cut, and it was pierced by at least thirty low, square doorways. I had never seen such a structure before.

"What is this?" I asked.

"Why, Praetor," said Silva, "these are ice caves."

"Oh, yes. You told me about these a few days ago. Who owns them?"

"The ice company leases them to various men of the city," said the guard captain.

"I want a list of all the lessees," I said.

"Why, Praetor?" Norbanus demanded. "One of them is mine, I freely admit. But why do you want to know this?"

"Because they strike me as a good place for a runaway slave to hide," I said, but that was only part of my reason.

He shrugged. "Very well. I can get you the list. There are several of these facilities around the city."

"This is the one that interests me," I said. "It will do."

I saw no more profit to be had in this place, so we returned to the city. By this time my new house was prepared. I sent the rest on about their business but I asked Cicero to tarry. He was clearly bored with life away from Rome and was following my progress out of curiosity.

"Join me for lunch, Marcus Tullius," I asked him. "I have no kitchen staff here yet but we can send out for some food."

"Gladly," he said.

"Thank you for backing me up with these plutocrats," I said as we took chairs in the house's excellent impluvium collonade. "In fact, I was not at all sure about my constitutional powers in this matter. It's not the sort of thing you get taught studying law."

"You're on quite solid ground in a municipality like this," he assured me. "Your imperium overrides all local authority, and your authority to use military force is unquestionable. Of course, that won't stop these people from suing you as soon as you step down from office."

"I'm not worried about that," I told him. "These men are so terrified at having their dealings investigated, they'll never go to Rome to hale me into court."

He grinned. "Isn't guilt a wonderful thing? Even when it has nothing to do with your investigation, it can get people to see things your way. By the way, it was very decent of you to arrange the rites for that poor girl."

"You mean very un-Roman of me?"

He frowned. "Not at all. The humane treatment of slaves is a bedrock of Roman custom. It is one of the things that distinguishes us from barbarians." He was dreaming, but I didn't mention it. "But there could be complications. I hear you've confiscated two of the priest's slave girls. He will construe your taking charge of this one's body as further unauthorized appropriation of his property. He will have grounds for suit."

"I took them to keep him from killing them. And they are evidence. Besides, he's as dirty as the rest of them—I can feel it. He's hiding something and I mean to find out what it is."

A short while later, Hermes returned from the market, trailed by a boy carrying a large basket crammed with goodies. I'd sent Marcus and the rest back to the villa for rest, doctoring, and to tell Julia what was going on. Over a humble but delicious lunch of sausage, seed cakes, fruit, and wine we discussed the latest twists.

"What sort of killer," I said, "goes to the trouble of murdering a slave girl, then lays her out with all possible dignity, as if she were a beloved relative, in one of the most beautiful sites the town has to offer?"

"A pervert," Cicero said without hesitation. "We've seen them in court often enough. The mad ones who kill repeatedly and perform little rites every time: perform unspeakable acts, take body parts, or else dress their victims in beautiful clothes or pose the bodies in grotesque ways or perform ceremonies of their own sick devising. It happens all too commonly."

"She was killed near water, like Gorgo," Hermes noted.

"Yes, that could be a connection," I agreed. "The mad killers Marcus Tullius referred to often employ such ritualistic repetitions. But why take such care with a victim, then strip her naked?"

We thought about this for a while, and it was Hermes who had the inspired answer. "When she ran, she must have had to stop frequently in the fields to rest. By the time she arrived at her protector's house, her clothes would have been filthy with dirt and blood. This friend must have given her new clothing."

"But why take it off—" Then I saw what he was driving at. "Of course! She was given slave livery. Many of the great houses here dress their slaves in distinctive uniforms. The killer couldn't afford to have her found in the livery of his own household."

"Very astute," Cicero approved. "You may have the answer."

"That leaves us the motive for her murder," I said.

"She may have simply known too much," Cicero said. "There has been a great deal of bloodshed around here lately. Plenty of reason to eliminate an inconvenient slave witness."

"Would she have fled to Gorgo's murderer?" I asked.

"She ran to someone she thought had reason to protect her," Hermes said. "She may have been wrong about that."

"If so," Cicero said, "she wouldn't be the first to learn, too late, that a friend can be treacherous."

A short time after this, a messenger came from Norbanus with the list I had requested. The ice company had leased caves to a number of familiar names: Norbanus, Silva, Diogenes the scent merchant; even Gaeto himself was among them.

"This doesn't narrow the search down any," I said disgustedly. "The only one missing is Diocles the priest. He isn't rich enough to afford such an exotic property and probably doesn't entertain enough to need one."

"You don't suspect him of killing his own daughter, do you?" Cicero said, shocked.

"Men have done it before," I pointed out. "Even Agamemnon killed a daughter when it seemed necessary. Diocles was conveniently 'away' that night. He had the opportunity and he may have felt she had dishonored him with her multiple liaisons."

Cicero laughed drily. "Decius, I do not envy you. It's hard enough to get a conviction when you prosecute one man you know to be guilty. But to sort out one or more guilty parties from such a crowd, that is a labor worthy of Hercules!"

A little later Julia and the rest of my party arrived. She greeted Cicero courteously but coolly. Cicero was known for his opposition in the Senate to Caesar's ambitions. Cicero took his leave and I brought Julia up to date on the day's happenings.

"I've brought Leto and Gaia. They can be the mourners at Charmian's funeral."

"Are they up to it?" I asked.

"Gaia is much recovered. Germans are tough. And Leto is greatly heartened."

"Heartened? Why?"

"They were concerned that Diocles might seize them. They were not entirely sure that a *praetor peregrinus* would be competent to protect them. I told them that they were in my personal charge, that I am a Caesar, and that anyone who dared to interfere with them must answer personally to Julius Caesar."

"Ah, that should do the trick," I said. A mere Metellus holding the second-highest office of the Republic was no bargain as a guardian, but Julius Caesar himself, that was another matter entirely.

"And it was an excellent gesture, to give Charmian a funeral."

"Cicero thought so, although he considered it eccentric."

"Cicero is just a jumped-up snob. I, on the other hand, am a patrician. I appreciate the obligations of *nobilitas*."

"I know a bit about *nobilitas* as well," I assured her. "My family, though plebeian, have been consulars for a good many centuries."

"My point exactly," she said with impeccable obscurity.

"On to more pertinent things," I said. "What do you make of the circumstances I've been investigating? In particular, the odd combination of smells on that girl."

Julia shuddered. "Just doing such a thing seems obscene, but I understand why you did it. In a way, I almost wish I had been there. My sense of smell is much more sensitive than yours."

"Well, she's still right over there at the Temple of—"

"Don't even suggest it!" she cried with an apotropaic hand sign to ward off evil. "The very thought fills me with revulsion. Now, if you are through making absurd suggestions—?"

"Quite finished," I assured her.

"Well, then. Assuming you are correct about Zoroaster's Rapture, and I am confident that you are, it occurs to me that the person with whom she sought refuge would have bathed her immediately. The scent may have been in the bath oil or in an unguent applied to her wounds. Like many of the costliest scents, that one is believed to have curative properties."

"Have you ever heard of a perfume that expensive being used on a slave?"

"This is Baiae. The oil or unguent may have been all that was convenient when she arrived."

"That makes sense. What of the horse smell?"

"Maybe she didn't take refuge in a stable. Maybe she had been riding a horse."

"Is that possible? In her condition?"

"We already know that she was incredibly resilient. Just surviving the beating in the first place, then escaping and making her way on foot to Baiae. What was one more ordeal to such a creature?"

I began to ponder, seeking to place the facts we had into some sort of coherent sequence of events, some possible process that might account for all, or most of them. I call this making a model. Julia preferred to call it a *paradigm*, because she was a snooty patrician and preferred to use Greek.

"All right," I said, "let's try this. The girl, with the collusion of Gaia, flees the temple. Somehow, hurt and bleeding, she makes her way to Baiae."

"She had to pass through a gate," Julia said. "Probably the Cumae gate."

"Good point. I'll look into it. Somebody may have seen her, although from what I've seen of the city guard, the Gauls could have marched in without waking them. So she got through the gate and went to the house of her friend protector, whatever you wish to call him. She is taken in, bathed, her wounds treated, given new clothes."

"Eventually," Julia said, following my line of thought, "she becomes a liability. Just why, we don't know. Perhaps she knew too much; perhaps he couldn't afford to have her discovered in his house. He tells her he's taking her somewhere else, somewhere safer."

"He mounts her on a horse," I speculated. "He leads her on another. But they go only as far as the municipal laundry, where he does away with her, removes the incriminating clothes, and goes away, probably back into the town."

"It's a possibility," Julia said, "but it leaves too much unexplained. Why did he kill her? Why the ritualistic disposition of the body? And just who did the girl think had a reason to protect her?"

"Almost anyone would be an improvement on Diocles," I said. "As for the rest, maybe Cicero's right and he's just mad."

"Madness is a too-convenient explanation for seeming irrationality. It is a way to explain away that which we do not understand. More likely, the murderer had a very good reason for each of these apparently inexplicable things—we just don't know what it might be."

"All too likely," I said.

Circe breezed in by dinnertime, with her cluster of personal servants and attendant luggage.

"This is the most entertaining trip I've ever taken," Circe cried as she rushed into the collonade. "Murders in strange places, pitched battles on the road! We'll be the envy of all our friends."

"You'll have an endless fund of stories to tell when everyone is back in Rome for the elections," I agreed. "I can't tell you how happy I am to be able to provide you with this bonanza of gossip."

A litter came right into the impluvium and was set down next to our table. In it Antonia was mopping the heroic brow of young Marcus with a damp cloth. He looked blissfully content.

"Marcus Caecilius Metellus!" I barked. "Get out of that litter and stand on your own feet! That little cut is on your arm and it hardly even bled, you malingering wretch. What am I going to do with you if we're called off to war? In the legions, you're expected to march forty miles a day if your legs are cut off at the knees!"

He crawled from the litter, grumbling, "Aren't you the grumpy one today."

"Can't you let a wounded hero enjoy a little pampering?" Antonia scolded. "You used to be known as the laziest rake in Rome."

"I earned my reputation the hard way," I told her. "Marcus is too young for such things. Decadence takes age and experience. He has neither."

Hermes came in from the town forum, where I'd sent him to collect gossip. "You'll be pleased to learn," he reported, "that there are calls to petition Rome for your recall, to send a band of local lawyers there to sue you for all manner of tyrannical and extraconstitutional practices, possibly to demand your execution."

"I see they're not a bit embarrassed that bandits attacked a Roman praetor on their city's doorstep," I noted. "And how were these incendiary harangues received?"

"Interestingly, the *duumviri* were the voices for moderation. They said that you are a meddlesome and high-handed senator, but that Roman justice must be allowed to take its course. Diocles says he's the man most offended, but he concurred with his friends the *duumviri*. And all of them are clamoring for Gelon's trial and speedy execution."

"Are they, now?" I fumed. "I never expected to have such trouble out of a pack of veritable provincials—"

"They aren't provincials, dear," Julia corrected me, "even if they are aliens. They have full rights of citizenship."

At last the discrepancy that had been lurking at the back of my mind broke out into my conscious mind. "Citizenship!"

"I agree it's something we hand out too freely these days," Julia said, "but why is it so significant now?"

"What I should have thought of immediately! Gaeto was a resident alien. Who was his citizen partner?"

"Whoever it was has been hiding," Hermes said. "Legally, this partner would have been Gaeto's patron. That means he was bound to help with the funeral preparations and attend the rites."

"And yet no local citizen appeared at the funeral," I said.

"It could be someone we've never heard of," Marcus commented. "Just some Italian who rents out his patronage for the convenience of foreign businessmen. If he was away from town when Gaeto died, he couldn't very well have attended the funeral."

"Nonetheless," I said, "I want to know who this patron is. Marcus, tomorrow I want you to go to the municipal archive and see who is registered as Gaeto's citizen patron."

"Why not just ask Gelon?" Julia suggested.

"Good idea," I concurred. "Where is Gelon, by the way?" Somehow I had lost track of the boy.

"He's at the villa," Circe reported, "seeing to the funeral rites for his two guardsmen who were killed this morning. They were his tribesmen and he is obligated to perform the traditional ceremonies."

"Oh," I said. "Does he wish us to attend the funeral?"

"No. They were desert men, simple warriors. Since they died in the morning, they must be cremated by nightfall and their ashes returned to their families in Numidia."

"I wish I had the firewood concession in this district," Marcus said. "With all the funerals lately, I'd be rich as Crassus."

11

WHEN GELON ARRIVED THE NEXT morning our interview was unproductive.

"Patron?" he said.

"Yes. Patron, partner, *hospes,* what have you. In order to practice business in Italy, he must have had one. You mean you were never introduced?" I was seated in the impluvium that morning. Since the town house was three stories high, this formed a veritable well, with the dining room, master bedroom, entrance hall, and so forth opening off the central collonade, the upper floors for storage and the household staff. It was bright and airy, with a beautiful fountain and many potted plants. But I was too frustrated to appreciate its charms.

"Not to my knowledge. If he had one, I am sure it was purely as a matter of convenience. No one was ever introduced to me as such."

"You mean he never mentioned that he had a patron, one who no doubt demanded a percentage of his profits? This is a grave oversight in an otherwise exemplary man of business."

Gelon jerked his head sideways, the Numidian equivalent of a shrug. "Nonetheless, he never spoke of such a person to me."

Marcus awaited nearby. I caught his eye and nodded. Silently he left the house, bound for the municipal archive.

Hermes' report was likewise unproductive. "This town's gates haven't been guarded since the rebellion of Spartacus more than twenty years ago," he said. "You should see the hinges. They're solid with rust. They couldn't get the gates shut if the Parthians invaded. Nobody keeps track of who enters or leaves the town at any hour. They don't want to do anything that might slow down business."

"Somehow this doesn't surprise me," I said. "Cato sounds like a wiser man by the minute."

An hour later Marcus returned, smiling so sunnily that I knew he had bad news to report. "The archivist was of no use at all."

"Gaeto's registration has to be on record there," I said. "Have you forgotten how to bribe a public slave? It's a simple transaction involving money."

"Oh, he was happy to be of assistance," Marcus protested. "You know how boring his job must be. It seems that the relevant documents are no longer there."

"Misplaced?" I suggested. In Rome, the archive slaves kept the filing system deliberately chaotic, so that only they could find anything. You had to bribe them generously if you wanted them to find anything for you.

"No, the archive is in impeccable order. They use the Alexandrian system, with the ends of the scrolls painted in various colors by category, and each category arranged by alpha-beta-gamma, so that any document can be found in seconds. He walked right to where it was supposed to be, but it wasn't among the registrations of alien merchants. And we quickly saw that it wasn't misfiled among other documents. It's just gone."

I kneaded the bridge of my long, Metellan nose. "My day is a shambles and it's not even mid-morning yet. I suppose the slave has no idea who might have appropriated this document?"

"He says he's only been there a year. It might have been taken any time before that."

"Or," Hermes said, "somebody might have gone there yesterday and bribed him to turn it over. He would hardly court a severe flogging by admitting it."

"Everyone here has something to hide," I said, "and the favorite thing to conceal seems to be any connection to Gaeto the Numidian."

This left me with one possible source of information: the grieving widow. Just after mid-morning I was at her front door, accompanied by my lictors. The janitor admitted us and Jocasta received me in the atrium.

"Official business today?" she asked.

"It isn't a court day," I told her, "but I have some informal questions I'd like to ask."

"Then please come this way." As I followed her within the house I admired the way she moved. She had a walk that was both graceful and provocative; its sway emphasized by her long, red hair, which was tied back that morning in a tail that hung down as far as her very shapely buttocks. These and her long legs were clearly delineated by the gown she wore; one of those sheer, close-pleated Greek garments you see in Greek vase paintings, not as shameless as the Coan cloth dresses but extremely bold by stodgier Roman standards. In fact, she was in full Greek regalia that morning, with armlets banding her bare upper arms, her hairstyle and her cosmetics—everything as Greek as Homer.

Instead of the impluvium, this time she led me to a small library that opened off the collonade. I scanned the titles in the honeycomb racks lining three walls. Her taste seemed to run to Greek playwrights and poets, no historians or philosophers. I had the impression that now, free of her husband, Jocasta was detaching herself from all things Numidian and Roman, reverting to her pure Greek heritage.

We took seats at a small table, and a slave set watered wine and a plate of fruit between us. I took a sip and, the amenities now taken care of, got down to the matter at hand.

"Jocasta, you've told me that when your husband was away from Italy, you handled all his business dealings."

"Yes, I told you that," she agreed.

"So you dealt with all his business associates?"

"I believe I did."

"Then you must know Gaeto's citizen partner."

She didn't pause a beat. "Oh, yes. It was a man named Gratius Glabrio." Just because she didn't pause didn't mean that she was not lying, of course.

"Glabrio? Is he a citizen of Baiae? Of Cumae or Stabiae or Pompeii, by any chance?"

"Oh, no. He lives in Verona. It will be days before he even knows that Gaeto is dead."

"Which would account for his absence from the funeral. Have you any idea why there is no record of the affiliation in the local archive? It is required by law."

"I've no idea at all. The partnership was established when my husband first set up business in Italy. That was several years before we were married. I've never met the man personally, although just last year I sent him his percentage of the year's profits."

Another dead end. Verona was nearly as far from Baiae as it was possible to go and still be on the Italian peninsula. By the time I could prove or disprove the existence of this Gratius Glabrio I would already have, hopefully, solved this case. And by that time Gelon might well have been tried, condemned, and executed for a murder I did not believe he had committed.

"You make much of Gaeto's outcast status," I said, "yet you are a woman of education and refinement. If I may be so personal, how does one of your breeding end up married to a Numidian slaver?"

"Haven't you guessed?" she said with a sultry tilt of her head. "Gaeto bought me."

"You were a slave?"

"Nothing quite as crude as that. I am from Athens. Like my mother and grandmother before me, I was raised to be a hetaera."

This explained much. Most Romans think that a hetaera is just a high-class whore, but the truth is more complex. The word means "companion," and they are just that: women raised from childhood to be fit companions for well-bred men. To this end they are educated far beyond the usual level allowed women. They must be able to converse knowledgeably and with wit on a wide range of subjects: politics, history, art, and so forth. They learn music and poetry and, of course, a great many sexual refinements.

It just goes to show you that not all Greek men are pederastic boy humpers. Some of them actually desire the companionship of intelligent, educated women and are willing to pay very high fees for the privilege.

"Gaeto was just a wealthy merchant in need of a refined wife for his Italian home. My mother named a price, and he paid it without haggling. The status of rich man's wife is not a bad one for one of my heritage. Of course, at the time I didn't know what his business was, nor about the other wife in Numidia. Still, it wasn't a bad arrangement. Amid great luxury I set about applying some polish to my new husband and I think you will agree I was successful in this."

"He was a charming as well as an imposing man," I concurred.

"Yes, and our union was a rather happy one as such things go. I can tell you for a fact that few of the women here in Baiae are as satisfied with their husbands as I was with mine."

And some of them were content with yours as well, I thought. "And was your husband at odds with any of the great men of the town?"

"If you mean the rich ones, he was not."

"What of the not so rich ones?"

"Well, the priest, Diocles—"

"The one you told me on our last interview you believe to be the go-between in a network of treasonous activity?"

She shrugged. "Just a suspicion, on the word of a few suborned slaves. And, anyway, Gaeto never had anything to do with that. No, the priest was extremely angry with Gaeto, even threatening. I believe it was because poor Gelon was paying court to the old man's daughter."

"Threatening? You said nothing of this at our last interview."

"My husband was alive at the time of our last interview. He would have taken a very dim view of my speaking of his feuds to an official. Numidians settle such matters personally."

"And did you not suspect Diocles of murdering your husband?" I demanded.

She snorted delicately. "That feeble old man kill a man like Gaeto? Only a strong man with a sure hand and eye could have struck that blow." She smiled. "At least you know it wasn't Gelon. He was in your custody when my husband was killed."

"So he was. What were relations like between father and son?"

"Probably better than between a Roman father and son. You Romans are known for your tyrannical attitude toward your children. Oh, Gelon chafed a bit under paternal authority. What spirited young man does not? But Gaeto adored him and indulged him shamelessly. You saw his horses, his trappings, his personal escort, like that of a young prince. No, Gelon had little to complain about."

"Did Gaeto forbid him to see the priest's daughter? I spoke to Gaeto about this personally, because I foresaw trouble in my district."

"I believe they exchanged some sharp words on the matter, but I heard nothing clearly. And if you foresaw trouble, you share the gift of the Cumaean Sibyl."

"Actually, I had no idea just how bad trouble could get in this district. But I am learning."

"You know," she said, subtly shifting her shapely body, "you are a very interesting man. I've heard how you all but wiped out those bandits by yourself."

"An exaggeration," I assured her. "I accounted for two of them. My men and Gelon's did for the rest."

"But Rutilia told me how you faced down the whole power structure of Baiae with a sword in each hand, drenched in blood from head to foot. She said it was a most stimulating sight. From the way she gushed on about it, you probably could have mounted her right there on the road in front of everybody and she'd have loved it."

"What is life but a series of missed opportunities?" I said.

She laughed gaily, apparently quite recovered from her recent bereavement. "You are just not what one expects in a Roman official. Most of them are such dullards."

"I try to be entertaining. So you have been socializing with Rutilia? I thought the local ladies cut you dead."

"Oh, in public they elevate their noses, but I fascinate them. Last night Rutilia called on me, ostensibly to console me in my loss. Of course she claimed that she truly wanted to attend the funeral, but Norbanus wouldn't hear of it. She really wanted to get all the details of the murder and learn what was to become of Gelon. Quadrilla had already been by earlier, on the same mission. I know them well, you see. Them, and the other society wives of Baiae. They come to learn from me."

"And what do you teach them?"

"Can't you guess? They want to learn how to best please their lovers. No woman is more accomplished than a Greek hetaera, after all. That is our reputation, at least."

"Their lovers, not their husbands?" I queried.

"Why waste fine technique on a husband? First, they'd wonder how their wives learned such depraved practices. Then, they'd just go and teach their mistresses how to do it."

"I thought we were cynical in Rome. You people make us seem like infants."

"You Romans vie with one another for world power, which is political and military. Here, men vie for local power, which is political and commercial. To that end they indulge in all manner of dirty politics, espionage, personal leverage, scandalmongering, slander, bribery—the list is a long one. Their wives and daughters please themselves while striving to improve their own positions. Rome and Baiae: the same game, just a different scale."

"And here you add a certain sophistication we lack in Rome," I said.

"Do you? Or is the famous Roman reticence, gravitas, stoicism, and so forth just a pose to cover the reality that you are a pack of voluptuaries as degenerate as any Sybarite?"

My conversations with this woman never seemed to manage to stay on the intended course, which was to find out what had happened when the priest's daughter and Gaeto had been murdered, what had been going on in the Numidian's house and business. She was continually diverging down irrelevant and suggestive paths. To my distress, I found that I had little objection to this. I decided to let her speak on. I've often learned revealing truths in what is intended to be inane or misleading conversation. And if, in the meantime, I enjoyed the spectacle, well, what Roman doesn't enjoy a spectacle?

"Actually," I told her, "we're just a community of Italian farmers who happened to be good at fighting. We worry a lot that, if we get too accustomed to luxury, we'll lose our military edge. When we conquered Sicily more than two hundred years ago, among the loot brought back were fine couches and pillows. The censors were convinced that such luxuries would turn us into a horde of indolent, decadent degenerates. There were also some statues and paintings in the loot, and it was feared that these would cause us to become effete art critics."

"Couches," she murmured, "pillows. Yet in spite of these menaces you are still conquering away like drunken Macedonians following their golden-haired boy."

"Personally, I think these fears of decadence are overstated. I truly enjoy luxury and so do most other Romans. Yet Caesar's legions are the toughest we have ever fielded. But we have never felt—I suppose we've never felt really *comfortable* with the easy, abundant life. We feel that we should be out sleeping on the ground, wrapped in a thin cloak, eating coarse barley bread and goat cheese, washing it down with sour wine that's half vinegar."

"Perhaps that's why you are so belligerent, so that people won't get the wrong idea."

"We do emphasize public image," I agreed.

"And how closely does public image conform to private reality?" she asked. "You Romans hold ruthlessness to be a virtue and female unchastity to be a great evil, but which causes more misery?"

"I didn't say we were logical. Logic is for Greeks. We value two things above all: military strength and our traditions. If the traditions are somewhat outdated, we love them anyway. As for wifely chastity, it was the attribute of our ancestral village women. These days, only the Vestals and Caesar's wife are above suspicion. The reigning queens of society are the likes of Clodia, Fulvia, Sempronia, and a score of others who are as scandalous as they are entertaining."

"What hypocrites you all are!" she cried.

"That's the advantage of being the greatest power in the world. You can be a hypocrite, take any pose, say what you like, and everyone has to smile and accept it."

"Power is a wonderful thing. Without it, what are we?"

"It strikes me that you are in a powerless position now, Jocasta. You are a widow; your husband's heir, your stepson, plans to abandon the business here and return to Numidia, where a woman's lot is not a desirable one, and I imagine that of a supernumerary widow is even less felicitous. Gelon may treat his mother with honor, but how will he, and she, treat you?"

"I have no intention of going to Numidia," she asserted, apparently quite unperturbed. "Gelon fancies a life there of living in tents, raiding the neighbors, endless riding and lion hunting, living on the flesh of gazelles, and trapping elephants and so forth. I'm sure it's all quite exciting, all something out of Homer. But while it may be a fine life for a man, it has few attractions for a woman, especially a woman of refinement like myself. I am quite capable of making my own way in the world. When Gelon leaves, I shall wave to him from the dock. Assuming, of course, that he is not executed for the murder of poor Gorgo."

"Speaking of which, that trial is coming up soon. At our last interview you speculated that your husband might forbid you to testify. That is no longer a factor. I shall summon you to speak."

She inclined her head. "As the praetor wishes, of course."

"And will your testimony serve to clear Gelon of the charge?"

"As I told you before, I saw him that evening and again the next morning. I shall testify to that."

"Most conscientious," I told her. "Expect my lictors to call upon you soon."

With a few more formal, meaningless politenesses, I left her and returned to the town house.

"You mean she is not even going to lie in court to save her stepson?" Antonia said, aghast. We were dawdling over lunch and I had given a somewhat abbreviated account of my interview with Jocasta.

"She will be under oath," Marcus said archly. "Perhaps she fears the anger of the gods."

Circe snorted. "She's a Greek. The Greeks think the gods admire a good liar. No, there must be a coolness between stepmother and stepson. Either she doesn't care if he's executed, or she actually wants him to die."

"If Gelon is executed," Julia said, "where does that leave his father's estate? If it passes to his local widow, that might be reason enough for her to want him to be executed."

"I've been considering that," I said. "My legal advisers tell me that the executor of a resident foreigner's will must be his citizen partner. I will have to summon this Gratius Glabrio all the way from Verona. By the time he reaches here, I will be in Bruttium or Tarentum. Then I will have to come back here to hear the case."

"If this Glabrio exists at all," Julia said. "And by then Gelon will be either executed or let go. I don't think much of his chances at the moment."

"What is her motive to lie about the partner?" Hermes wanted to know.

"One," Antonia said, "to cover her ignorance. She says she's been managing Gaeto's affairs in his absence. If he kept the identity of his partner secret, she may not want anybody to know it, so she makes up a fake one who is safely distant. As you say, by the time she's caught in the lie, this matter will be settled one way or the other." She popped a honeyed cherry onto her mouth, chewed, and spat out the pit. "Two, she knows, but she and the partner have an agreement to keep the arrangement secret for the time being."

"Why?" I asked, intrigued at this line of reasoning.

"You'll know that when you learn the contents of the will," she said. "but it will have to be something advantageous to both Jocasta and this partner, and it will require that Gelon be out of the way."

"I'm beginning to be glad that we brought you along on this trip," I said to her. She had a natural grasp of the ins and outs of devious, deceitful behavior. A typical Antonian, really. Her brother, the soon-to-be triumvir Marcus Antonius, was as close to a decent human being as that family ever produced, and even he was a criminal on a world scale.

"By the way," Julia said, "just where is the will and why hasn't it been read already?"

"It's deposited in the Temple of Juno the Protector in Cumae," Hermes reported. "That's the local custom. It won't be released while the dead man's son is under arrest, but the praetor can subpoena it for the trial."

"See that it's done," I said. "I want a look at it."

"Time is pressing," Julia said. "We have fewer than ten days before we must be in Bruttium for the scheduled assizes. When will Gelon be tried? You really can't stall much longer."

"The city council has already notified us," Hermes said. "Tomorrow is the day of a local festival and all official business is forbidden. The next day is a court day, and after that you have to hold court in Stabiae, so the day after tomorrow is the only day Gelon can be tried."

"At least the docket is otherwise clear," I said. "We can devote the whole day to the trial. Who will prosecute on Diocles' behalf?"

"A citizen named Vibianus," Hermes informed us. "He studied law with Sulpicius Galba and has won a number of important cases."

"And who will speak for Gelon?" Julia asked. "It seems that his father didn't live long enough to engage a lawyer."

"I may have to select one myself," I said. "Marcus, you could use some practice before the bar. Would you like to defend Gelon?"

"Impossible!" Julia protested. "For a member of the *praetor peregrinus's* own party to take part would seriously compromise the trial."

"Why?" Circe asked. "It happens all the time in Rome. Just last year I saw a Claudius prosecute a Claudius with a third Claudius defending and a fourth sitting as praetor."

"Rome is hopeless," Julia said, "but we must set a better example for the municipalities and the provinces."

"I suppose so," I concurred. "Pity Cicero wouldn't consider it."

"What about his brother?" Marcus asked.

"He does what Cicero tells him to," Hermes said. "But what about Tiro? He's a freedman now and a full citizen, so he can plead in court, and as a freedman it would not be a disgrace for him to defend a slaver's son. He's been Cicero's secretary since the beginning of his career, so he must know the law just as thoroughly. Plus, Cicero could coach him during the trial."

"Brilliant!" I approved. "I'll talk to Cicero this afternoon."

I wondered why I had not thought of it already. With Cicero defending through a proxy, Gelon would have a decent chance. Just as important, the trial was sure to be entertaining. A good legal spectacle might be just what was needed to restore the district to its customary mood of slothful good humor.

THAT AFTERNOON I CALLED ON CICERO. He was socializing at the baths with a number of cronies and no few sycophants. In the Baiaean game of social one-upmanship, having the famous ex-consul among your intimates was a coup. And Cicero, for all his superiority of intellect, was not immune to such sycophancy.

The very fact that he was petitioning the Senate for a triumph was a sign of his declining powers of self-criticism. If ever Rome had produced a man of high political capacity who was utterly lacking in soldierly qualities, it was Cicero. His inflation of some trifling successes in Syria to a victory worthy of a triumph was a matter for considerable amusement in high political circles. The man who had saved the Roman situation there was young Cassius Longinus, and he had received no recognition at all.

My arrival was greeted with enthusiasm, for while my high-handedness had rankled the *duumviri* and a few others, my bloody brawl with the bandits had raised me in the esteem of most. After a long soak I got Cicero aside and made my proposal. He was at first astonished, but quickly came around to my point of view. He summoned his brother and Tiro and we discussed the matter.

"So you really think the boy is innocent?" Cicero said.

"Something is just not right. He is too convenient and there are too many other contenders."

"Decius always has good instincts in these matters, Brother," said Lucius, "and Tiro could certainly use the exposure. Trying a capital case in Rome might be too ambitious a start, but Baiae is just right—plenty of wealth without the distraction of great political power."

"I agree," Cicero said. "How about it, Tiro? Would you like to launch your career as a barrister here?"

"Well," Tiro said, "as a former slave myself, I might be reluctant to defend a slaver's son. However, since he plans to renounce his father's business and become a respectable thief and raider, how can I refuse?"

We were just leaving the baths when a clatter of hooves announced the arrival of my reinforcements. The forum crowd gawked as a full *turma* of thirty cavalrymen rode in, their scarlet cloaks streaming gaily. They wore glittering mail coats split at the sides to facilitate riding and scarlet-crested helmets of shiny bronze. Instead of the long, oval shields carried by Caesar's cavalry, these had the old-fashioned *pompanum* shield, so-called for its resemblance to the round, bossed cake used in sacrifices. Their long, slender spears waved gracefully. They were fine-looking young men and had all the earmarks of the sons of wealthy *equites* of southern Italy, too well-bred to slog around behind a shield in the legions. Still, they were full of spirit and verve.

Their leader was an even handsomer youth who wore a bronze cuirass sculpted to resemble the torso of Hercules. It was an immensely uncomfortable thing to ride in, as I knew from sore experience, but a splendid thing to see. His helmet was skinned with silver artfully embossed to resemble a head of curly hair. He reined in and spoke to Cicero.

"I am Marcus Sublicius Pansa, *optio* of the Ninth *Turma*, attached to the eleventh Legion, now being raised at Capua by the proconsul Gnaeus Pompeius Magnus. Have I the honor of addressing the *praetor peregrinus* Metellus?"

"No, you address the proconsul Marcus Tullius Cicero," I told him. "I'm Metellus." Technically, Cicero was still proconsul while he awaited his triumph, and would not lay down his office until he reentered Rome. The boy had made a natural mistake but he looked mortified.

"My apologies, sir! I thought—"

"Quite understandable," I told him. "It's only natural to think the most distinguished-looking man with a purple stripe is the one in charge. As it occurs, I am the one who sent for you. Who is your commander?"

"Sextus Pompeius, sir, the proconsul's son." The young man's diction reeked of the Greek rhetoric schools that were considered essential for a public career.

"Marcus Sublicius," I said, "we've had an outbreak of banditry in the region. I was personally assaulted and I take that as an insult to the dignity of Rome. I want them scoured out, and a few brought back alive for questioning. They are most likely on their way to the crater of Vesuvius, although they probably won't venture inside until the current venting dies down. Do you think you can handle that?"

He grinned. "It will be good training for the boys." The boys. He had to be all of nineteen years old.

"Good. Go first to the Villa Hortensia and get the horse master there. His name is Regilius and he's an old cavalryman and scout. He knows this countryside intimately and will guide you where you need to go. You have my authority to requisition supplies, grain, and remounts if need be anywhere in this district. With or without those men, be back here on the morning after tomorrow, in case I need you to keep civic order here."

"It shall be as you command, Praetor." He saluted, whirled, and rode out with his *turma* clattering at his heels.

"They seem to be a likely band of young men," Cicero said. "What do you think, Decius? You served with Caesar's cavalry. How would these match up to Caesar's?"

I didn't have to think about it long. "They're smartly turned out. Lots of glitter and panache, but they look like the horsemen of Scipio Africanus two hundred years ago. Caesar's cavalry look like bandits who plundered their gear off a battlefield. If it came to a fight, they'd eat those boys alive."

Cicero sighed. "That was what I was afraid you'd say."

12

THE LOCAL FESTIVAL WAS AN ANNUAL celebration in honor of Baios, the helmsman of Ulysses, whose tomb I had been shown outside the gates. It commenced with a sacrifice at the tomb, accompanied by much pomp and ceremony. This I attended as a visiting dignitary. All the priests of the region turned out, many of them dressed in regalia peculiar to the district. Diocles was there, representing the Temple of Apollo, looking no more solemn than usual.

Young girls robed in white danced before the tomb and draped it with wreaths and garlands of flowers, and libations of wine and oil were poured over the altar. Then the girls led the procession back into the town amid loud singing from the civic chorus, scattering flower petals lavishly.

In the forum, stages had been erected upon which dancers and actors performed stories connected to the epic voyage of Ulysses, many of these extremely salacious. Calypso was portrayed by a Spanish dancer from Gades whose joints seemed to bend in all directions. We also learned that Circe and her attendants still had uses for Ulysses' men even after they were transformed into beasts.

The performances were followed by another of the lavish public banquets we had grown accustomed to. It occurred to me that, had it not been for all this chasing about after murderers and the occasional fight with bandits, this stay in southern Campania would be making me very fat.

The *duumviri* went out of their way to be conciliatory. There was, after all, no profit to be had from resisting Rome, and much to be gained by cooperation. The bandit attack had embarrassed them and my act of calling in the troops had sobered them. As for Gelon, the trial would be on the morrow and all would be settled then. Besides, nothing should stand in the way of a good party.

In that spirit, we ate and imbibed and enjoyed the proceedings as if no dark cloud hung over us. Of course, a very palpable cloud did just that. Vesuvius was belching out a particularly profuse and noxious plume of smoke that day. Luckily, the prevailing wind kept the soot and ashes away from Baiae. Most of it seemed to be falling into the Bay of Neapolis, but an occasional shift of wind brought us a hot-iron odor laced with the stench of burning sulfur. It was rather like those aforementioned skeletons people use as decoration in banquet rooms, reminding all and sundry that death is always near and we might as well enjoy life while we can.

As if Baiaeans needed encouragement to enjoy life. During dinner famous Greek rhapsodes sang us the *Odyssey*, their Attic Greek so flawless, their renditions so filled with spirit and emotion that you could hear the oars creaking in the tholes and the splash of the great stones cast by Polyphemus at the fleeing ship of Odysseus (old Baios at the helm, no doubt.) Cognoscenti compared these performances with those of past years and, naturally, some claimed to have heard it done better. I never had.

When the festivities were over, Julia and I were entertained at the home of Publilius the jewel merchant. The last thing we needed was more food and wine, and by local standards this gathering was all but austere. Instead of another bout of gluttony, we were treated to an evening of that rarest and most delightful of diversions; sparkling conversation. Publilius had invited the wittiest and most eloquent men and women of the district, people noted for their skill at repartee. There were only two rules to observe: It was forbidden to talk about politics, and nobody was to talk too long about anything. Each of us was provided with a basket of buns, which we were to throw at anyone who waxed too loquacious.

It seemed that even a jewel merchant could be a person of taste. I have rarely enjoyed myself more, and would scarcely have believed that an evening could be so satisfying in the absence of a great deal of food and wine, tumblers and acrobats and dancers or at least a good fight. Topics ranged from the nature of the volcano in the distance to the true identity of Homer to whether dancing or oratory was the greater art. Discussion continued long into the night, illumination being provided by yet another Baiaean innovation: candelabra magnified by polished silver reflectors, supposedly an invention of Archimedes but adapted by the Baiaeans for purposes of luxury.

As we were making our farewells and calling for our litters, Hermes arrived with the latest load of bad news.

"There's been another," he said.

"Not another murder!" I cried. "No! I absolutely forbid it!"

"I fear some things are beyond even the power of a Roman praetor," said our host. "Who is it this time?"

"Quadrilla, wife of the *duumvir* Silva," Hermes reported. "You'd better come quick."

"Where?" I said. "Their villa?"

"No. The town house. It's only a few streets from here."

"Julia," I said, "return to our lodgings. Try to keep Circe and Antonia from meddling in this. You'll get a full report upon my return."

She nodded wordlessly, tight-lipped. Earlier in our marriage she would have insisted on accompanying me, and longed to do so now, but she was trapped by her own vision of how a praetor's wife should behave, and an unseemly fascination with bloody doings was not among the qualities she thought she should display.

We made our way to Silva's house without delay. The city's street lighting made torches unnecessary so our walk took no more time than it would have in daylight, a thing unthinkable in Rome. We found a crowd of citizens outside the door with a handful of the city guard keeping out the rabble. They stood aside for me. Inside, we found the *duumviri* in the atrium. Norbanus spoke in soothing tones to his distraught colleague. Manius Silva was pale and agitated. His Cretan colleague, Diogenes, stood nearby.

"Well," I said, "we should be getting used to this. Manius Silva, please accept my condolences for your loss, but matters are getting out of hand. We must dispense with the sad conventions for the moment. We will observe them later, I promise. Now, tell me what has happened."

They were too stunned to object. Once again, my authority here was on shaky ground, but by bulling in forcefully and taking charge as if I were born to command, I got my way. This is a useful tactic that should be practiced diligently by all governors and magistrates sent to the hinterlands. People will usually cede authority to one who demands it with sufficient brazenness.

"I—I found her when I returned—" Silva was stammering, either sorely distressed or faking it very well.

"Returned from where?" I asked.

"We were—" Diogenes began, but I cut him off.

"I wish to hear this from Manius Silva. Please continue."

"I was at the annual banquet of the perfumer's guild, of which I am head. It is held every year on this date." He had gone from the lavish public banquet earlier in the day to another banquet. How typical of Baiae. "When I reached home, all seemed as usual—"

"Quadrilla did not attend this banquet with you?" I asked. I had seen her with him at the earlier event.

"No. Most years she goes with me, but she pleaded that she was not feeling well and wished to spend the evening at home."

"So, when you returned?"

"When I returned—this was perhaps an hour ago, maybe less—all seemed as usual. The janitor opened the door for me, the majordomo greeted me and reported all was well in the house."

"Did you speak to any of the other servants?"

"No. The rest had all retired. I do not require them to wait up for me when I am to return late."

I turned to Hermes. "Find the janitor and majordomo and isolate them in separate rooms. I will question them later." He nodded and went to do my bidding. "Now, Manius Silva, if you will tell me how you found your wife?"

"Well, from the atrium I walked back to our sleeping quarters. Hapi—that is the majordomo's name—walked with me. I don't believe we said much. I just spoke of how well the banquet had gone, I think. I opened the door as I do every night. I was immediately struck by a—a strange odor."

I knew that odor well. "You saw nothing at first?"

"Nothing. It was very dark. I assumed Quadrilla had snuffed the lamps. I knew something was terribly wrong. I called her name, but there was no answer. Hapi ran to fetch lamps and we went in. Quadrilla was lying—well, you shall see, Praetor. I saw immediately that there was nothing to be done for her. I ordered Hapi out of the room and backed out myself. Nothing has been touched in there. She is as I found her. I immediately sent messengers to summon you and Norbanus and the civic magistrates." People were learning how I conducted an investigation.

I placed a hand on his shoulder. "Manius, you've shown great presence of mind under the most distressing of circumstances. I appreciate your foresight. I will make my inspection as quickly as possible, then we can have the *libitinarii* in to give Quadrilla the proper rites." He nodded dumbly.

Hermes returned moments later. "I've done as you ordered, Praetor." By this time a small group had assembled in the house, mostly the other civic officials.

"Very good. Here is how we shall proceed. Only I, my assistant Hermes, and the *duumviri* will enter the room where Quadrilla lies. This is not a spectacle but an official investigation. All will keep silent until I speak, and then they will speak only to answer my questions. I abjure you to remember what you see and what words are spoken. This will be a matter for court testimony soon. Is that understood?"

"Yes, Praetor," they said.

"Very well. Let's see what is to be seen."

Silva conducted us to the room, which opened off a central courtyard. Nervous slaves stood by with lamps. "Hermes," I said, "take the lamps inside and place them yourself. You know how to do it." By this I meant that he had long practice at not disturbing a crime scene.

"Yes, Praetor." He took the first lamp and walked in very carefully. Then he returned for another, taking them in one at a time until he had placed eight or ten within. When the room was illuminated, I walked in.

Immediately I was conscious of the smell that Manius Silva had noted—the sordid smell of death. Quadrilla lay on the bed amid luxuriant, disordered pillows. She was quite naked and had that deflated look common to the newly dead, like a wineskin that has been drained. She was a handsome woman of advancing years and clearly had once been a great beauty. Her overstretched navel gaped obscenely, the sapphire gone from its setting. I looked around the room and did not see it anywhere.

"Manius," I said, "where did Quadrilla keep her—her abdominal sapphire?"

He pointed to an ivory box upon a table. "She had a number of them."

"Hermes," I said. He opened the box to reveal around twenty sapphires. Some were rimmed with gold, some carved intaglio, even one with a pearl set in its center. They were nestled in yellow silk, each in its own depression. One depression was empty. "Which one is missing?"

"The largest," Silva said. "It was her favorite."

"Was she wearing it earlier today?"

"She was."

"It may be in the bedding," I said. "We'll have it searched once her body is attended to."

There was no mystery about how she had died. She lay in an untidy sprawl, her head twisted to one side. The hilt of a miniature dagger protruded from the base of her skull, at what my physician friend Asklepiodes would term the insertion point of the neck vertebrae.

"Manius, do you recognize this weapon?" I asked. "Is it from this house?"

"Never saw it before," he said. From without, I heard whispering to the effect that Quadrilla had been killed in the same fashion as Gaeto. Hermes shushed them.

Beneath the smell of death I detected another fragrance, one with which I had grown familiar of late. "Manius, I suppose you can identify this perfume?"

He stepped closed and sniffed with a sick look on his face. "Of course. It is Zoroaster's Rapture. It was her favorite, and incredibly costly. Even I was able to procure only small amounts of it. She wore it for special occasions."

"And was she wearing it when she left you earlier?"

"She was not," he said grimly, not missing the implication.

I walked carefully around the room. There was no disorder save on the bed, where the cushions and coverlets were in some disarray, possibly as a result of the death struggle, but I doubted that.

I examined the lamps that had been in the room before we entered. Each had a good supply of oil. Either they had been snuffed out, or they had not been lit that night.

"There is no more to be done here," I said. "Call in the *libitinarii*. I want to know if that sapphire is found. Now I will talk with the majordomo."

Hermes had put the man in a small room opening off the triclinium. As his name would indicate, he was Egyptian. Hapi is the twin god of the Nile. He was middle-aged, bald, and pudgy, possibly a eunuch. When I walked in, he was sweating profusely.

"Praetor!" he piped. Yes, definitely a eunuch. "Praetor, I had no idea— I don't know what—"

"Just tell me what you *do* know," I commanded. "To begin with, when did your mistress return from the festival?"

"Just after sunset, Praetor." He wrung his hands, eyes darting in all directions save toward me.

"Was she alone?"

"Well—well, she arrived in a litter. A closed litter."

"Then I will want to speak to the litter bearers."

"It was not my lady's litter, Praetor. Her own litter had returned perhaps an hour earlier. She had dismissed her bearers, telling them that she wished to stroll in Diana's Grove, and that she would walk home, since it was such a fine evening."

"I see. And did you recognize this litter or its bearers?"

He looked down at the floor as if his salvation lay there. "No, Praetor. It was costly, and the bearers were all black Nubians."

"And she did not explain how she came to return in this fashion? Were you not curious?"

"One—one learns not to ask, Praetor."

"I understand. Tell me exactly what happened."

"At an hour past sunset, as I said before, the litter arrived at the front gate. The janitor admitted it, and when I came into the atrium, my lady told me that she was going to her bedroom and I was to dismiss her girls to their quarters."

"Did you see who else might be in the litter?"

"No. My lady only put her head out and held the curtains close around her. The bearers took her right back to the bedroom, and a few minutes later they left with the litter."

"And you didn't— Yes, I know, one learns not to ask. Did you hear anything unusual from the bedroom?"

"No, Praetor. She said that the master would be at the guild banquet until very late and I might as well retire to my own quarters. It was not a suggestion, Praetor. I know when I am receiving a command, however gently it is put."

"Do you remember anything else?"

"Just that my lady seemed—very happy, Praetor."

The janitor was of no help at all. He was an elderly Bruttian who was barely able to speak and whose intelligence seemed just about equal to his duties. One doesn't need much in a slave who does little but open and shut the front door.

By the time I left it was determined that the sapphire was nowhere in the bedroom.

"I rather liked the woman," I told Julia when I returned to our town house. "I am sorry that she is dead."

"At this rate," Antonia observed, "there will be no one left alive to give you any trouble."

"The last one still alive will be the killer," said Marcus helpfully. "That makes it simple, at the very least."

"If there's only one," I grumbled. "There may be a whole pack of them."

"Quadrilla was killed by Gaeto's murderer," Julia said. "The method was the same."

"Or somebody is copying this homicidal technique to cover up an unconnected murder," I speculated. "In the bad old days in Rome, when senators were being proscribed, many men used the confusion to settle old scores."

"Nonsense," Julia said. "Quadrilla smuggled a lover home and the lover killed her and took that sapphire."

"Why?" Circe queried. "I mean, why take that sapphire, fabulous though it was? There was ten times its value in the box that held her other navel adornments."

"The killer was taking a souvenir, a keepsake," I said.

"That's insane," Julia said.

"Clearly, this murderer is not quite sane, however clever," I said.

"Gorgo was killed haphazardly, and perhaps the killer did not go to meet her with murder in mind. Gaeto and Quadrilla were killed with an incredible cold-bloodedness. And then there was the bizarre, ritualistic way Charmian's body was laid out."

"Assuming there is just one killer," Julia said. "If it is just one, and he is not sane, we may never find out his identity."

"Why do you say that?" Antonia wanted to know.

"Because people usually kill from greed or jealousy," she answered. "A madman does not act from such motives. Do you remember that madman in Lanuvium a few years ago?"

"Oh, I remember that one!" Antonia said, clapping her hands with delight like a little girl. "Was it twenty or thirty bodies found in his well?"

"Twenty, I think," Julia said. "He testified that he heard Pluto calling from the bottom of his well, demanding human sacrifices. He threw one in every full moon for almost two years. Other than that, he seemed like a normal, rational man."

"I remember Cato saying that it was a terrible thing to do to a good well," I said.

"Our killer may be acting according to motives that make sense to him alone," Julia said, "and if that is the case, we may never discover who it is or who will die next."

"And I have to conduct a trial tomorrow," I said.

"Is there no way to delay it?" Julia asked.

"None," Hermes said. "Even if the augurs find the omens unpropitious, they'll just throw Gelon into the local lockup until the praetor can find time to return here, or until the next *praetor peregrinus* comes down from Rome."

"We can't have that," I said.

"Then go to bed," Julia ordered. "It's almost sunrise now."

"Very well," I said, suddenly feeling unutterably tired. "But I want to be wakened immediately if those cavalrymen return with some live bandits."

13

THE HORSEMEN RETURNED EARLY IN THE morning, as I was rubbing my bleary eyes and plunging my face into a basin of cold water. I was not in a good mood, and my disposition was not improved by their report.

I went into the atrium to find Sublicius Pansa, glittering in his polished cuirass and helmet, awaiting me.

"Praetor!" he cried joyfully. "I am happy to report that the bandits have been scoured out and will menace the district no more." You'd have thought that he'd conquered the Parthians single-handedly.

"Excellent. Now where are your prisoners? I want to question them."

"Ah, well, Praetor, you see, the boys were very keen to avenge your honor and the honor of Rome. After all, these vile creatures had raised profane hands against a serving praetor, insulting both to Rome, and to—"

"You didn't take any alive?" I said, disgusted but not at all surprised. Actually, I was somewhat astonished that they had managed not to get themselves massacred by the bandits.

"What did you bring me?" I asked, resigned.

"If you will come this way, Praetor." He strutted out into the street, where his *turma* awaited. Besides the cavalrymen there were seven horses draped with corpses. I took a close look but saw no familiar faces. The bandits smelled no prettier dead than they had alive.

Regilius sat his horse a little aside, looking disgusted. I signaled him to me and he rode over and dismounted.

"All right. Tell me what happened."

"We found three dead while tracking them," he said. "They'd been wounded in the fight with your lot. Caught up with the rest of them at the foot of the volcano. These twits treated it like stag hunting on their fathers' estates, whooping and chasing them down with lances. Could've got you your prisoners easy enough, if they hadn't been having so much fun." He spat on the unoffending pavement. "Found something for you, though."

"If so, I am grateful."

He led me to a small horse tethered behind the ones carrying the bodies. It was a handsome animal but very tired.

"This is the one we've been looking for. Knew it as soon as I saw their tracks." He caught my look. "It wasn't ridden by your murderer. He was a big, ugly brute that was no horseman. That's one reason it was so easy to ride them down. This is a fine beast, but she shouldn't have been carrying so much weight. Whoever rode her to the grove and to the slaver's house was the right weight for her."

"So she was pay," I said. "The murderer gave her as part of the bandits' fee for getting rid of us."

"Makes sense," Regilius said. "Bad bit of luck, though. I was hoping I'd be able to track her to the bugger's stable."

"It would have been conclusive evidence," I affirmed. "But our murderer is very good at getting rid of evidence." How good, I was just beginning to appreciate.

Although I considered the bandit-hunting expedition to have been a disaster, the townspeople felt otherwise. The sight of the dead bandits put them in a good mood and they hailed the cavalry as if they were conquering heroes. It did not hurt that they were Pompeian forces, Campania being one of Pompey's strongholds.

IN THE EARLY MORNING, THE TOWN forum was packed with people come to witness the trial. Not just the town was there but also people from nearby towns and the surrounding villages. They had all come for the previous day's festival, and were staying on an extra day to see the splashy trial everyone had been talking about for days.

With my lictors clearing the way before me, I took my seat in the curule chair on the dais. At my nod the day's proceedings began with sacrifices and the taking of auguries. To my relief, there was no examining the livers of sacrificial animals, for there was little Etruscan influence so far south. Rome, on the very border of Tuscia, has always been plagued with these liver readers. Instead, the local augurs took the omens decently, by observing the flight and feeding of birds and by determining the direction of lightning and thunder. Whatever methods were used, the omens were deemed propitious and we were permitted to proceed.

A chorus of hisses and execrations greeted Gelon, who rode in escorted by my own men. If his acquittal depended on crowd approval, he was already a dead man. Beside him rode Tiro. The two had spent the previous day closeted together, preparing the defense. Tiro looked confident, but that is part of a lawyer's job.

Next the jury was empaneled, some forty comfortable-looking *equites* who blandly took frightening oaths before the gods, happy in the knowledge that the gods, too, can be bribed.

One of my lictors led the witnesses to their benches. There were a good number of these, among them Diocles the priest, some nervous-looking temple servants, and Jocasta. Just before all was arranged, a man wearing a white tunic and the winged red hat of Mercury came running into the forum, holding aloft a little golden caduceus. He had tiny silver wings affixed to his sandals, and the crowd made way for him. He halted before the dais and took a small scroll from the wallet slung over his shoulder.

"The Temple of Juno the Protector at Cumae sends this to the *Praetor Peregrinus* Decius Caecilius Metellus the Younger, holding assizes at Baiae, in accordance with his subpoena." Hermes took the scroll and tipped the messenger as the crowd muttered, wondering what this might mean. Hermes tucked the scroll into his tunic and returned to my side.

I held up a hand for silence and received it. I nodded to young Marcus and he stepped forward, a picture of Roman gravitas. Around his arm was tied a bandage far larger than was justified by the wound beneath. "People of Baiae, attend!" he intoned. "Today the *praetor peregrinus* hears the case of Gelon, son of Gaeto the Numidian, accused of the murder of Gorgo, daughter of Diocles, priest of the Temple of Campanian Apollo. Long live the Senate and People of Rome!"

"Counselors, attend me," I said. The two advocates approached my curule chair. I nodded to Tiro. He turned to face the crowd and raised his right hand, palm to the sky.

"By Jupiter, Best and Greatest, dispenser of justice and protector of the innocent, I swear that I will prove the innocence of the accused. I am Marcus Tullius Cicero Tiro, freedman of the great proconsul Marcus Tullius Cicero."

At my nod the other now turned and raised his hand. He was a tall man with a face of great distinction, about forty-five years of age. His toga was draped in the fashion set by Quintus Hortensius Hortalus, a wonderfully effective look for delivering rhetoric.

"By Jupiter, Best and Greatest, punisher of the guilty, I swear that I will prove the guilt of Gelon, son of the notorious slaver, murderer of Gorgo, daughter of our revered priest. I am Aulus Julius Vibianus, citizen of Rome and Baiae."

This surprised me. I had no idea that the Julian gens had a branch in Baiae. The only Julians you ever heard of in Rome were the ones sur-named Caesar, and there were few of them. They never used the praenomen Aulus. I looked at the man's sandal and it was red, with the ivory crescent at the ankle, so he was a genuine patrician. I glanced toward Julia and she shrugged. She'd never heard of them either, it seemed.

Julia, of course, had no official capacity, and some in Rome might have thought it rather scandalous that she would even be present at one of my trials. But nothing was going to keep her away from this one, just as no law or custom prevented her from occasionally leaning over to whisper something in my ear. As long as she never spoke aloud, no one could ac-cuse her of female interference, or me of being swayed by my wife's ad-vice.

Julia sat behind the dais, accompanied by Antonia and Circe and their whole gaggle of handmaids and pages. At the foot of the dais to my right Tiro and Gelon huddled with Cicero and his brother, getting some last-minute coaching. To my left, Vibianus stood with a group of men, doubtless some of the town's leading legal minds.

We began with the ritualistic denunciations, in which Tiro and Vib-ianus execrated each other and their respective clients, accusing them of all manner of crime and degeneracy. This is a traditional practice using many stock phrases and is so familiar that I will not bother setting down the vituperative details. Once this was over, the serious part of the trial began. The lots were cast and Tiro got to speak first. Since there were no other cases to be heard that day, I dispensed with the water clock and al-lowed each advocate to speak as long as he liked, stipulating that the pro-ceedings must be concluded by sundown.

Tiro came forward, his toga draped in the simple, ancestral fashion favored by Cicero. Tiro's posture and assurance of bodily address were so dignified that no one would have guessed that he had ever been a slave had he not freely admitted to that state.

"Citizens of Baiae," he began, "I am here before you to prevent a gross injustice from being done. Gelon, the newly bereaved son of the late

Gaeto of Numidia, has suffered grievously. In the first place, he lost the young woman to whom he was paying court." There were angry mutters from the crowd, but he bore on. "Yes, I know that many of you judged him to be unworthy to approach so highborn a lady, but on what grounds do you judge him? Because his father dealt in slaves? It is a legal business of great antiquity, else how could he practice it openly among you? And this young man has never worked in that trade. Indeed, his dearest wish is to return to Numidia and take up the life of a gentleman of that land." He wisely forebore to mention that this life was, by Roman standards, one of banditry.

"As you all know," he went on, "I have been a slave for most of my life, yet I find no fault in this young man. And, not only did he lose the maiden he loved but also now finds himself unjustly accused of her murder! There is no justification for this calumny! The only reason he finds himself suspect is the spite of Diocles, priest of Apollo. I sympathize with Diocles. Who would be so hardhearted as not to feel the grief of a father for a beautiful and blameless young daughter? But in his grief he has made an unjust accusation. His *only* cause for believing Gelon is the murderer is that he deemed the boy unworthy to approach his daughter.

"He forbade the girl to associate with Gelon, and he barred Gelon from the temple and its precincts. Gorgo, dutiful girl that she was, obeyed her father. Gelon persisted in his suit." Here Tiro gestured gracefully toward that imperiled young man. "And yet, can one expect otherwise of high-spirited youth? Since the earliest tales of the Greeks it has been acknowledged that the impetuous affections of youth are proof against the rancorous disapproval of parents.

"Behold him!" Here Tiro swept his hand up and down, indicating the totality of the boy's comely form. "Is he not as handsome as a god? Has he not the dress and bearing of a young prince? In the days of his freedom, did not all here see him riding in splendor upon his caparisoned steed, followed by his tribal guards, beautiful and noble as Alexander riding into Persepolis?"

He won applause for his eloquence. There were nods and even

shouts of agreement that the boy was indeed a fine sight, and how could one so comely be adjudged guilty? I have long noted that the prettier you are, the more likely you will be found innocent. There is something in us that wants to believe that ugliness signifies guilt and beauty is proof of innocence. Yet it has been my experience that lovely women and handsome men can be the foulest criminals. Nonetheless, it made an effective argument in court.

"To add to his sorrows," Tiro went on, "while under arrest, his own father was murdered! Attacked by an unknown assailant, while his son was unable to protect or avenge him, and only through the kindness of the praetor who held him in custody was he allowed to carry out the obsequies for his father. Is this justice?" Many seemed to agree that the boy had been done a bad turn.

"And it does not end there!" Tiro cried, trembling with lawyerly indignation. "While riding back toward the praetor's villa, the party was set upon by bandits, at the very gates of this city! The clear object of these desperadoes was the death of Gelon. Indeed, two of his loyal tribal guards died defending him! Are we to believe that this attack and the murder of the blameless Gorgo are unconnected?" Here there were growls of agreement. I glanced at the jury. They didn't seem greatly impressed.

"Those outlaws were set upon that party in which Gelon rode, and only the valor of Roman arms and the loyalty of the fierce Numidians saved him! Nor did Gelon seek to take advantage of the situation to escape. Mounted on his splendid horse, such a course was quite feasible. Yet he meekly submitted to the authority of the praetor, trusting that Roman justice would prove his innocence. Is this the act of a murderer?"

He went on in this vein for some time, extolling the virtues of his client, stressing his splendid appearance, that he just did not *look* like a guilty man. Even the impassive *equites* of the jury at last seemed to be swayed, perhaps more by the obvious wealth of the accused than by his appearance.

Tiro summed up with a few more oaths as to his client's innocence, then it was the prosecutor's turn.

Vibianus strode to the front of the dais and adjusted the elaborate draping of his toga with studied absentmindedness. "People of Baiae," he began in a splendid voice, "our esteemed Tiro, known to you all for many years, has done well by his client, as any lawyer should. He has pointed out to you the boy's greatest asset, which is his fine figure." Here he paused and flicked some imaginary dust from his toga. "Well, I have a very handsome horse. Nonetheless, it has kicked me more than once." This got him a good laugh.

"So let us dispense with these irrelevancies and examine the realities of the matter at hand, shall we?" Head high, he scanned the crowd in lordly fashion, seeking and finding approval. The man knew how to conduct a prosecution, I had to admit. I hoped the rest of his performance would not be as competent.

"First, I would like to eliminate from consideration the lurid incident of the bandit attack. By the way, in case you have not heard, those rogues have been exterminated, thanks to the swift action of the young horsemen of Sextus Pompeius!" Here the crowd cheered. I wanted to shout that I'd done for two of those bandits myself and my men and Gelon's had killed most of the others and that I'd sent for the *turma* myself and they'd only killed four. But it would have appeared churlish to say so, and I held my tongue.

"As for the motives of the bandits," he went on, "what motive do bandits ever need save robbery? How were they to know that this was a well-armed band on that foggy day? The Numidians quite rightly placed themselves between their master and the attackers, some of whom most certainly assaulted the slaver's son. And why? Was it because they were hired to do away with him?" He paused and waited, looking around and timing his next line. "No! They went for him because he was riding the finest *horse*! The beast itself was a desirable prize and who would be riding such an animal save a man with a fat purse, one who would fetch a rich ransom!"

There were loud cries of agreement at this, and that it only stood to reason and why hadn't someone thought of this before?

"This man knows his business," Hermes muttered.

"Studied under a master, so they say," I commented.

"Why," Vibianus said when the hubbub died down, "would anyone go to such lengths to kill Gelon, a man destined for the cross already? If someone put those bandits up to their attack, might the intended victim not more likely be our esteemed *praetor peregrinus*?" He did not point at me in vulgar fashion but merely indicated me with a wave of his hand.

"Explain yourself," I said.

"Noble Praetor, you seem to us the most just and blameless of men, and who can deny your valor, when you took a personal part in the fighting despite your praetorian dignity? Yet yours is a very great family, one important in the public life of Rome for many generations. What family of such eminence lacks enemies? We all know very well that yours does not. Some years ago you personally investigated the death of the illustrious Metellus Celer, your kinsman, and did you find any lack of suspects with motive to slay him?"

He did not wait for an answer but whirled to face the crowd. "Citizens, these are perilous times in Rome, when lines are being drawn and sides taken. In such times great men always walk in danger, often only because of their family affiliation. A Caecilius Metellus like our praetor, scion of one of the most powerful senatorial families, has many such enemies. Thus I feel confident in dismissing that unfortunate attack from serious consideration as indication of some sort of criminal conspiracy toward the defendant. Let us look rather into the circumstances of the murder itself."

He made a gesture indicating an invitation to calm and rational discourse. "All know that Gelon was infatuated by the beauty of Gorgo. No one has claimed that she in any way encouraged or acknowledged this attention. Her father disapproved in the strongest terms. As a good and dutiful daughter, she agreed that these unwelcome advances must not be allowed. Therefore, she went out on that fateful night to tell him that he must cease his futile courtship." He paused and surveyed his audience solemnly. "Citizens, it seems that the boy did not take this rejection calmly."

He straightened and readjusted his toga. "Now, in similar circumstances, you or I might take such news ill. In fact, I daresay many of us *have* been the recipients of just such unwelcome tidings, when we were young men courting ladies who perhaps did not share our youthful passion. How did we react? Certainly with chagrin. Perhaps with anger and harsh words. But with violence? Never! We behaved as gentlemen and as Romans. At least, I hope we did.

"But over there"—he leveled a beringed finger at Gelon—"you do not see a Roman or a gentleman. Look past those pretty features and you see a foreigner, a barbarian! Ignore his princely airs. For all his wealth and fine horses he is still just a primitive tribesman with no more concept of civilized behavior than a caged beast! He could ape the manners of his betters, but he is nothing but the son of a barbarian slaver! He could imitate the graces of a wellborn youth courting a lady of his own class, but when she rejected him, he behaved like the savage he truly is: with rage and the lust to punish and kill one who had insulted him!"

The crowd growled and shouted. My lictors pounded the butts of their fasces on the dais for order, but the crowd was in no mood to pay them any attention. I snapped my fingers and one of Julia's pages came forward with a *lituus*: a long, straight, bronze trumpet sharply curved at its sounding end, so called for its resemblance to the hooked augur's staff of the same name. It is the horn used for signaling in the cavalry. He placed its mouthpiece to his lips and winded a long blast. At the eerie, high-pitched note the crowd stilled. Then amid a clatter of hoofs, the glittering *turma* rode into the forum with the even more glittering Sublicius Pansa in the lead. They ranged themselves before the dais, facing outward.

"Praetor!" Vibianus cried. "This is not necessary! There is no danger."

For the first time I stood. "I intend to see that there will be no danger. I will have order in this court and I will enforce it. All spectators will keep their voices down." It was quite futile to demand that Italians of any sort keep entirely silent. "At the first call for violence or mob action, I will set these men on you. If you think that I speak idly, recall that I have car-

176

ried through on everything that I have said during my stay among you and that I do not shrink from taking the strongest action." I gazed around and saw discontent but no open defiance. "Now, Vibianus, please continue, but I abjure you to refrain from inflammatory rhetoric."

He inclined his head. "As the praetor commands," he said coldly. He adjusted his toga again. "Now, where was I before the troops were called in? Oh, yes, the plain and evident guilt of young Gelon here. I have already demonstrated that he had the motive to murder Gorgo. I will now demonstrate that he had ample opportunity.

"On the night that Gorgo was murdered, many of the most distinguished men of this district, including the praetor, were attending a banquet held at the house of the *duumvir* Norbanus. Even the late Gaeto, the defendant's father, was there. Diocles, father of the victim, was in Cumae. The coast was clear, so to speak, for a meeting between the two; Gelon hoping to consummate his lust for the girl, Gorgo to forbid him her presence. Praetor, I wish to question the woman Jocasta, widow of the slaver Gaeto."

"Proceed," I said.

Jocasta came forward, dressed in a modest Greek gown and discreet jewelry. Today only her streaming hair was flamboyant. She took the usual oath and waited calmly. Her face was unreadable.

"Jocasta," Vibianus said, "on the night in question, where were you?"

"In my town house in Baiae."

"And was your stepson there as well?"

"He was."

"He was there the *whole* night?"

"He was there early in the evening. We had dinner together. After that I retired to my bedroom."

"And did Gelon remain in the house after that?"

"I—I cannot say. I assumed so."

"Assumptions are of very little weight in a court of law," Vibianus said. "Can you testify that Gelon was there the entire night?"

"No. No, I cannot." This raised a murmur.

"In fact, my fellow citizens," Vibianus said, "you will find that *nobody* can testify to seeing Gelon that night. This woman says that she saw him early in the evening. He was not seen again until the praetor's men came to arrest him the next morning. Does no one besides me find it odd that this—this 'princely' young man was not out with friends that night? He had many, you know. Surely it is the rule that socially active men dine at the houses of friends, perhaps even carouse a bit among the manifold delights of Baiae. Does it seem likely that such a one would waste a fine evening having dinner with his stepmother, then retiring early? It certainly wasn't my practice at that age!"

He shook his head ruefully, as if baffled by the deceitfulness of mankind. "No, my friends, this barbarian youth had plans for that evening. Plans that required stealth, and darkness, and privacy. He intended to steal away to the grove of Apollo and meet Gorgo there. I do not say that he intended to commit murder there. But I can say with perfect confidence that murder was exactly what he did there."

With a flourish he dismissed Jocasta and summoned Diocles. The old priest stood there with a tragic face and spoke of the death of his blameless daughter, of how he had forbidden her to see Gelon, how she had agreed and promised to forbid the boy ever to see her again, how he returned home to find her murdered. The crowd showed great sympathy for the old man. Vibianus dismissed him with thanks and turned to me.

"Now, honored praetor, I wish to demonstrate the actions of poor Gorgo on that fatal night. Her personal handmaiden, Charmian, is dead and therefore unable to testify. However, there were two other slave girls with her that night, named Gaia and Leto. I understand that these are in your custody. I wish to summon them to testify."

I stiffened. "You wish to put them to torture?"

He seemed puzzled. "Is that not the custom? Surely I do not need to lecture a Roman praetor on Roman legal practice. The ordeal is quite mild, as such things go."

"I have confiscated these slaves as evidence in this case," I said.

"The girl called Charmian was beaten almost to death before she escaped from the temple. The other two are in poor condition and I will not have them put to the ordeal."

"You refuse to surrender them?" he said, eyebrows going up.

"I do."

"Praetor, I protest!" Vibianus cried. "From the very first day of this case, you have shown the most inexplicable bias in favor of the slaver's boy, the deepest hostility toward our priest Diocles. You have ignored the strongest evidence for Gelon's guilt. Instead of letting the city lock him up in the civic ergastulum, you have kept him in comfort, nay, in luxury, in your own house, as if he were your honored guest instead of your prisoner! You interfered in Diocles' disciplining of his own household and confiscated his property in the form of two slave girls, Leto and Gaia, in defiance of Roman legal practice and custom. You have gone personally to question witnesses, seeking only exculpatory evidence, never the proof of Gelon's guilt. And now you refuse to surrender these two slave girls so that they may testify in a trial over which you preside! Praetor, we have grounds here for bringing charges of corruption against you in Rome!"

There was a collective gasp from the crowd. They didn't get entertainment like this every day. I heaved up from my curule chair, so enraged that I swayed from dizziness. "Have a care, lawyer! I'm of a mind to have you flogged from this court!"

"Roman citizens may not be scourged," he said haughtily.

"That Metellus Celer you mentioned had a reputation for doing just that," I replied.

Tiro stepped in smoothly. "Praetor, please resume your chair. Your color is very bad. We'd hate to have you taken from us by apoplexy."

"Listen to him!" Julia hissed.

Slowly, glaring at Vibianus, I sat back down. "You've talked long enough, Vibianus. Tiro, proceed with your defense."

Vibianus retired to his corner with a triumphant smirk. Not only had he conducted a very competent prosecution argument but also had made me lose my temper and probably convinced most of those present that I was a corrupt, bribe-taking magistrate. Since these were a large majority of Roman judges, nobody needed much convincing. This was looking bad. Not just bad for Gelon, bad for me.

Tiro launched into another oration, giving me time to calm down. Wisely, he did not call Jocasta or any of the other witnesses. They had nothing to say that might help to clear Gelon. Instead, he attacked Vibianus's arguments as specious, denouncing each point with Ciceronian sarcasm. These arguments held little real weight, but Italians and Greeks have always prized eloquence above logic. He wound up with another round of vituperation.

Then it was Vibianus's turn to do the same. He used stock phrases but with excellent composition and timing, and with a great deal of spirit. In spite of myself, I almost enjoyed the performance. When the lawyers retired, I rose to address the jury.

"Citizens," I said, "I now invoke my authority to give special instruction to the jury. This is not commonly done, but I feel that this is a very special case, one in which there is a great deal of ambiguity and in which too much guilt is being loaded upon the head of a single unfortunate man, Gelon son of Gaeto.

"To begin with, he is accused of a murder in what is actually a chain of related murders. The slaying of Gorgo was only the first. No sooner was the son in custody than the father was murdered. Gaeto could not have committed that crime. Next came the death of Charmian, the only possible witness of her mistress's murder. Gaeto could not have killed her. Quadrilla, wife of the *duumvir* Silva was murdered as well. Her connection to the other killings is unknown, but she was murdered in the very same, highly unusual fashion as Gaeto. Gelon could not have killed her.

"I almost hesitate to bring up the bandit attack, since, as the learned, distinguished, and eloquent Vibianus has pointed out the ambiguities of that incident. I can testify, however, that one of the bandits was mounted on the same horse ridden by the murderer of Gorgo and the slayer of Gaeto." I gazed around and saw Julia wince. She didn't think much of this argument. Well, you use what you have.

"The horse was a Roman-shod mare, such as Numidians never ride. This steed was a part of the bandit's hire!" The crowd muttered, impressed. They lacked skepticism. Not so the jury, who looked skeptical beyond measure.

"There is a final piece of evidence I believe should be made public before the jury retires to its deliberations." I gestured to Hermes and he took the scroll from inside his tunic and handed it to me. I held it high.

"This is the will of Gaeto of Numidia. It was deposited for safekeeping in the Temple of Juno the Protector at Cumae, after the custom of this district. I subpoenaed it for this trial and did not see it until it was delivered by messenger this morning. As all can see, the seal is unbroken." I passed it to the little group of local magistrates and they examined the seal. Quite carefully, in fact. They were not unfamiliar with documents that had been tampered with. At last they passed it back, affirming that the seal was authentic and intact.

"I will now have the document read. I feel certain that it contains evidence that bears on this case." It certainly couldn't make things much worse, I thought. I passed it to Marcus and he broke the seal and unrolled the scroll with the verve of a man about to read news of a victory to the Senate. He scanned the contents briefly.

"This is written in Greek," he said.

"You can read Greek," I told him, "and most people here understand Greek. For the benefit of those who don't, I will provide a translation into Latin. Begin."

And so, pausing every few lines for me to translate, Marcus read the will.

"'*I am Gaeto,*'" it began, "'*a native of Numidia, of the line of Juba, a prince of the Tarraelian Berbers.*'" There followed a number of oaths to Gods Greek, Roman, Numidian, and, I believe, Carthaginian. There attested that he was sound of mind and body and not under the baleful influence of witchcraft, curse, or divine displeasure.

The actual will began with the manumission of certain faithful

181

slaves of long service. In Roman wills these testamentary manumissions are usually at the end, but perhaps things are done differently in Numidia. Then he got to the meat of the matter.

"'To my beloved son, Gelon, I bequeath all my lands, estates, tribal titles, and hereditary clientships and loyalties in the land of Numidia, and commend to him the care of his mother and all my concubines.'" The crowd seemed to find this last clause a rare jest.

"'To my second wife, Jocasta,'" he went on, "'I bequeath my lands, houses, properties, and business interests in Italy.'" This was a cause for some astonishment. Under Roman law widows and daughters can of course inherit property, but one does not expect such a thing of a barbarian, certainly not one with a surviving son. Gelon looked astounded. Jocasta was quite impassive. Well, I thought, the boy hadn't wanted to trade slaves in Italy, and now it looked like he would get his wish. He'd probably expected to be able to sell up, though.

"'My beloved second wife,'" the document continued, "'has been my helpmate in all my business dealings, for which my son shows no aptitude nor desire. She is Greek, and a life in Numidia would be a cruel imposition. I assure her comfort and position thus.'"

Now here was a puzzle. A man does not often justify himself in his will. There is no need, unless he wants to cut out some obnoxious heir and wishes to append an insulting comment to make it worse.

Marcus read off a few final oaths, then displayed the seal of Gaeto to all and sundry. Then he handed it to me. Crowd, lawyers, and jury all looked at me, mystified. Finally, Vibianus spoke.

"Honored Praetor, does this odd document in your opinion supply some new and conclusive sort of evidence?"

"I feel that it does," I said, frustrated.

"Will you impart it to us?" he asked so impassively that you could hear the sneer. When I did not answer he said, "Is there any reason to delay further the deliberations of the jury?"

"There is none," I said.

The jury retired within the basilica while I sat and brooded over the will. Surely, I felt, the answer was here. It was my last hope. I began to wonder why I even bothered. What was a slaver's son to me? And what true reason had I for believing him innocent other than that he made such an agreeable first impression and that I had so little liking for Diocles and the others involved in this sorry business? The red ink and Greek lettering had an odd familiarity, but I set the will down when the jury returned.

"They weren't gone long," Hermes said. "That's a bad sign." He didn't have to tell me that.

I stood. "President of the jury," I said, "how do you find?"

The man stepped forward with the traditional vase and dumped its contents on the court secretary's table. In Baiae they used a variation of the Greek ostracon. Here, instead of potsherds, they used little tile disks the size of scallop shell: white for innocent, black for guilty.

Every tile was black. "We find the defendant, Gelon of Numidia, guilty of the murder of Gorgo, daughter of Diocles, priest of the Temple of Campanian Apollo."

The boy's face drained of color, turning his usual high olive complexion a dirty yellow gray. I had ruled out crucifixion and the lions, but even a gentlemanly beheading is not an easy thing to contemplate.

I was about to pronounce that sentence, knowing that the crowd wouldn't like it and not caring, when Julia touched my arm and pointed at the will, lying at my side. She whispered: "It's the same hand that wrote those poems."

Like ice breaking up on a German river in the springtime, things began to shift and loosen in my mind. New possibilities opened up. Nothing was truly clear yet, but I knew I now had all the pieces to the puzzle. What I needed more than anything else was time and it had run out. Then I remembered the conditions I had stipulated at the outset of the trial. I squinted up at the sun. It was barely past midday.

"The jury has spoken and Roman justice will be done," I said. "I will render my judgment at sundown."

There were many exclamations of surprise. Why should I need several hours to send a guilty felon to his death?

"Why delay?" Vibianus demanded. Diocles stood beside him, his face furious.

"I said that this court must be concluded by sundown and that is when it shall end! No back talk from any of you! I now order all here to disperse to their homes and to reassemble here at sundown to hear my judgment. Sublicius Pansa, keep the forum clear and patrol the streets. Disperse any groups larger than four."

There were shouts of outrage at this abuse of authority.

"If any of you defy me," I shouted, pointing at Vesuvius smoking in the distance, "you'll wish that mountain had blown up instead!"

14

THE ATMOSPHERE IN OUR TOWN HOUSE could best be described as tense. Nobody knew what was happening, nobody knew what I was up to. I posted my lictors at the street door and ushered everyone inside. Antonia and Circe chattered away, excited as always by discord. Julia was grim faced; all the men of my party except Hermes looked at me as if I had committed political suicide. That would have suited Hermes fine. He'd have been overjoyed if I had run down to the harbor, seized a ship, and turned pirate.

"There'll be big trouble over this in Rome," Marcus predicted.

"With the uproar that prevails in Rome," I said, "who is going to notice? Now be silent. I have to think some things through." I sat in the courtyard and a servant brought wine and lunch.

"I was hoping you'd thought things through already," Julia said.

"Oh, we should be able to sort things out well before sundown," I told her. I took out the will. "Now, about this document. You are sure that it's the same hand?"

She went to our bedroom and returned with the little scroll. We spread both of them out on a table. There was no doubt of it.

"Gelon," I said, "did you know that your father was having an affair with Gorgo?"

"Impossible!" he cried, now recovered enough to feel indignation over something besides his impending execution.

"Why impossible?" I demanded. "It wouldn't be the first time a father swept a sweetheart out from under his son, so to speak. Look at these papers. He was writing some very intense, erotic poems to the girl. She had them hidden in her handmaid's chamber."

Gelon strode to the table and stared, dumbfounded at the documents. "My father never wrote these!"

"How can you be sure?" Julia asked him.

"Because he couldn't write Greek! Or Latin, either, for that matter. He could read and write in Punic, which is a language good for keeping accounts and little else."

I looked at Julia and she looked back at me, the possibilities revolving in our heads. As so often, we were treading the same path together.

"Hermes," I said, "fetch that little dagger that killed Gaeto."

Mystified, he did my bidding, returning in moments with the minuscule weapon. I handed it to Julia. "Tell me, my dear," I said, "how would you use this to kill me?"

While the others stood or sat with mouths agape, she studied the dagger in her palm. Then she smiled. "Here is how I would do it."

That day her hair was dressed in the most demure fashion, parted in the middle, drawn back and knotted at her nape, the remainder trailing in a long tail down her back. She reached behind her neck and threaded the little dagger into her hair, trying several different ways until she was satisfied. When her hands fell away, the weapon was not visible. She turned to our rapt little audience, smiling.

"You may now assume that I am naked, about to embrace my loving husband." Even Antonia and Circe kept silent as Julia approached me. She wrapped her arms around my neck and drew my head down for a kiss. In Rome, for a wife to kiss her husband before witnesses was something of a scandal, but we were all Baiaean libertines by now. I felt her fingertips resting at the back of my skull, then I felt a tiny pricking sensation in that spot. One of our watchers—Circe, I think—gasped slightly.

"You will notice," Julia said, "that I withdrew the dagger just as our faces came together. Even with his eyes open, my unsuspecting spouse couldn't see what was going on behind me. I placed the tip of the thing between the fingers of my left hand and guided it to that very vulnerable spot where the neck joins the skull. No unerring eye was needed. I could have done the whole operation with my eyes shut. Next—"

I jerked as she smacked me very sharply on the back of the neck. Antonia and Circe jerked as well. The men were made of sterner material, but they looked a little sick, doubtless thinking of all the women with whom they had let their guards down.

"Had I not snatched the dagger away in time," Julia said, "I'd have driven it in to the hilt. No powerful arm required, either." She stepped back, pleased with her performance.

I glared at Hermes. "I blame you for putting that idea into our heads," I told him. "You were the one who first said it had to be a strong man with the eye of a swordsman." He just shrugged and rolled his eyes.

"I should have seen it sooner," Julia said. "I told you there was something odd about that writing and that verse. If it had been in Latin, I'd have noticed it sooner. Those verses were written by a woman. When I first saw them, I said they read like something out of Sappho."

"Just a minute," Antonia said with horrified delight. "Are you saying that it was Jocasta who was having an affair with that girl? Jocasta who killed her?"

"She wasn't the only one sharing a bed or a grassy hummock with poor Gorgo," I said, "but she killed her."

"No!" Gelon cried, distraught. "She could not have!"

"Just as Gorgo and your father were not the only ones enjoying the intimate delights of Jocasta's body," I said. "Hermes said that you were half asleep when he called on you that morning, and more stunned than might have been expected when you got the terrible news. Did Jocasta drug you?"

The boy sat huddled in a heap of misery, covering his face with his hands. "She—she must have! It was not something we did often, but sometimes I couldn't help myself, and she always acted as if she did it only to please me. That night, Father was away, the house was empty of all save the two of us. I thought we'd just had too much wine with dinner—"

"But you woke up in her bed with the lictors pounding on the door, eh?" I said. "Must have been a shock."

Hermes stared at him, aghast. "You mean you were putting it to your father's *wife*?" This was pretty strong stuff, even for Rome.

"Oh, don't be so hard on him," Antonia said. "It's not like she was his *mother*! She was just a second wife, more like a concubine. He was going to inherit the old man's concubines anyway."

"It is a terrible crime in Numidia," Gelon said. "If word of it reaches there, I can never go back!"

"Don't complain so much," Antonia advised. "The praetor has already spared you the cross and the beasts of the arena. Now it looks like you won't even be beheaded. You're ahead of the game any way you look at it."

"Spoken like a true Antonian," I said.

"But why kill Charmian?" Julia said, "And Quadrilla?"

"Charmian!" Hermes said, anxious to cover up his earlier gaffe. "It was to Jocasta's house that she fled. Jocasta was her 'protector'!"

Circe snorted. "Some protector."

"We'll find out about the rest," I said. "We know enough for now. Time to talk to the woman herself."

"I'll take the lictors and go arrest her," Hermes said.

"No," I told him. "I don't want her to have time to concoct a story. I want to go and brace her before she knows she's been exposed."

"I'm not missing this for anything," Julia said. "Praetorly dignity be damned. I'm going with you."

"Me, too!" cried Circe and Antonia in unison. I know when I am outnumbered.

In a small mob we made our way to Jocasta's town house. On the way we encountered Sublicius Pansa, patrolling the streets as I had ordered.

"Am I not supposed to disperse gatherings of more than three?" he said, grinning.

"I didn't mean me," I growled. "And I don't require an escort." I didn't want the woman to hear approaching hoofbeats.

Baiae being the small town it was, we were at her door in minutes. It was not locked, and the lictors rushed in with us close behind.

We found her seated at the rim of the pool of her impluvium, toying with a lotus flower that floated therein. She wore another of her silk gowns. This one was black, perhaps in recognition of the solemnity of the occasion. She looked up at me and saw instantly that it was all over for her. A lictor placed a hand ceremonially on her shoulder.

"Jocasta," I said, "I arrest you for the murders of Gorgo the daughter of Diocles; of your husband, Gaeto; of Charmian the slave of Gorgo; and of Quadrilla, wife of the *duumvir* Manius Silva." I almost added the rest of the formula, "Come with me to the praetor," but realized in time that I *was* the praetor.

She sighed. "You are such a stubborn man. If you had just executed that fool"—she jabbed a finger toward Gelon—"you would have been too embarrassed to come after me, even if you figured out the truth later."

"I have a high tolerance for embarrassment," I told her. "I wouldn't have let you get away with it."

"If you say so. But you are very sensitive, for a Roman. Not many would have gone to such lengths for a slaver's son. And you are wrong about one thing. I didn't kill Charmian."

"Then how did she die?" I asked her.

"Perhaps," Julia said, "you should tell us all that happened."

Jocasta stared at her with eyes grown haggard, a face abruptly aged. "Aren't you forward for a Roman wife?"

"She isn't a Roman wife," I told her. "She's a Caesar." I found a nearby chair and sat as a praetor should when hearing a case. The rest of my party remained standing, even Julia.

"Why should I tell you anything?" Jocasta demanded. "I'm to die whatever I say."

"I'll make you the same promise I made Gelon: No cross, no beasts in the arena. A quick beheading and it's over. But only if you explain it all. I owe this to Manius Silva and to Diocles and to the shades of the dead. They can cross over the river and know peace when this matter is settled and they are avenged."

"You owe Diocles *nothing*!" she hissed with shocking malice.

"All right," I said. "Let's start there. What was Diocles' part in all this?"

"He was Gaeto's partner! I lied about the man in Verona. When Gaeto first set up in Baiae he needed a citizen partner, and he needed one of impeccable lineage. Slaving can be a chancy business, you know. He might have bought kidnapped Roman citizens by mistake, and then he would have been in terrible trouble. The penalties are fearsome, as you know well. He had to have a highly placed partner to speak up for him in court."

"Why would the priest of Apollo go into partnership with a slaver?" Julia wanted to know.

"For money, of course! Far higher than the usual percentage. And he wasn't a priest back then. His father was still the priest, and he had an older brother. But the brother died first, and then Diocles inherited the priesthood and he was too respectable, too noble for the likes of us. But he took the money. Year after year he demanded his cut, and year after year he snubbed us and treated us like offal beneath his feet!" The woman had great reserves of bitterness, that much was clear.

"And your talk about Greek malcontents meeting at the temple to talk against Rome, that was just magician's smoke to confuse my investigation?"

"Oh, such meetings were held, but nothing would ever have come of them. It was the drunken ramblings of resentful men. They all had too much at stake to risk revolutionary action. They were just disgruntled at having Rome lording it over them. But Diocles did help them out when they had financial troubles. He could afford to, with the money he raked in from the slave trade."

"You said you had a spy in the temple," I said. "Was it Gorgo or Charmian who told you about these meetings?"

"Charmian," she said sadly. "Poor Charmian. She was so lively and strong, so intelligent. No, Gorgo had little going on in her head and a great deal going on between her legs."

Circe astonished me by saying; "Did you love her?"

Jocasta jerked around, surprised. "No. She was a sweet, stupid girl and she was pleasant to be with, but I could not love such a creature."

"But those passionate poems—" Julia began, then she stopped, her eyes going wide. "You wrote them to Charmian!"

"We speculated such a thing at first," I said. "We found the poems in the girls' quarters. But we were fixated on Gorgo."

"She loved you, though," Julia said, her voice hardening. "She put on her best jewelry, anointed herself with your favorite perfume, Zoroaster's Rapture—surely you gave her the jewelry and the perfume?"

"Oh, yes, they were my gifts. But I wrote poems only for Charmian."

"So was Charmian your go-between with Gorgo," Antonia asked, "or was it the other way around?"

Jocasta regarded her with eyes worldly enough to give even an Antonian pause. "Why do you think it had to be one or the other?"

"You mean," Antonia said, "all three of you?" Her face filled with wonder. "You were getting up to some serious debauchery out in Apollo's grove!"

"Very Greek in all respects," I said. "But she didn't wear her very best jewelry to that last meeting. She didn't wear this." I took the huge necklace from within my tunic and let it drop to its full length, the jewel-studded golden lozenges rattling faintly. Jocasta jerked slightly at the sight, glaring. "Gaeto gave her this, didn't he?"

"Yes!" She packed a world of hatred into one short word.

"Is it why you killed her?"

"No, it's just a bauble. But it portended worse things. Charmian told me about it, that Gaeto was meeting Gorgo and bringing her fabulous gifts."

"Poor little Leto said Gorgo returned to bed smelling differently after various assignations. Sometimes it was Jocasta's perfume, sometimes it was healthy male musk, Numidian variety."

"You are being vulgar, dear," Julia chided.

"And the girl was fickle," Jocasta went on. "She was beginning to fancy Gelon, who was closer to her own age."

I stole a glance at Gelon. He seemed to have turned to stone. Maybe he wasn't going to be executed, but he was getting a double ration of suffering.

"You mean," Hermes said, "you were bedding the father, the son, the woman they both loved, *and* her slave girl?"

"Let's not forget Quadrilla," I said, "but we'll get to her later. You said the necklace portended worse things. What did you mean?"

"I think I can answer that," said my wife, who had turned out to be unsettlingly handy with a dagger. "He was looking for a younger wife, wasn't he? One better placed than a Greek hetaera."

Jocasta smiled bleakly. "Pray you don't learn what it feels like. Yes, he wanted Gorgo for a wife. Unlike Gelon, he could have forced Diocles to his will. Killed him if necessary. Under all the polish I gave him, he was a brute. And Diocles wasn't much of a partner any more. The great men of the town were borrowing from Gaeto as well as from the priest. Any of them would have agreed to be a partner, as long as discretion was observed."

"So you got rid of her," I said. "Did Charmian help you?"

"No, both girls were asleep when I strangled her. With a scarf, it can be done so gently that the victim passes into death without ever wakening. Wives sometimes hire *hetaerae* to do away with their husbands in such a fashion. They seem to have passed away from overindulgence."

"But the scream—" Julia began. Then, "Oh, that was Charmian, wasn't it?"

"Yes, when I awakened her and told her her mistress was dead. She was distraught for a while, tried frantically to revive her. But she recovered quickly."

"So that accounts for the disordered state of the body, despite your humane method of assassination," I noted. "Now tell me how you killed your husband."

She thought for a while, and we did not prod her. One doesn't hear so elaborate a confession often.

"I prepared for this long ago," she said. "Gaeto depended on me for many of his business dealings. I write well in Latin and Greek, languages in which he was illiterate, though he spoke them well enough. He dictated his will, in which he left most of his property to Gelon, with provisions he thought would satisfy me. I wrote it the way I knew it should read. When I knew he would soon be making a new will, it was time to act. At such times you have to act swiftly and decisively. You can't hesitate.

"With Gorgo dead, I knew that he would deduce what had happened within a few days. He was not a stupid man. I hadn't realized that Diocles would suspect Charmian so swiftly. He'd suspected her of spying for a long time, it turns out. When she escaped, she came straight to me, of course. She'd been hideously beaten, but she insisted on coming with me when I went to kill my husband. I didn't want her to—she was too badly hurt—but she was like iron. Besides, there was a problem with my plan."

"You needed to stand on your horse to get atop the wall," I said. "But somebody had to hold it while you were inside, so that you could make your escape." This accounted for the smell of horse I'd detected on the girl's body.

"I told myself that it was all right. It wasn't a long ride, after all. I washed and dressed her and we rode out after dark. There was no problem getting into the compound. I was very familiar with the place and its routines. Gaeto was surprised to see me, but he thought I'd just come in through the front gate. I disrobed and let him know that I was overcome with passion. He was a man. He was flattered. I put the dagger in him and dressed and left."

So much for her inconvenient husband.

"But as we neared the city before dawn, Charmian doubled over in terrible pain. It was the beating. I never should have let her ride with me. That vicious priest killed her!" For the first time she wept. This was the only death that touched her. She dried her tears and went on. "I took her as far as the laundry park and she could ride no farther. I laid her down on the grass and she died before sunrise. I did the best I could by her, and it was such a beautiful place." She was weary, now, all but drained.

"But you had to strip her and leave her naked," I said, "because you'd dressed her in your household livery."

"Aren't you the clever one," she said tonelessly.

"Actually," I told her, "Hermes figured that one out. He has his moments. That leaves only Quadrilla. Why did you kill her?"

"The dagger."

"What?" I said.

"She'd taught me that trick with the little dagger, hiding it in your hair. Greek hetaerae don't use it, you see. They don't stoop to common, brutal clients. They're too expensive. But Italian whores know the trick, and Quadrilla had been forced into prostitution when she was a young girl, after her father was ruined. Like so many of the wives around here, she came to me to learn refinements. In return, she taught me some of the baser realities of a whore's life. Just in case I should ever be cast aside, you see."

"But she smuggled you into her house," Julia said. "You were sleeping with her, too."

"With quite a few of the local ladies, actually. As I said, they came to me for lessons. What better way to teach? But Quadrilla began to tease, to let me know she knew I'd done away with Gaeto. Maybe she would have kept silent. But I couldn't risk it."

"And the bandits?" I said. "How did you contact them?"

She livened a bit. "By pure luck. They found me arranging Charmian's body. They'd been driven from Vesuvius by the smoke and ash and were foraging in the countryside. They wanted the horses. I told them go ahead and take them. Then I told them that I could pay them handsomely of they'd get rid of a Roman praetor and his prisoner for me. You're such a troublesome snoop. I told them when Gaeto's funeral would be and which road you would be on."

"How did you know I'd let Gelon go and that I would attend?"

"Because I'd already seen what a dutiful man you were, what an examplar of Roman *pietas,* when you were so generous about Gorgo's funeral. You were so punctilious about matters of religion and ritual. I never thought you'd be so handy with a sword. I was very impressed."

"But why," Julia asked, "did you take Quadrilla's sapphire?"

She looked at my wife, and for the first time her eyes revealed the madness within. "As a keepsake. I truly liked Quadrilla."

"Why didn't you kill Diocles?" Antonia asked.

"He was next," Jocasta told us. "But Diocles presented difficulties. He would never let me get close. The others allowed me to get close."

There was silence for a while, then I rose from my chair. "It is almost sundown and I told the town that I would render judgment by then. Let's go to the forum and set this matter at rest."

"Actually," Jocasta said, "I don't wish to provide a spectacle for all these Campanian snobs. But I don't mind letting a Caesar and a Metellus see this." Her right hand went to her hair.

"Stop her!" Julia shouted.

But Jocasta was too swift for our stunned senses and she hadn't run out of daggers. This was not one of her needlelike weapons. It was no larger, but its blade was flat and double-edged, with a keen point. It flashed across and went in beneath her left ear. She jerked it across, all the way to the other ear. The she stood there, with her blood flowing like a waterfall. Throughout, she glared at us with defiance, standing erect, letting us know who was the true aristocrat here. Then the light went out of her eyes.

I sat again, ignoring the wails and sobs of the women, the strangled noises made by the men.

"I should have had her stripped and her hair searched," I said. "I must be getting old." But I was truly not unhappy that I would not be condemning her to death. In spite of all she had done, I did not want her blood on my hands.

"I LOST THE CASE BUT MY CLIENT WAS exonerated," Tiro mused. "I am not sure how I feel about that."

"Feel happy," Cicero advised. "The law is a chancy business. I was exiled for the finest legal judgment I ever delivered." He shook his head. "This district is so pleasant it's hard to believe it's such a sink of corruption."

"I like it anyway," I assured them. "They know how to have a good time, and you can't get fish stew like this just anyplace."

We were lounging in a dining room of the Villa Hortensia while my household packed up for the trip to Bruttium. We were dipping crusts of bread into the last of the stew, having put away a prodigious amount of it.

"Did you hear?" Hermes inquired. "Diocles opened his veins last night."

"With all his guilt," I said, "what he couldn't stand was for people to know he'd been the slaver's partner. This is one funeral I'll pass up."

"So ends the line of priests of Campanian Apollo," Julia said sadly.

"They'll find another one," I assured her. "Bloodlines aren't everything."

"But such an ancient lineage!" she said. "It seems a shame."

"This was just a little change in a little town," Cicero said. "I fear that far greater things are about to change very soon."

And so they did.

THESE THINGS HAPPENED IN SOUTHERN Campania in the year 704 of the City of Rome, the consulship of Lucius Aemilius Lepidus Paullus and Caius Claudius Marcellus.

GLOSSARY

(Definitions apply to the year 704 of the Republic.)

ala   Literally, "wing." A squadron of cavalry.

arms   Like everything else in Roman society, weapons were strictly regulated by class. The straight, double-edged sword and dagger of the legions were classed as "honorable."

The *gladius* was a short, broad, double-edged sword borne by Roman soldiers. It was designed primarily for stabbing. The *pugio* was also a dagger used by soldiers.

The *caestus* was a boxing glove, made of leather straps and reinforced by bands, plates, or spikes of bronze. The curved, single-edged sword or knife called a *sica* was "infamous." *Sicas* were used in the arena by Thracian gladiators and were carried by street thugs. One ancient writer says that its curved shape made it convenient to carry sheathed beneath the armpit, showing that gangsters and shoulder holsters go back a long way.

Carrying of arms within the *pomerium* (the ancient city boundary marked out by Romulus) was forbidden, but the law was ignored in troubled times. Slaves were forbidden to carry weapons within the City, but those used as bodyguards could carry staves or clubs. When street fighting or assassinations were common, even senators went heavily armed, and even Cicero wore armor beneath his toga from time to time.

Shields were not common except as gladiatorial equipment. The large shield (*scutum*) of the legions was unwieldy in narrow streets, but bodyguards might carry the small shield (*parma*) of the light-armed auxiliary troops. These came in handy when the opposition took to throwing rocks and roof tiles.

augur An official who observed omens for state purposes. He could forbid business and assemblies if he saw unfavorable omens.

balnea Roman bathhouses were public and were favored meeting places for all classes. Customs differed with time and locale. In some places there were separate bathhouses for men and women. Pompeii had a bathhouse with a dividing wall between men's and women's sides. At some times women used the baths in the mornings, men in the afternoon. At others, mixed bathing was permitted. The *balnea* of the republican era were far more modest than the tremendous structures of the later Empire, but some imposing facilities were built during the last years of the Republic.

basilica A meeting place of merchants and for the administration of justice. Among them were the Basilica Aemilia (aka Basilica Fulvia and Basilica Julia), the Basilica Opimia, the Basilica Portia, and the Basilica Sempronia (the latter devoted solely for business purposes).

client One attached in a subordinate relationship to a patron, whom he was bound to support in war and in the courts. Freedmen became clients of their former masters. The relationship was hereditary.

compluvium An opening in the roof of a Roman house through which rain fell to be gathered in a basin called the impluvium. Eventually, it became a courtyard with a pool.

crucifixions   The Romans inherited the practice of crucifixion from the Carthaginians. In Rome, it was reserved for rebellious slaves and insurrectionists. Citizens could not be crucified.

curule   A curule office conferred magisterial dignity. Those holding it were privileged to sit in a curule chair—a folding camp chair that became a symbol of Roman officials sitting in judgment.

duumvir   A duumvirate was a board of two men. Many Italian towns were governed by *duumvir*. A *duumvir* was also a Roman admiral, probably dating from a time when the Roman navy was commanded by two senators.

ergastulum   Locked room in which to imprison one's slaves.

euergesia   The obligation laid upon the wealthy to provide public works and entertainment for the people.

euergetes   One who provides public works and entertainment for the people.

families and names   Roman citizens usually had three names. The given name **(praenomen)** was individual, but there were only about eighteen of them: Marcus, Lucius, etc. Certain praenomens were used only in a single family: Appius was used only by the Claudians, Mamercus only by the Aemilians, and so forth. Only males had praenomens. Daughters were given the feminine form of the father's name: Aemilia for Aemilius, Julia for Julius, Valeria for Valerius, etc.

Next came the **nomen.** This was the name of the clan (gens). All members of a gens traced their descent from a common ancestor, whose name they bore: Julius, Furius, Licinius, Junius, Tullius, to name a few. Patrician names always ended in *ius*. Plebeian names often had different endings. The name of the clan collectively was always in the feminine form, e.g., Aemilia.

A subfamily of a gens is the **stirps**. Stirps is an anthropological term. It is similar to the Scottish clan system, where the family name

"Ritchie" for instance, is a stirps of the Clan MacIntosh. The **cognomen** gave the name of the stirps, i.e., Caius Julius Caesar. Caius of the stirps Caesar of gens Julia.

The name of the family branch **(cognomen)** was frequently anatomical: Naso (nose), Ahenobarbus (bronzebeard), Sulla (splotchy), Niger (dark), Rufus (red), Caesar (curly), and many others. Some families did not use cognomens. Mark Antony was just Marcus Antonius, no cognomen.

Other names were **honorifics** conferred by the Senate for outstanding service or virtue: Germanicus (conqueror of the Germans), Africanus (conqueror of the Africans), Pius (extraordinary filial piety).

Freed slaves became citizens and took the family name of their master. Thus the vast majority of Romans named, for instance, Cornelius would not be patricians of that name, but the descendants of that family's freed slaves. There was no stigma attached to slave ancestry.

Adoption was frequent among noble families. An adopted son took the name of his adoptive father and added the genetive form of his former nomen. Thus when Caius Julius Caesar adopted his great-nephew Caius Octavius, the latter became Caius Julius Caesar Octavianus.

All these names were used for formal purposes such as official documents and monuments. In practice, nearly every Roman went by a nickname, usually descriptive and rarely complimentary. Usually it was the Latin equivalent of Gimpy, Humpy, Lefty, Squint-eye, Big Ears, Baldy, or something of the sort. Romans were merciless when it came to physical peculiarities.

fasces   A bundle of rods bound around with an ax projecting from the middle. They symbolized a Roman magistrate's power of corporal and capital punishment and were carried by the lictors who accompanied the curule magistrates, the *Flamen Dialis,* and the proconsuls and propraetors who governed provinces.

first citizen   In Latin: *princeps.* Originally the most prestigious senator, permitted to speak first on all important issues and set the order of debate. Augustus, the first emperor, usurped the title in perpetuity. Decius detests him so much that he will not use either his name (by the time of the writing it was Caius Julius Caesar Octavianus) or the honorific Augustus, voted by the toadying Senate. Instead he will refer to him only as the First Citizen. *Princeps* is the origin of the modern word "prince."

flagellum   A multistranded whip, whose thongs were cords or leather; *flagrum* was a flagellum whose thongs were were strung with bones, circles of metal, or hooks.

forum   An open meeting and market area.

freedman   A manumitted slave. Formal emancipation conferred full rights of citizenship except for the right to hold office. Informal emancipation conferred freedom without voting rights. In the second or at least third generation, a freedman's descendants became full citizens.

games *ludus*, pl. *ludi*   Public religious festivals put on by the state. There were a number of long-established *ludi*, the earliest being the Roman Games *(ludi Romani)* in honor of Jupiter Optimus Maximus and held in September. The *ludi Megalenses* were held in April, as were the *ludi Cereri* in honor of Ceres, the grain goddess and the *ludi Floriae* in honor of Flora, the goddess of flowers. The *ludi Apollinares* were celebrated in July. In October were celebrated the *ludi Capitolini*, and the final games of the year were the Plebian Games *(ludi Plebeii)* in November. Games usually ran for several days except for the Capitoline games, which ran for a single day. Games featured theatrical performances, processions, sacrifices, public banquets, and chariot races. They did not feature gladiatorial combats. The gladiator games, called *munera*, were put on by individuals as funeral rites.

gravitas   The quality of seriousness.

hospitium   An arrangement of reciprocal hospitality. When visiting the other's city, each *hospes* (pl. *hospites*) was entitled to food and shelter, protection in court, care when ill or injured, and honorable burial should he die during the visit. The obligation was binding on both families and was passed on to descendants.

imperium   The ancient power of kings to summon and lead armies, to order and forbid, and to inflict corporal and capital punishment. Under the Republic, the imperium was divided among the consuls and praetors, but they were subject to appeal and intervention by the tribunes in their civil decisions and were answerable for their acts after leaving office. Only a dictator had unlimited imperium.

iudex An investigating official appointed by a praetor.

janitor A slave doorkeeper, so called for Janus, god of gateways. In some houses they were chained to the door.

legion They formed the fighting force of the Roman army. Through its soldiers, the Empire was able to control vast stretches of territory and people. They were known for their discipline, training, ability, and military prowess.

libitinarii Rome's undertakers. Their name comes from Venus Libitina, Venus in her aspect as death goddess. Like many other Roman customs associated with the underworld, the funeral rites had many Etruscan practices and trappings.

lictor Bodyguards, usually freedmen, who accompanied magistrates and the *Flamen Dialis,* bearing the fasces. They summoned assemblies, attended public sacrifices, and carried out sentences of punishment.

lupanar A brothel.

military terms The Roman legionary system was quite unlike any military organization in existence today. The regimental system used by all modern armies date from the Wars of Religion of the sixteenth century. These began with companies under captains that grouped into regiments under colonels, then regiments grouped into divisions under generals, and by the Napoleonic wars they had acquired higher organizations such as corps, army groups, and so forth, with an orderly chain of command from the marshal down through the varying degrees of generals, colonels, majors, captains, sergeants, corporals, and finally the privates in the ranks.

The Roman legions had nothing resembling such an organization. At the time of the SPQR novels the strength of a legion was theoretically 6,000 men, but the usual strength was around 4,800. These were divided into sixty centuries. Originally, a century had included one hundred men, but during that time there were about eighty. Each century was commanded by a centurion, making sixty centurions to the legion. Six centuries made a cohort. Each centurion had a *optio* as his second in command. The centurionate was not a single rank, but a complex of hierarchy and seniority, many details of which are obscure. We know that there were first-rank and second-rank centurions. The senior centurion of the legion was *primus pilus*, the "first spear." He was centurion of the first century of the first cohort and outranked all others. Centurions were promoted from the ranks for ability and they were the nearest thing a legion had to permanent officers. All others were elected or appointed politicians.

Legionaries were Roman citizens. They fought as heavy infantry fully armored and armed with the heavy javelin (*pilum*), the short Spanish sword (*gladius Hispaniensis*), and the straight, double-edged dagger (*pugio*). They carried a very large shield (*scutum*) that at that time was usually oval and curved to fit around the body. Besides holding the center of the battle line, legionaries were engineers and operated the siege weapons: catapults, team-operated crossbows, and so forth.

Attached to each legion were usually an equal number of *auxilia*, noncitizen troops often supplied by allies. These were lightly armed troops, skirmishers, archers, slingers, and other missile troops, and cavalry. The legion had a small citizen cavalry force but depended upon the *auxilia* for the bulk of the cavalry. Through long service an auxiliary could earn citizen status, which was hereditary and his sons could serve in the legions. *Auxilia* received lower pay and had lower status, but they were essential when operating in broken terrain or heavy forest, where the legions could not be used to advantage. In battle they often held the flanks and usually, with the cavalry, were charged with pursuing a broken and fleeing enemy, preventing them from reforming or counterattacking.

There were other formations within a legion, some of them obscure. One was the *antesignani*, "those who fight before the standards." Already nearly obsolete, they were apparently an elite strike force, though how it was manned and used is uncertain. Apparently exceptional bravery was required for assignment to the *antesignani.*

There were awards for valor. Greatest of these were the crowns. The Civic Crown (*corona civica*) was awarded for saving the life of a fellow citizen in battle. The Wall Crown (*corona muralis*) was awarded to the first man atop an enemy wall or battlement. The Grass Crown (*corona graminea*) was awarded by the centurions to a general who had won a great victory. It was braided from grass growing on the battlefield. There was great competition among officers for the crowns, because they made election to higher office a near certainty. The citizens loved them. For the rankers there were bracelets awarded for valor. Among Roman men only soldiers wore bracelets, and these only as decorations for bravery. Torques, twisted Gallic neck rings in miniature form, were also awarded in pairs, slung over the neck on a scarf. Centurions might be awarded *phalerae:* seven or nine massive silver discs worn on a harness atop the armor. Apparently these were for exceptional service rather than a single feat.

In Decius's time the legions were still formed as a unit, served for a number of years, then discharged collectively. Even when on many years' service, they were ceremonially disbanded, then reformed every year, with the soldier's oath renewed each time. This archaic practice was extremely troublesome, and when a few years later Augustus reformed the military system, legions became permanent institutions, their strength kept up by continuous enlistment of new soldiers as old ones retired or died. Many of the Augustan legions remained in service continuously for centuries.

The commander of a legion might be a **consul** or **praetor,** but more often he was a **proconsul** or **propraetor** who, having served his year in Rome, went out to govern a province. Within his province he was commander of its legions. He might appoint a legate (*legatus*) as his assistant. The legate was subject to approval by the Senate. He might choose a more experienced military man to handle the army work while the promagistrate concentrated upon civil affairs, but a successful war was important to a political career, while enriching the commander. For an extraordinary command, such as Caesar's in Gaul, or Pompey's against the pirates, the promagistrate might be permitted a number of legates.

Under the commander were Tribunes of the Soldiers, usually young men embarking upon their political careers. Their duties were entirely at the discretion of the commander. Caesar usually told his tribunes to sit back, keep their mouths shut, and watch the experienced men work. But a military tribune might be given a responsible position, even command of a legion. The young Cassius Longinus as tribune prosecuted a successful war in Syria after his commander was dead.

munera   Special games, not part of the official calendar, at which gladiators were exhibited. They were originally funeral games and were always dedicated to the dead.

offices   The political system of the Roman Republic was completely different from any today. The terms we have borrowed from the Romans have very different meanings in the modern context. "Senators" were not elected and did not represent a particular district. "Dictator" was a temporary office conferred by the Senate in times of emergency. "Republic" simply meant a governmental system that was not a hereditary monarchy. By the time of the SPQR series the power of former Roman kings was shared among a number of citizen assemblies.

Tribunes of the People were representatives of the plebeians with power to introduce laws and to veto actions of the Senate. Only plebeians could hold the office, which carried no imperium. **Tribunes of the Soldiers** were elected from among the young men of senatorial or equestrian rank to be assistants to generals. Usually it was the first step of a man's political career.

A Roman embarked upon a public career followed the **"cursus honorum,"** i.e., the "path of honor." After doing staff work for officials, he began climbing the ladder of office. These were taken in order as follows:

The lowest elective office was **quaestor:** bookkeeper and paymaster for the Treasury, the Grain Office, and the provincial governors. These men did the scut work of the Empire. After the quaestorship he was eligible for the **Senate,** a nonelective office, which had to be ratified by the censors; if none were in office, he had to be ratified by the next censors to be elected.

Next were the **aediles.** Roughly speaking, these were city managers, responsible for the upkeep of public buildings, streets, sewers, markets, brothels, etc. There were two types: the **plebeian aediles** and the **curule aediles.** The curule aediles could sit in judgment on civil cases involving markets and currency, while the plebeian aediles could only levy fines. Otherwise their duties were the same. The state only provided a tiny stipend for improvements, and the rest was the aediles' problem. If he put on (and paid for) splendid games, he was sure of election to higher office.

Third was **praetor,** an office with real power. Praetors were judges, but they could command armies, and after a year in office they could go out to govern provinces, where real wealth could be won, earned, or stolen. In the late Republic, there were eight praetors. Senior was the *praetor urbanus,* who heard civil cases between citizens of Rome. The *praetor peregrinus* (praetor of the foreigners) heard cases involving foreigners. The others presided over criminal courts. After leaving office, the ex-praetors became **propraetors** and went on to govern propraetorian provinces with full imperium.

The highest office was **consul,** supreme office of power during the Roman Republic. Two were elected each year. Consuls called meetings of the Senate and presided there. The office carried full imperium and they could lead armies. On the expiration of the year in office, the ex-consuls were usually assigned the best provinces to rule as **proconsul**. As proconsul, he had the same insignia and the same number of lictors. His power was absolute within his province. The most important commands always went to proconsuls.

Censors were elected every five years. It was the capstone to a political career, but it did not carry imperium and there was no foreign command afterward. Censors conducted the census, purged the Senate of unworthy members, doled out the public contracts, confirmed new senators in office, and conducted the *lustrum,* a ritual of purification. They could forbid certain religious practices or luxuries deemed bad for public morals or generally "un-Roman." There were two censors, and each could overrule the other. They were usually elected from among the ex-consuls.

Under the Sullan Constitution, the quaestorship was the minimum requirement for membership in the Senate. The majority of senators had held that office and never held another. Membership in the Senate was for life, unless expelled by the censors.

No Roman official could be prosecuted while in office, but he could be after he stepped down. Malfeasance in office was one of the most common court charges.

The most extraordinary office was **dictator.** In times of emergency, the Senate could instruct the consuls to appoint a dictator, who could wield absolute power for six months, after which he had to step down from office. Unlike all other officials, a dictator was unaccountable: He could not be prosecuted for his acts in office. The last true dictator was appointed in the third century B.C. The dictatorships of Sulla and Julius Caesar were unconstitutional.

optimates Supporters of a continued senatorial dominance, *optimates* were an aristocratic party in Republican Rome.

orders The Roman hierarchy was divided into a number of orders (*ordines*). At the top was the Senatorial Order (*Ordo Senatus*) made up of the senators. Originally the Senate had been a part of the Equestrian Order, but the dictator Sulla made them a separate order.

Next came the Equestrian Order (*Ordo Equestris*). This was a property qualification. Men above a certain property rating, determined every five years by the censors, belonged to the Equestrian Order, so named because in ancient times, at the annual hosting, these wealthier men brought horses and served in the cavalry. By the time of the SPQR novels they had lost all military nature. The equestrians (*equites*) were the wealthiest class, the bankers and businessmen, and after the Sullan reforms they supplied the jurymen. If an *eques* won election to the quaestorship he entered the Senatorial Order. Collectively, they wielded immense power. They often financed the political careers of senators and their business dealings abroad often shaped Roman foreign policy.

Last came the Plebeian Order (*Ordo Plebis*). Pretty much everybody else, and not really an order in the sense of the other two, since plebeians might be equestrians or senators. Nevertheless, as the mass of the citizenry they were regarded as virtually a separate power and they elected the Tribunes of the People, who were in many ways the most powerful politicians of this time.

Slaves and foreigners had no status and did not belong to an order.

palla   A cloak, a cover.

patrician   The noble class of Rome.

pietas   The quality of dutifulness toward the gods and, especially, toward one's parents.

priesthoods   In Rome, the priesthoods were offices of state. There were two major classes: pontifexes and flamines.

Pontifexes   were members of the highest priestly college of Rome. They had superintendence over all sacred observances, state and private, and over the calendar. The head of their college was the ***Pontifex Maximus***, a title held to this day by the pope.

The **flamines** were the high priests of the state gods: the *Flamen Martialis* for Mars, the *Flamen Quirinalis* for the deified Romulus, and, highest of all, the *Flamen Dialis*, high priest of Jupiter.

The *Flamen Dialis* celebrated the Ides of each month and could not take part in politics, although he could attend meetings of the Senate, attended by a single lictor. Each had charge of the daily sacrifices, wore distinctive headgear, and was surrounded by many ritual taboos.

Another very ancient priesthood was the ***Rex Sacrorum,*** "King of Sacrifices." This priest had to be a patrician and had to observe even more taboos than the *Flamen Dialis*. This position was so onerous that it became difficult to find a patrician willing to take it.

Technically, pontifexes and flamines did not take part in public business except to solemnize oaths and treaties, give the god's stamp of approval to declarations of war, etc. But since they were all senators anyway, the ban had little meaning. Julius Caesar was *Pontifex Maximus* while he was out conquering Gaul, even though the *Pontifex Maximus* wasn't supposed to look upon human blood.

Princeps (First Citizen)   This was an especially distinguished senator chosen by the censors. His name was first called on the roll of the Senate, and he was first to speak on any issue. Later the title was usurped by Augustus and is the origin of the word "prince."

sistrum   Percussion instrument consisting of a handheld frame to which small metal disks are attached, rather like those on a tambourine.

SPQR *Senatus Populusque Romanus*   The Senate and People of Rome. The formula embodied the sovereignty of Rome. It was used on official correspondence, documents, and public works.

stola   A long woman's dress, generally fastened with pins at the shoulders and worn belted at the waist.

Toga   The outer robe of the Roman citizen. It was white for the upper class, darker for the poor and for people in mourning. The *toga candidus* was a specially whitened (with chalk) toga worn when standing for office. The *toga praetexta* bordered with a purple stripe, was worn by curule magistrates, by state priests when performing their functions, and by boys prior to manhood. The *toga trabea,* a striped robe, was worn by augurs and some orders of the priesthood. The *toga picta,* purple and embroidered with golden stars, was worn by a general when celebrating a triumph, also by a magistrate when giving public games.

Triclinium   A dining room.

Triumph   A ceremony in which a victorious general was rendered semidivine honors for a day. It began with a magnificent procession displaying the loot and captives of the campaign and culminated with a banquet for the Senate in the Temple of Jupiter, special protector of Rome.

Vestal Virgins   Virgin priestesses, chaste like the goddess Vesta, six of them served for thirty years, any violation of the vow of chastity was punished by burial alive. Vesta's shrine was the most sacred object of Roman religion.